DIAMONDBACK

A TAYLOR MADISON MYSTERY

ELIZABETH DEARL

Hard Shell Word Factory

To Joe, who made it all possible. I love you.

A huge thank you to Jude Morris who read each chapter the moment I produced it and provided encouragement and feedback.

Copyright 2004 Elizabeth Dearl
eBook ISBN: 0-7599-3162-3
Published February 2005

ISBN: 0-7599-3178-X
Trade Paperback
Published May 2005

Hard Shell Word Factory
PO Box 161
Amherst Jct. WI 54407
books@hardshell.com
www.hardshell.com
Cover art © 2005 Dirk A. Wolf

Chapter One

MY VOLKSWAGEN WHEEZED in weary protest as it encountered yet another rise in the road. Houston's terrain is as flat as a sheet of paper, not counting a man-made incline or two on the freeway system, and the ancient little car was never going to forgive me for introducing it to the hills of west Texas. The transmission groaned as I downshifted and began the climb, my ears popping from the slight change in altitude.

On the passenger seat, my backpack stirred and Hazel presented a quivering nose.

"Not dinner time yet," I informed her, and the nose withdrew, twitching in disgust.

The setting sun shimmered against the asphalt, glancing off the beer cans and tin foil strewn along the roadside. This section of highway evidently hadn't been "adopted" by any civic-minded group. I was beginning to wonder if anyone beside me even knew it existed. It had been at least an hour since I'd passed another car.

I had made an interesting discovery during my five hundred mile journey. Desolate stretches of road had a charismatic effect on my right foot. The lonelier the landscape, the harder my foot pressed the accelerator, as if to hurry me back to human companionship. The two speeding tickets in my glove compartment convinced me that cops out here in the boonies had discovered the phenomenon long ago, and made use of it to pad the coffers of tiny towns with names like Rising Star and Pancake.

A sign flashed by:
PERDUE 10 Miles
LUBBOCK 54 Miles

Lubbock is farm land, as flat as Houston, and it amazed me that Perdue was surrounded by craggy hills, rising out of nowhere with startling suddenness.

I nudged the backpack and a tiny black nose emerged inquiringly. "Tell me something, Hazel. Have I lost my mind? Why am I doing this?"

She yawned.

"Never mind. Go back to sleep."

Floor it, suggested a reasonable little voice inside my head. *Just keep on going right through Perdue, all the way to Lubbock. You can sell this old rattletrap for a few hundred, hop on a plane...*

"Sell my car?" I shouted. The voice had overstepped its bounds. I had worked odd jobs all the way through high school to earn the money for my precious VW, and I'd keep it long enough to be buried in it, if I had my way. It had been my graduation gift to myself, and buying a used car had left enough money to pay for my first semester at U of H. So what if it was fourteen years old? I patted the dashboard fondly. It had, in fact, been my *only* graduation present. Mom hadn't even bothered to show up at the ceremony.

Something long and dark slithered into the road ahead, and I reacted before I realized what it was. Jerking the steering wheel sharply to the right, I stomped on the brake. The car careened sideways into the ditch that constituted the road's shoulder, and lurched to a halt. A cloud of red dust billowed up through the rust holes in the floorboard. I coughed. Hazel sneezed.

Still shaking, I turned in the seat to peer behind me. The snake was squirming into a tangle of brush on the opposite side of the road.

"Lovely countryside," I muttered, and turned the key.

The engine stuttered and caught, sounding as cranky as I felt, but that was as far as the matter went. The steering wheel moved awkwardly and apparently no longer held any influence over the tires.

I squinted through the bug-smeared windshield. Straight ahead, a large sign informed me that I had reached: Perdue City Limits, Pop. 2,948.

"Well, at least we made it to our destination," I told Hazel, who sneezed again. Gathering my backpack and windbreaker, I stepped out into the red dust.

I had spoken too soon. By the time I reached the first indication of civilization, I was wishing for a fur coat (and to hell with Greenpeace). If not for the intervention of my neighbor, George, I probably wouldn't have tossed the windbreaker onto the front seat, so anxious had I been to set out on this idiotic quest before sanity could take hold. But George, bless his heart, had reminded me that the entire state of Texas doesn't share Houston's near-tropical climate. The temperature had hovered in the mid-eighties on the morning I said good-bye to the house where I'd grown up. Here, I'd guess it to be in the lower fifties at the most, and a strong north wind pushed me along, whistling down my collar.

The jacket's thin nylon pockets offered little protection; my fingers were already numb by the time I reached the dubious shelter of Forman's Gas Station—which, by all indications, had been closed since circa 1939. The two gas pumps would have brought a fortune in an antiques auction, and I had to wonder how the building itself had managed to remain standing. The wood was weathered and cracked, silver with age, and the entire structure tilted precariously. A well-aimed spitball would have toppled it.

"Okay, Hazel, what now?" But Hazel, curled in the bottom of my backpack and snug in a nest of tissue, didn't offer a reply. I resumed walking.

By the time I reached the true outskirts of Perdue, my ears ached, my eyes burned, and my breath came out in solid little chunks that shattered as they dropped to the asphalt.

I pushed my way into the first building I saw, which turned out to be Hope Feed and Hardware. A wave of deliciously warm air caressed me like a lover, and I made a beeline for its source: a cast-iron, wood-burning stove that squatted comfortably in one corner of the room.

When the scuffed, wooden floorboards creaked beneath my sneakers, a bald head popped up from behind the counter.

"Sorry, miss, I'm gettin' ready to close."

I tried to answer, but all I could manage was the sound of chattering teeth.

"Why, you poor kid!" The man was at my side in a flash, hustling me closer to the stove. "You just sit yourself down in that old rocker—atta girl—and I'll pour you a nice, hot cup of coffee. Cream and sugar? No? Here, now, put your feet closer to the stove, unless you think them fool plastic shoes will melt. Haven't you youngsters ever heard of boots? Good pair of leather boots'll last a lifetime. And what kind of coat is that for winter? Dadburn plastic clothes..."

Throughout this nonstop monologue, he had settled me into the wooden rocker, eased the backpack off my shoulders, tucked a quilt around my knees, shoved another log into the already blazing fire, and poured coffee from a battered tin pot simmering atop the stove. I took a swig of something that tasted like the liquid derived from boiling old tires. It was heavenly.

He pulled up a stool and sat. "Now, then, suppose you tell me what you're doing wandering around in a blue norther, and dressed for a spring picnic?"

"Car broke down." I was relieved to find some feeling had returned to my lips. "I walked here from out near the city limits sign."

"Jeez Marie, that's two, three miles! Why didn't you stop at old

Jack's gas station? You had to pass right by it to get here."

"I did. No one was there."

He shook his head. "Jack's been feeling poorly lately. He's gonna have to hire someone if he wants to keep the place going. That, or sell it." He chuckled. "Can't shut it down, for sure. Only gas station in town."

"Great," I mumbled. "So, who's going to fix my car?"

"Oh, Jack don't fix cars. He only pumps gas. When he's open, that is. You need Roger."

"Roger?"

"Yeah. He's got an old pickup rigged for towing, and he's real handy with tools."

I sighed. "Roger it is, then. Could you call him for me?"

"Nope, Roger ain't got a phone. Oh, now, don't pull a face. We'll get your car fixed up. On your way to Lubbock, are you?"

"Uh, no. Actually, I was on my way here." I didn't explain further, not sure how much I wanted to tell a total stranger, even one who had probably saved me from frostbite.

My host brightened. "You came for the festival, I'll bet! You're early, though. The hunt don't start till tomorrow." He winked. "Officially, that is, though between you and me, I know a few early birds getting a little head start on the proceedings. Cheatin', some would say."

I had lost the thread of this conversation fairly early on. "I don't know anything about a festival. I came to...visit my aunt."

"You got kin in Perdue? I'll be. How come I've never seen you around before? I know most everybody here, lived here all my life. Tell you one thing, I never saw hair that color." He covered his mouth with one hand. "Guess I shouldn't have said that. Nothing wrong with hair color in a bottle, and none of my business, anyway. Just trying to place your looks, was all. What did you say your name was?"

"Taylor Madison." I figured an introduction might stop the questions. I had heard the hair color comment too many times throughout my life to be offended by it. My hair is pale blonde, almost white. I've even been asked, once or twice, if I were an albino.

He shook my proffered hand. "Rude of me not to have said so before, honey. I'm Hank Barton. I own this place." He gestured proudly around the store, which was stacked with sacks of feed, seed, and manure, and crowded with items ranging from gardening gloves to a small John Deere lawn tractor parked near the door. A couple of miniature rabbits watched me from their cage, and I was glad Hazel couldn't see them. I had never put her to the test but, after all, it was in her genes to chase rabbits.

"Barton? I thought it was Hope's Hardware."

Hank laughed and pulled a handkerchief from the chest pocket of his overalls to mop his bald pate. He moved away from the stove a bit, and I would have done the same if I could have gotten untangled from the tightly tucked quilt.

"Hope, not Hope's," he explained. "That was my granddaddy's little joke. He started this store back when Derrick County was barely a scattering of dirt farmers and sheep ranchers. Said he didn't know if a hardware store out in the sticks would ever turn a profit, but he could always hope."

"Well, it's obviously been a success, Mr. Barton."

"Call me Hank. Here I've been jabbering away, and you've got places to go. Wish I could drive you myself, but my wife took the car tonight. I know! Stay put while I make a call. Have some more coffee."

"Thank you." Now that I was warm, no amount of torture could have induced me to drink more of the awful brew. "Do you mind if I smoke?" I had quit for almost two years, but the first thing I'd done after reading the letter was go out and buy a pack.

"Why should I mind?" He handed me an old-fashioned glass coaster to use as an ashtray, then left me alone. I took advantage of his absence to scoot the rocker away from the stove and sneak a peek at Hazel, who was still sound asleep in her makeshift burrow. I could hear Hank talking on the phone, but couldn't make out what he was saying.

"Sheriff's on his way," he said cheerfully upon his return. "Won't take him long. He's right across the street."

I gaped at him. "The sheriff?"

He shrugged. "Sure. Perdue don't have a taxi service, you know. Sheriff's the next best thing. I reckon if he can drive old Mrs. Archer to the grocery store once a week, he can sure tote a pretty little gal to her aunt's house." He peered at me. "Who'd you say your aunt was, again?"

Why was I hesitating? "Tessa Potter," I told him. "Do you know her?"

"Why, of course I do! Everybody knows Tessa and Wood." He examined me more closely, then slapped his knee. "Gosh sakes, that must mean Sarah had a kid. Well, I'll be. No one's heard a peep out of her since she high-tailed it to Houston—when? Must be nigh onto thirty years ago. How's she doin'?"

"She's dead," I said flatly.

"I'm right sorry to hear that." He looked over my shoulder and waved at someone. "There you are, Miles! Gettin' sneaky in your old age. I didn't even hear the door open. This young lady needs...Miles? Hey, you all right?"

I turned, locking eyes with a tall, middle-aged man wearing a brown uniform. His angular face had been tanned to a permanent bronze by the west Texas sun, but at the moment, he somehow managed to look pale.

"Lordy, Miles, sit down before you fall down." Hank went into his bustling routine again, finding a clean mug and pulling the stool closer to the fire.

The sheriff made his way to the stool and sat. After a moment, he blinked and shook his head.

"I'm okay, Hank, so stop fussing. No, I don't want any of that melted tar you call coffee." He turned back to me and stuck out a hand the size of a catcher's mitt. "Miles Crawford, Miss...?"

"Madison. Taylor Madison." I watched the hand swallow mine briefly before dropping back into his lap.

"Sorry about the dramatic entrance. I'm getting over the flu, and on top of that, I haven't eaten since breakfast." He summoned a weak smile.

"Then you ought to be at home. I'm sure I can find someone else to drive me."

"No need. I have to pass right by Tessa's house on the way to mine."

"How about that, Miles?" Hank broke in. "Sarah Ross's little girl, can you believe it? She says her mama's passed away, though. Now, that's a shame. Was it her heart or something? She couldn't have been but forty-five or six."

"She was forty-nine." I began extricating myself from the quilt. "It was a hit-and-run accident, not an illness. Mr. Barton—I mean, Hank—how can I thank you? You saved my life."

Hank grinned. "Hardly that. Now, you get you some good boots and a heavy coat, hear?"

"I'm sure she'll take your advice, Hank." The sheriff nudged my arm. "If you're ready, Miss Madison?"

"Taylor, please. I'm ready." That was a lie. Blue norther notwithstanding, the worst still lay ahead of me.

I had expected a patrol car, but was instead helped into a bright red Toyota sedan. The sheriff had left the engine running, and a warm interior greeted me.

"My county car's in the shop," he explained as if he had read my mind, tossing a tan felt Stetson into the back seat to make room for me.

"Roger's?" I asked. "Speaking of that——"

"Yeah, Hank told me you needed a tow. Tell you what, give me your keys. I'll drop you off at Tessa's, then track Roger down and get him to pull it in tonight."

"Great. Listen, there's a laptop computer shoved under the front passenger seat. Could you make sure it's locked up somewhere?"

The sheriff stopped for a red light (the only one I had seen so far, so perhaps the only one in town) and glanced at me. "Locked up?"

"Well, it's pretty valuable."

"This isn't the big city, Miss Madison. Lots of folks around here still leave their doors unlocked. But I'll make sure your little computer is safe."

"Thanks," I said, feeling somehow rebuked.

After only a few blocks, the sheriff pulled into the driveway of a two-story house. I couldn't make out any details in the dark, but a front window shed muted light. At least someone was home.

The sheriff cleared his throat, and I realized I had been gazing at the house for quite some time. I opened the car door, surprised when he got out as well.

"I'll walk you to the porch," he said, and I nodded gratefully. This was going to be harder than I had expected.

"I thought they lived on a ranch," I said, as we climbed the front steps. I was beginning to shiver again, though I was pretty sure it wasn't from the cold wind this time.

He nodded. "They just moved into this place about six months ago. Wood had a stroke, and Doc wanted to get him into town for a while, closer to the clinic."

I felt an unexpected flare of concern for someone I'd never met. "Is he all right?"

"Getting along. The physical therapy seems to be helping. He can walk with a cane now." His expression remained impassive in the dim light, but I knew he had to be wondering why I wasn't aware that my uncle had been gravely ill. "Well?"

I started. "Well, what?"

"You might try ringing the bell," he suggested.

The front door opened while my finger was still on the button. A plump woman peered out at me, one hand lifting to shove a dangling hairpin back into her gray bun.

"Yes?" She noticed the sheriff and gave him a puzzled smile.

"Why, hello, Miles."

I waited for him to respond, but he obviously felt his duty had been done by bringing me here, and he was now ready to throw me to the wolves. In fact, I couldn't figure out why he hadn't already beat feet for his Toyota.

"I'm looking for my aunt." The goose bumps on my arms were hatching goslings. "Tessa Potter," I added when she didn't reply.

The woman's dentures threatened to pop out of her mouth. "Tessa has a niece? I had no idea. My stars, you think you know a person! Well, come on in, child. Haven't you got enough sense to wear decent clothing in weather like this? Miles Crawford, why on earth didn't you lend the girl your jacket? And here I thought you were the last remaining gentleman in the state. I've never seen the like. Poor thing freezin' to death, and you stand there like a bump on a log. There now, Tessa will be home in a bit. I'm mindin' Wood while she runs to the grocery store. Are you comfy?"

During this incredible speech, she dragged me into the living room, settled me into a gigantic wing chair so close to the fireplace that I could feel the fine hairs on my arms singe, and bustled off to fetch a pot of tea. The sheriff, drawn along in our wake, sat down in a matching chair. I leaned closer to him.

"Is she, by any chance, related to Hank?" I whispered.

Crawford snorted a laugh. "That's Mabel Donnely. She's a retired nurse, and Doc recommended her to help out with your uncle."

"Oh." The fire crackled through another silence. "Thanks for bringing me, Sheriff Crawford, but you really don't have to stay."

Before he could reply, Mabel returned, lugging a loaded tea tray. "You'll stay too, won't you, Miles?"

"Wouldn't turn down your famous tea, Mabel."

I swear he shot me a satisfied smirk. Obviously, even the high sheriff wasn't immune from small town curiosity.

"Tessa's niece," the nurse marveled, plunking herself down on the sofa. "I've known the woman for twenty years, and you think she'd mention a niece. Where are you—oh, my God!" To my amazement, she was climbing the couch like a tree, her screams coming in breathless little bursts.

Baffled, I turned to Crawford. He was watching my backpack, his eyebrows almost disappearing into his hairline. I followed his gaze, suddenly certain what I would see.

Sure enough, a furry little face had poked its way from beneath the flap, and Hazel's bright eyes were taking in her new surroundings.

Mabel's screams intensified.

"A rat!" she shrieked. "Don't sit there like a lump, Miles Crawford. Do something! Shoot the filthy thing!"

"Don't you dare!" I shouted, torn between indignation and hilarity. Mabel would have made a great go-go dancer in her younger days, the way her rubber-soled nursing shoes trounced that couch.

Easing Hazel from the pack, I cuddled her protectively. "She's not a rat, she's a ferret. She won't hurt you, Mabel, I promise."

"What in blue blazes is going on in this house?" came a voice from the foyer. We all froze, Mabel in mid-bounce, which must have been difficult.

My aunt stood in the archway.

Oh, yes, I knew she was my aunt, despite the fact I had never laid eyes upon her until that moment. Her resemblance to my mother was astonishing. Same petite frame, same light brown hair, though Tessa's held far less gray than Mom's had. I got to my feet, absently handing Hazel over to Crawford.

Mabel, somewhat recovered now that the sheriff had the "rat" in custody, clambered down from the sofa, smoothing her dress.

"Tessa, dear, look who came to visit! Why didn't you ever tell me you had a niece?"

Tessa dropped the grocery sack. It hit the tiled floor, something inside tinkling as it broke. She held out both hands, not in welcome, but rather as if she were making a sign to ward off evil.

Mabel's mouth dropped open and she rushed to gather the scattered groceries. "Guess you're as surprised as I was, aren't you? I'll just put these things away for you, Tess, while you sit down and have tea with your pretty niece."

"Thank you, Mabel," Tessa said quietly. "Is Wood all right?"

"Sleeping like a baby," Mabel assured her and hurried out of the room, cradling the dripping bag.

Ignoring me for the moment, Tessa picked up the teapot with a hand that trembled noticeably, splashed some tea into the cup Mabel had been using, and downed it like a shot of bourbon.

"Get out of my house," she ordered in a low, deadly tone. "Right now."

She didn't stay around to make sure I obeyed, but disappeared up the staircase. Crawford dragged me out the front door before Mabel could emerge from the kitchen to find out what was going on.

Mercifully, the sheriff didn't ask me any questions. He just drove, jacking the car's heater up to the hellfire setting in an attempt, I'm sure,

to stop my trembling. Hazel wormed her way up to my shoulder and I
nuzzled her gratefully, her long whiskers tickling my chin. Eventually,
I came to realize that we had passed the same lighted church steeple at
least twelve times.

"Sorry," I said. Whatever that meant.

Crawford turned down a residential street, where he found a place
to pull over to the curb. We sat there for a while, listening to the
whoosh of the heater and Hazel's occasional chattered comment.

"Want to tell me what that was all about?" he asked finally.

"I have no idea. And I'd rather not speculate right now, if you
don't mind." I noticed that his car's ashtray had been used, so I felt safe
in digging out my cigarettes. He pushed in the lighter for me when I
couldn't find my matchbook, and I rolled down the window, letting the
cold air wash over my cheeks. "You know, I've spent all my time in
this town either freezing or roasting. Don't you people know what
happy medium means?"

"A cheerful psychic?" he suggested, deadpan, surprising me into a
weak laugh.

"We can't sit here all night, Miss Madison. You'd better at least
tell me what's next on your agenda."

"What are my alternatives?" I returned, taking a drag of smoke.

"Well, there's always the bus station, but that might present a
problem with your car. Tow charges from here to Houston would be
pretty steep."

"True." I tossed the glowing butt out the window, wondering
wearily if he'd charge me with littering. I damn sure wasn't going
anywhere without my car, but didn't see any reason to inform him that
I wasn't planning to leave at all until Tessa answered at least one
question. "Okay, then, would you mind dropping me off at a motel?"

"I wouldn't mind at all, except for one minor thing. Perdue
doesn't have a motel."

"Perfect. Where do people stay when they visit this godforsaken
place?"

"We have a boarding house."

"Fine."

"Afraid not. It's all booked up for the festival."

*The damn festival again. Didn't take a lot to get the local yokels
excited,* I thought sourly.

"This is about the only time of year that we get any tourists," he
went on. "The boarding house fills up fast, and then a lot of the citizens
like to rent out spare rooms to catch the overflow. Works out pretty

good for everyone. The homeowners get a little extra cash, and the tourists get home-cooked meals. 'Course, a lot of the tourists nowadays bring motor homes or trailers. We've got a big area set up out near the auditorium for camping."

"Darn, and I left my motor home parked next to the mansion. What you're telling me is, there's no room at the inn. Any of the inns."

He pulled away from the curb. "I think we can find you something."

I was puzzled when he parked in front of Hope Hardware, but kept my mouth shut and followed him inside.

Hank greeted me like an old friend, and started nodding even before Crawford had finished his request. "Sure, I'll set up a rollaway bed in that little storeroom upstairs." He turned to me. "Will that be comfortable enough?"

At that moment, I probably would have agreed to sleeping on a bed constructed of rocks and cactus. "Sounds great."

Crawford managed to suppress the dozen or so questions he must have been dying to ask me, and took his leave. I trailed Hank up the stairs.

The room he opened was at the end of a long hall, and might have measured eight by twelve feet if you removed some of the junk stacked along the walls. It had a single window overlooking the rear of the store, and an extra door that led, Hank informed me, to the bathroom belonging to the small apartment next door.

"My grandparents lived there when they started the store," he told me as he bustled around, setting up the bed, finding an old brass floor lamp to put beside it, and plugging in a space heater. "My wife and I have a real house now, so I rent the apartment out. What the hey, a little extra money never hurts, and I've got a good tenant. Nice and quiet, no wild parties." Hank peeked at his watch. "He'll be working until midnight at least, so feel free to use the bathroom."

It wasn't until he'd gone that I realized he hadn't asked any questions either, though he must have been wondering why I hadn't stayed with my 'kinfolk.' I could see I'd have to shake the notion that small town folk are genetically unable to subdue their natural nosiness.

I fed Hazel from the Ziplock bag of dry cat food in my backpack, spread out a few layers of newspaper for her to use as a potty, then ran myself a tub full of hot water. After prudently making use of the hook and eye lock on the door that led into the apartment next door, I eased myself into the claw-footed tub and finally allowed myself to think. Tessa's reaction had shocked me, but it really shouldn't have. The letter

I'd found certainly made it clear that she and my mother hadn't been on good terms. She probably didn't even know Mom had died. Who would have informed her? After all, I hadn't known Tessa existed until the week after the funeral.

I felt myself slipping into a doze, and stood to towel off before I drowned.

Hazel had climbed onto the sheets and was curled into a ball next to my pillow. I left her there, drifting into sleep with her musky scent in my nose.

Chapter Two

THE SUN SLANTED in at an outrageously early hour. As I tried to tug the sheets into a position that would block the light, excited voices from outside lured me to get up and take a peek out the window. Okay, so who said only small town folk are born with the nosiness gene?

A tiny wood-framed house, badly in need of paint, squatted on the lot behind the store. Children of all sizes spilled out the back door, like clowns from a trick circus car. I had to wonder how they all managed to sleep in that house. Sardines in a can sprang to mind.

A broad-shouldered man—obviously the brood's daddy—followed on their heels, brandishing a pole that looked something like a golf club, with a loop of heavy wire at one end and some sort of trigger built into the handle. The children all carried burlap sacks and the oldest, a boy in his teens, also toted a five-gallon gas can. Daddy flipped open the cargo hatch of a rusted station wagon and the munchkins piled in, clutching their odd treasures and squabbling for pride of place. The teenager caught sight of me at the window. He waved. I waved back, and watched the wagon leave a plume of red dust as it took off down the street.

Since my luggage was still in the car, wherever that might be, I'd just put on the jeans I'd worn the day before. Fortunately, my backpack contained a clean set of underwear, and I added a bra beneath the t-shirt I'd slept in, thinking to at least spare the citizens of Perdue my usual undignified jiggling. After giving Hazel another helping of food, some water, and a fresh layer of newspaper, I left her free run of the little room. Her cage was also in the car, but since ferrets don't chew furniture or sharpen their claws, I figured Hank's property was safe enough.

The store hadn't yet opened for business. I exited through a self-locking door in the back and made my way up the alley to the main street. Turning south, I noticed that, while there was still a nip in the air, the gale of the night before had settled down to a breeze. My windbreaker succeeded, finally, in living up to its name.

The Investor's Bank of Perdue shared the block with the hardware store. Across the street, the town's central square was occupied by the county courthouse, a hulking three-story building fashioned from native rock and embellished with elaborately carved gingerbread trim. It looked like a piece of architecture conceived by Frank Lloyd Frankenstein. The one charming touch was a gigantic brass bell that replaced the more usual clock at the top of the central tower. I wondered what type of event would occasion its ringing.

At the corner, I had a choice to make. I could continue straight across, which would deliver me to the offices of the *Derrick Gazette*, Your Weekly Source of County News. Or I could jaywalk on the diagonal, which would put me at the door of Lucy's Café—Good Food.

No contest. I couldn't even remember the last time I had eaten.

A skinny redhead stepped from behind the counter and offered me a booth. I declined, preferring to perch on one of the counter's high stools where I could take advantage of the heat wafting from various griddles and toasters. I took a grateful sip of the coffee she set before me, the steam from the mug thawing the tip of my nose. Most of the booths and stools were occupied by flannel-shirted men, most likely farmers. The waitress and I were the only females present.

She topped off my coffee. "You're the one Sheriff Crawford picked up yesterday, aren't you?"

I ignored the awkward phrasing that made it sound as if I were a conquest he'd made at a singles bar. At least, I hoped it was only awkward phrasing.

"Yes, that was me. Could I have one of those bear claws?"

The waitress put one on a plate for me—the pastry was freshly made and still warm—then resumed wiping the already spotless counter right under my nose. "Honey, how on earth can you use that much bleach without turning your hair to straw?"

I took this as an attempt on her part to make conversation, so I obliged. "I take it you're Lucy?"

"Lucy?" She looked puzzled.

I pointed to the mirrored wall behind the counter, where the name of the place was etched in gold lettering.

She chuckled. "Reckon I forgot that you're a stranger. Lucy was the lady who started the cafe, but that's been twenty years or so. I'm Rita."

"Nice to meet you. But why didn't you change the name?"

"You'd have to ask Fred about that."

I fortified myself with a sip of coffee. "And who is Fred?"

"He owns the place now. Before that, it was Lottie Simpson, but she tried serving tea and cookies instead of real food, so she didn't last long. And before Lottie, it was a pool hall, but they couldn't serve beer since this is a dry county, so none of the guys would hang around."

"I get the picture. Simpler to leave the sign alone."

She grinned, displaying widely spaced teeth. "That's about it. 'Scuse me, I've got customers."

I finished my pastry, watching in the mirror as she escorted a chubby couple to a booth and handed them menus. Noticing an old chrome-and-glass jukebox in one corner, I slid off the stool, digging some change from my pocket. The couple greeted me as I passed, and I remembered to return their polite words. These people were making me feel like a city snob.

The jukebox selections proved that Perdue was slowly, and probably unwillingly, easing out of the mid-fifties. Madonna and M.C. Hammer shared space with singing sensations on the order of Little Jerry Haggerty and the Dixie Swans, the Homer Tiddle Fiddle Band, and the immortal Nelson Sludge. I settled for an old Linda Ronstadt ballad, unwilling to sample Nelson Sludge, but equally unwilling to offend the clientele.

Dropping in a dime—a dime? I'd have to check out the nearest pay phone and see if it still had a nickel slot—I turned to find myself eyes-to-Adam's apple with Sheriff Crawford. For one blinding moment, I thought he was going to ask me to dance. He stepped back to peer down at me, his pure white hair glistening in the light of the overhead fluorescents. At five-foot-ten, I wasn't used to men being so much taller than me, but Crawford had to be at least six-five. His color was healthier than it had been the night before, but his pale eyes were cradled by dark circles as if he hadn't gotten much sleep.

"We meet again." He winced a little as Linda crooned an impossibly high note. "Can I buy you a cup?"

"Only if there's coffee in it." I followed him to one of the red vinyl booths, where Rita refilled our coffee mugs and took his breakfast order.

I looked up from stirring cream into my coffee and caught him watching me. "Fly on my nose?"

"What? Oh, sorry. I was thinking how much you remind me of Tessa."

"No kidding." In a pig's eye. I was about eight inches taller than my aunt, blonde to her brunette, angular where she was curved. "And I'll bet you thought Laurel was Hardy's twin brother."

"Come again?"

I shook my head. "You were obviously trying to flatter me, so thanks. Speaking of thanks, I think I forgot last night. To thank you, that is. For dragging me all over town."

He kept his gaze on the table. "Not a problem."

Rita showed up with his plate of pancakes, waving the coffee pot over my already brimming mug. I caught her sleeve as she turned away. "I don't suppose you could use an extra waitress in here?"

Her mouth dropped open. "You? Honey, you wouldn't want to work here. Lordy, I go home at night with my bottom pinched raw. Besides, old Fred is as tight as a Tupperware seal. I only get minimum wage because he rakes off half my tips." That seemed to settle it, and she hurried off to dispense more coffee to the farmers.

Crawford had paused with a forkful of pancake halfway to his mouth, and syrup was drizzling down his tie. I dipped a paper napkin into my water glass and handed it to him. He shoved his plate out of the way and dabbed at the stain. "You weren't serious, were you? About wanting a job here?"

I shrugged. "A job's a job. I've been a waitress before, among other things."

"But you do have a job back in Houston, don't you?"

"Sort of. I think I do, anyway, but as pissed as my agent is at me right now, it doesn't bode well for the future. She was dead set against me taking this trip. See, I have a shot at a hardback sale, but the publisher wants the entire manuscript.

"Under the circumstances, I've tried to get her to let the paperback house have this one, too, so I could get my advance on the basis of the first three chapters, but Annie's being stubborn. She doesn't seem to care that I'm broke. Tyrant." I sighed. "And I really am flat broke at the moment. I've had a lot of unusual expenses lately. Like my car, for example." *And my mother's funeral,* I added silently.

He cocked his head. "So, you're a writer?"

I nodded. "Mystery novels."

"Madison. Taylor Madison. My God." He gaped at me. "Maddy Taylor? Are you Maddy Taylor?"

"That's my pen name."

"Well, I'll be dipped in hog fat! Maddy Taylor. I've read all of your novels."

I didn't quite know how to respond to that. The phrase 'all of your novels' made me sound as prolific as Stephen King. "I've only published two so far."

"Good, then I haven't missed any." He picked up his fork and mashed his pancakes thoughtfully.

"Sheriff, I'd like to talk to you about something," I began, when a new voice cut in.

"Sorry to interrupt your breakfast, Sheriff, but Mrs. Gleason is in the office, and she's spittin' blood."

I stared. I couldn't help it.

Blonde men have never attracted me, maybe because of my own coloring. Two blondes together tend to look like escapees from a cheerleader convention. But this one was so drop-dead gorgeous that I found myself wiping my chin, checking for drool. "Spitting blood?" I repeated stupidly.

He smiled. My God, he even had dimples. "Ever see a horned toad when it's mad?"

"I've never seen a horned toad when it's happy," I admitted. "What's a horned toad?"

"Looks like a bumpy gray lizard," Crawford put in. "They shoot blood out of their eyes when they feel threatened, but most people think they spit it. Taylor Madison, Deputy Lester Forman."

"Meetcha," he said amiably, extending a hand. I shook it absently, still appalled by the thought of blood-spitting lizards.

"What's got Dora Gleason's tail in a twist?" Crawford asked.

"Same as last year. Snake hunters on her property."

The sheriff sighed and wiped his mouth, sliding out of the booth. "Would she rather live with the snakes? Don't answer that. I'll go talk to her. Everything okay at the festival grounds?"

"So far, so good. Cal was helping 'em hang the banner when I left. Craft and food booths are all assembled, tanks are filling fast. Everything should be ready for the official opening on Friday."

"We'll have to increase overnight security to make sure kids stay away from the tanks. You and Cal work out a schedule. Speaking of Cal, what's he doing out there already? He didn't get off duty until two this morning, did he?"

Lester shrugged. "We're all workin' overtime, Sheriff. We're one man short, you know."

"Yeah, I know." Crawford donned his Stetson and looked at me. "Miss Madison, give me half an hour or so to get rid of the Gleason woman, then come by the office, if you will. I haven't had a chance to talk to you about your car."

"Sure," I said. "But what's all this about hunting snakes?"

"Lester looks like he could use a cup of coffee. I'll let him tell you." Giving his hat brim a final tug, the sheriff left.

Lester took the seat Crawford had vacated. "Best assignment he ever gave me."

Rita hustled over with the coffee pot, then lingered, adjusting the sugar bowl and creamer so he wouldn't have to strain his arm reaching for them, pulling a fresh napkin from the dispenser to wipe an already clean spoon, offering him a slice of apple pie, on the house. No? How about cherry? He finally shooed her away.

Her less-than-subtle flirtation gave me the opportunity to study him more closely. I discovered that his nose was a shade too long, his green eyes were set a tad too closely together, and his chin was on the weak side. I was relieved. Perfection is disconcerting.

"Snakes," I prompted as he added an ice cube from his water glass to his steaming coffee.

"Yeah. Mrs. Gleason is sorta anti-social, doesn't want the hunters or anyone else on her land. Including, I suspect, Mr. Gleason."

"But why would anyone want to hunt snakes in the first place? I'd think it would be a lot healthier to run in the opposite direction."

He laughed. "You're probably right, but this time of year, everyone hunts them."

I looked at him blankly.

"Don't you know about our festival?"

"I've heard people talking about it, but what's that got to do with snakes? Isn't it just a little county fair, or something?"

"It's that, too, but more."

I leaned back, lighting my first cigarette of the day, and waited for an explanation.

"The Rattlesnake Festival is our big annual event, modeled after the one they hold in Sweetwater every March. We chose April so there wouldn't be a conflict with the tourists, since a lot of folks go to both. Ours is a lot smaller than theirs, but we attract a decent-sized crowd. Good for the local economy."

I wondered if I had stumbled into one of those backwoods religious cults. "And you hunt snakes?"

"Sure. The locals started this morning."

"I see." A horrible suspicion occurred to me as I remembered the munchkin family I had watched through the window. The weird golf club, the burlap sacks. I told Lester about it, and he nodded.

"Yep. What you do is find a likely spot for the rattlers to be holed up, and spray gasoline into the den to flush 'em out. Folks used to smoke them out, but that can be dangerous when it's been dry, and gas fumes work even better. That pole you saw is used to catch them alive. The wire is looped around the snake's neck, then tightened using the trigger." He shrugged. "Drop the critter into a sack, and that's all there is to it."

I thought about asking how you determined where a snake's 'neck' was, but decided against it. "Great fun, huh?"

"A lot of people think so, but it's also a form of self-preservation. Ask any rancher how many sheep, especially lambs, he loses every year to rattlers." He squinted at me. "In case you're a card-carrying environmentalist—we get our share of protestors—I'll tell you right now that we don't even put a dent in the rattlesnake population. Those little buggers breed faster than rabbits."

"Hooray for them," I muttered, and picked up my windbreaker. "I'd better go see what the sheriff found out about my car."

He looked amused. "If I promise not to talk about snakes any more, can I walk you across the street?"

"Only if you solemnly swear," I warned him. Snakes and blood-spitting lizards! Made Houston's muggers and junkies seem tame. If I owned a pair of ruby slippers, I would have tapped the heels together right then and there.

I peeled off my jacket before we were halfway across the street. The bank boasted a digital clock/thermometer below its sign, and I was surprised to note that the temperature had climbed into the upper sixties.

"Good thing that norther blew by," Lester said. "The snakes might have gone back into hibernation if it had stayed cold."

So much for promises. "Fine Boy Scout you'd make," I grumbled.

"Sorry." But his grin stayed in place. He led me around to the back of the courthouse, where a door was marked: Derrick County Sheriff's Office.

Inside, a skinny redhead was seated at an L-shaped counter that took up one corner of the outer office. At first, I thought it was Rita, and was trying to figure out how she'd gotten here ahead of us when Lester called out a greeting. It was a boy who turned away from the typewriter—a kid, maybe eighteen years old—and I hardly needed an introduction to know that Billy Jackson was Rita's brother.

Billy lisped a shy, "Hello," and glanced out the window. "Hey, Les, isn't that Paula?" I followed his pointing finger and saw a young woman climbing down from the cab of an old pickup truck.

Les frowned. "What's she doing here? 'Scuse me, Taylor. I'll be right back." He hurried out the door, intercepting the woman before she was halfway up the walk.

"That's Lester's wife," Billy informed me, and my budding fantasies crumbled.

I studied her through the window glass, but all I could really determine was that she was petite, dark-haired, and wore sunglasses so big they barely balanced on her tiny nose. Because she was standing in direct sunlight, I could also see she was wearing far too much makeup for someone her age, pale foundation applied with a heavy hand. I've never understood why some women think more is better. A door near the desk opened, and Sheriff Crawford appeared, his hand cupping the elbow of a woman who had surpassed mere obesity long ago. Her entire collection of chins waggled as she glared up at him.

"This is your last chance, Sheriff. Either they stay off my property, or they'll feel the sting of my daddy's shotgun. I haven't forgotten how to use it."

"You put up those No Trespassing signs like I told you, and we'll handle it from there, Dora. Don't put us through the expense of widening the cell door."

She gaped at him for a moment, then broke into rolling guffaws. "Was that a threat, Miles?"

"Call it a friendly warning."

"I shoulda married you instead of that old coot, Wally. He never took me dancin' again after the wedding, that's why I got so fat."

"I'll see you at the festival dance," he told her seriously. "Save one for me."

"Hell, I'll save 'em all for you!" She laughed her way out the door.

Billy shook his head. "You've put your foot in it now, Sheriff. She'll hold you to it."

"Small price to pay for preserving the peace. Besides, maybe it'll make Wally jealous enough that he'll take up dancing with her again. Hi, Ms. Madison...be right with you."

He moved to close the door and caught sight of the pair outside. "Well, hey, Paula!" he called, and ambled out to join them.

People-watching is one of my favorite hobbies, but it's a lot more interesting if you can eavesdrop, too. I settled back in my chair and was idly contorting a paper clip into the outline of a pig when Crawford burst back inside, Les in tow.

"We had an agreement, Lester," Crawford was saying. "You swore you wouldn't miss any more classes. I think you'd better step into my office so we can talk about this."

When the door closed behind them, Billy and I were left in awkward silence. He got busy with a bottle of correction fluid, and I pretended interest in the decor of one of the two holding cells.

"Would you like to sample the view from the inside?" someone drawled in my ear. I jumped.

"Who the hell are you?" An impertinent question, since he was wearing a county uniform and obviously belonged there more than I did. But I hate people sneaking up on me.

His dark eyes assessed me. I thought it odd that clean-cut Crawford let him get away with wearing his hair so long he was able to draw it into a stubby ponytail.

"I'm Deputy Sheriff Cal Arnette," he answered solemnly. "Is there something I can help you with?"

"I have an appointment with Sheriff Crawford."

"I'll get him for you."

Billy swiveled in his chair. "Uh, Cal—"

"He's occupied at the moment," I informed the newcomer frostily. "I don't mind waiting." Which was a lie. Billy and I both flinched as angry voices rose from the back room.

"I see." Arnette settled himself on a corner of the big desk. "You're new in town, aren't you?"

I was torn between irritation and laughter. Laughter won.

"Do you realize you sound like a bad script from a spaghetti western? Next, you'll be telling me that this town ain't big enough for both of us, and to be on the noon stage outta here."

He crossed one booted foot over the other and graced me with a thin smile. "Not at all. And what was your name?"

Billy apparently felt the need to step into the fray. "Miss Madison, Cal. I forgot her first name, but it's something kinda weird." He blushed to the tips of his ears and looked at me in mute horror.

I smiled. "That's okay, Billy. It's definitely an unusual name. Would you please tell the sheriff that I had to leave—"

At that moment, the door to the inner sanctum swung open and Lester slouched out, closely followed by Crawford. The younger man looked sullen as he hurried out the door.

Crawford watched him go, then gave Arnette a light slap on the shoulder. "How's it going, Cal? Sorry about the overtime. Taylor, I'm glad you're still here. Y'all been introduced?"

"Sort of," I muttered.

"Fine. Come on back. Cal, why don't you put on a pot of coffee?"

The sheriff's cubicle was crowded with furniture and reeked of pipe smoke, despite the open window beside his desk. Rusty filing cabinets hunched in a corner, and an old army cot stood against one wall.

"I sometimes spend the night here if we have a prisoner out front," Crawford explained, noticing my interest. "Saves wear and tear on the deputies. Especially now, since I'm shorthanded. Nelson picked a hell of a time to retire, right before the festival."

I shuddered. "Lester told me about your, ah, annual event."

"Didn't appeal to you, huh? Well, it's not as bad as it sounds, and it sure pumps up the county economy." He pushed a paperback book aside to reach for his humidor, and I noticed the title. *Cat Among the Pigeons.*

"You're a Christie fan?"

"Devoted. Dame Agatha and I are old friends. You?"

"For as long as I can remember. But—"

Crawford leaned back in his chair, tamping tobacco into his pipe. "I seem more the Robert Ludlum type, is that it? Sex, blood and guts?" He considered me for a moment, holding a flame to the pipe bowl and puffing smoke from one corner of his mouth. "Critics today claim Christie's work was sadly lacking in any real literary quality. Beats me. She concocted some good puzzles, don't you think? And what I admire most is the ability she had to bring her characters to life. Some writers, even well respected ones, never quite pull that off." He lifted one white eyebrow. "Take your novels, for instance."

I tried not to feel immediately defensive. "What about them?"

"Your characters are terrific. Shirley? In the last one? Oh, yeah, I've known women just like her. That was tough to do without turning her into a stereotype, but you pulled it off."

I relaxed a little. "Thank you."

"Far as I can tell," he continued, "the only problem you have is with cops."

I fumbled out a cigarette and lit it, squinting at him through our mingled smoke. "You didn't like my cops." It wasn't a question, and I really didn't expect, or want, an answer.

"Who the hell *would* like your cops?" he asked. "Arrogant, stupid bastards. Did a cop steal a candy cane from your stroller or something?"

"I don't have anything against the police." My defenses were melting into genuine concern. "Is that really the way they come across? No one ever mentioned it before."

"Maybe most people see us that way." He leaned back a little further, the chair tilting precariously. "Which brings me to my proposition."

I smiled a little. "Hey, I'm a Houston girl, remember? Should I reach for my Mace?"

"Keep it in your pocket...it's not that kind of proposition. What I'm trying to do is offer you a job. Temporary, of course."

I blinked. "Me? What kind of job?"

"Deputy sheriff."

Chapter Three

MY FINGERS SPASMED, and the cigarette dropped to the floor. I made a dive for it.

"Deputy?" I panted, rising from beneath his desk.

"Why not?"

"There's a long list of why nots. I'm not qualified, I have no training. Good Lord, you can't pin a badge on a virtual stranger."

"As the high sheriff, Ms. Madison, I can deputize the grade school janitor, if I've a mind to. In fact, I did just that last year at festival time. He, um, doesn't care to do it again."

"Why not?" I asked suspiciously. "Did a snake bite him?"

Crawford laughed. "Nothing like that. Come on, Ms. Madison, how about it? You said you needed a job, and I could sure use the help right now."

I didn't know what to say.

The sheriff tapped ashes into the trashcan. "You think it over and let me know, but soon, okay? I really think you might enjoy it, and you just might learn something about cops that would help with your future novels."

Belatedly remembering why I had come to his office, I opened my mouth to ask, but he beat me to the punch. "By the way, your Volkswagen has a broken axle, among a few lesser problems. Roger estimates between eight and nine hundred dollars."

I groaned. I thought of Mom's funeral expenses, which had wiped out my paltry savings account; of the soft real estate market in Houston, which meant it would probably be months before I found a buyer for her house; of Annie's outright refusal to send me an advance until I'd coughed up the final three chapters of my latest work. And, most important, I considered my absolute determination, deranged though it might be, to remain in Perdue until someone—if not Tessa, then someone else—could answer one very pressing question for me. I had worked a lot of odd jobs over the years, first to put myself through college, and then to cover expenses while I peddled my first novel. Freelance reporting, census taking, delivering phone books, telephone soliciting for a dance studio. Name it, I had done it. But I had never been a cop. Well, why the hell not?

I sighed. "This deputy job. How much does it pay, and where do I sign up?"

Beaming, Crawford swore me in before I could change my mind.

Arnette brought in two cups of coffee as the sheriff dug a spare badge out of his desk drawer. Crawford instructed him to stick around for a few minutes, pending assignment, and the deputy nodded, curiosity oozing from every pore. When he'd shut the door again, the sheriff gazed out the window for a moment as I pinned the star to my t-shirt.

"Do I get a uniform?"

"Probably not," he said distractedly. "Ms. Madison—"

"Come on, aren't we past that stage by now? It's Taylor."

"Okay. Taylor, then. Up to now, I've done my best not to poke my nose into your business, but I think the time has come for you to tell me what brought you to Perdue."

"I explained that last night."

"Yeah. And I was with you last night when your aunt tossed you out of her house, remember?" He leaned across the desk. "I've known Tessa Potter since fifth grade. Wood, too. Neither of them has ever mentioned having a niece. Granted, Tessa and I had a falling out some years ago, and it was only about six months ago that we started patching things up. We're pretty good friends now, in fact. But she's never said a word to me about you."

I took a breath. "My mother—"

"I called her Sadie," he put in. "She and Tessa were only two years apart in age, and I was a year ahead of Sarah in school." He cracked a grin. "Now, I'd have been lettin' down the male species if I hadn't gotten to know the two prettiest girls in Perdue."

Still trying to decide how much I wanted to tell him, I stalled with a question. "You said you and Tessa had a falling out. What about?"

He suddenly became very busy refilling his pipe. "Sarah."

I choked on my coffee, which was preferable to drinking it. It wasn't as bad as Hank's, but it would still gag a maggot. "Mom? What about her?"

"I dated her in high school. Matter of fact, we went steady our senior year."

"Really?" This was fascinating. Mom had never talked about her youth. I tried to picture my stern, irascible mother as a giggly teenager, wearing this man's class ring on a chain around her neck, smooching in the back seat of his Chevy. "I take it you broke up. What happened?"

He flushed. "Tessa. She, um, grew up."

I took a sip of the gruesome coffee to hide a smile. "I get it. Bratty little sister fills out. It's an old story."

"Is it? Well, it wasn't to me. Took me totally by surprise." He sighed. "Poor Sarah was so hurt. And furious with Tessa, as if she'd deliberately stolen me away."

"Well, did she?"

"Hell, no. Tessa was so mad at me for breaking Sarah's heart that it was two years before she'd have anything to do with me. Sarah had moved away right after graduation, and Tessa blamed me for that, too."

"Could that be it? God, I never would've imagined something so trivial."

He cocked his head. "What are you talking about?"

I dug in my backpack for the letter and handed it over without another word. I could have quoted it to him verbatim, I had read it so many times in the past week.

Dear Sarah,

I find it hard to believe that the tiny infant I once held in my arms is now a grown woman. I have no doubt you've been a perfect mother, just as you've been perfect in every other aspect of your life. Oh, dear, that sounded like a snipe, didn't it? Guess we're getting too old for sibling rivalry. I'm enclosing another check. Please don't send this one back. The ranch is doing very well, and Wood never stints on my spending money. Use it to buy her something nice for a graduation gift. If she's planning to go on to college, let me know, and I'll send more to help cover the tuition. I have a right to help her, Sarah. Your pride is misplaced if you use it to deprive Taylor of the monetary assistance I can so easily provide.

I wish you would write to me, but please, can't we drop the old argument? I'll come to Houston any time you like, but the two of you simply cannot come here. Not now. Why can't you understand?

Send a picture of Taylor, would you? She must be beautiful. You and I were certainly pretty at that age, and her father is a very handsome man.

Oh, Sarah, can't you stop holding grudges? We could be close again, if only you'd let go of the past.
Your sister,
Tessa.

Crawford handed the letter back to me, his expression unreadable. "This was dated ten years ago."

I nodded. "My eighteenth birthday. Mom must have torn up the check, or sent it back. I scratched for every penny, all the way through college." He nodded for me to go on, so I did, feeling the secret's weight easing from my shoulders as I finally shared it with someone else. "After Mom died, I was packing up her things so I could put the house on the market. I've helped her keep up the payments for years, but I knew I wouldn't be able to swing it on my own. I found this letter tucked under the lining of her jewelry box. What's baffling is why she didn't throw it away, if she really hated Tessa so much."

"Maybe she wanted you to find it. Someday."

"Maybe." I doubted it.

"So, you came to meet an aunt you never knew you had, is that it?" I had the strange feeling that he was hanging on my every word.

"Not really," I said. "I came to find out from Tessa who my father is. It's obvious from the letter that she knows."

"You mean you don't?"

I shrugged. "Mom wouldn't talk about him, except to say he had abandoned us while I was still in diapers." I took a deep breath, striving for calm. "You said before that you and Tessa had become friends again. I hate to ask, but do you think you could find out why she won't talk to me?"

He was shaking his head. "Already tried. I phoned her this morning to get the scoop on what that little scene last night was all about."

"And?"

"She hung up on me. Twice."

I felt the anger rising again. "Damn it, Sheriff, I have a right to know his name, don't I? Don't you think I'm entitled to at least that much? I have no idea what Tessa's problem is, and at this point, I'm not sure I care. But she'll tell me what I came to find out, or I'll stay in Perdue until we both rot."

A knock at the door interrupted whatever he might have been about to say, and Billy stuck his head in. "'Scuse me, Sheriff, but Cal needs to be goin', and you'd told him to hang around."

"Thanks, Billy. We'll talk later, Taylor. Come on."

Billy seemed pleased when Crawford told him the news. "You're mighty pretty for a deputy," he told me.

I smiled at him. "Thank you." I trailed him into the front office. "So, Sheriff, do I wear jeans or what?"

"Better keep your shirt on, too," advised an amused voice at my shoulder. "We have decency laws in this town." Damn the man, always sneaking up on me.

"Cut it out, Cal. Jeans are fine, Taylor, but I can't let you carry a handgun yet."

"Yet?" I wasn't sure I was thrilled by the prospect, now or in the future. I had researched guns for my work, but had never so much as held a real one in my hand.

Crawford misinterpreted my reaction. "Don't get me wrong. You're a real deputy, and you're entitled, but I'd rather wait and let Cal take you out practice shooting a little first. He's a certified instructor."

"Glad to, boss," Cal said.

"Uh, yeah, great." I wasn't sure I wanted to be around Cal with a weapon in my possession. The sheriff was already shorthanded.

"So, Cal, how about taking Taylor out for a tour of the festival grounds? Get her used to the idea. We can't have our newest deputy fainting away at her first sight of a snake."

"Thanks heaps," I mumbled.

The patrol car was a nondescript beige sedan with an old-fashioned red bubble set on top, like a large maraschino cherry. Inside, a metal grill separated the front seat from the back, and the mingled odors of urine, sweat, and vomit permeated the upholstery. I immediately rolled down the passenger side window.

"Damn," Cal muttered as he got behind the wheel. "I hate this car."

I couldn't say I blamed him.

"Is there a 7-11 nearby?" I asked as he eased into the street. "I'm out of cigarettes."

"Nearest 7-11 is in Lubbock, but I'll swing by Posey's."

Posey's turned out to be a small grocery store situated in a prime location at one corner of the square, its interior an odd blend of modern convenience and old-time general store. Bright fluorescent lights illuminated most of the nooks and crannies, but the cash register was of the hand-crank variety. A sleek freezer section was well stocked with frozen pizzas and Lean Cuisine entrees, but the canned goods were lined up on floor-to-ceiling shelves behind the counter. A metal display bin was crammed with Mars Bars and Snickers, while a row of huge glass jars lined the countertop, brimming with gumballs, rock candy, and soft taffy wrapped in twists of waxed paper.

An elderly woman perched on a high stool near the cash register, her nose buried in a tattered paperback entitled *Lust's Naked Passion.* She looked up reluctantly as we came in, nodded at Cal, then examined me unabashedly, her beady eyes taking in my badge. Her interest in me was demonstrated by the rapidity with which she slammed shut the book, not even bothering to mark her place.

Cal obliged with introductions.

"Call me Bo," cooed Bonita Posey. "I'll be eighty-two next Monday."

"Congratulations," I offered. Cal was engrossed in a display of corn nuts, leaving me to my own resources.

"You're supposed to say that I simply can't be that old," Bo informed me. "Everyone else does. Trying to stay on my good side, you know. I hold a lot of folks by the short hairs around here."

I was startled into a laugh, and she cackled along with me, a large wart on her chin bobbing.

"Well, you don't look a day over eighty, and I'd like a pack of cigarettes, please."

She shook a gnarled finger at me. "Shouldn't smoke. It'll kill you." Scrabbling beneath the counter, she produced a pack of unfiltered Camels and lit one, blowing a perfect smoke ring. "How old are you, gal? Twenty-three?"

"Twenty-eight."

"I reckon you've got a few years to go. What brand?" As she placed my choice on the counter top, I gave in to an irresistible impulse and requested a can of green beans. Cal looked up in surprise, but Bo nodded briskly and produced a long-handled hook. Quick as a cat's sneeze, she snagged a can from the top-most shelf. It toppled obediently, and she made a neat left-handed catch.

"Wow," I marveled. "A genuine can of corn."

"Beans," Cal pointed out, looking confused.

Bo's cheeks crinkled like withered apples. "Obviously not a baseball fan," she said, cocking a thumb at Cal. "But you are, right, sweetie?"

"And Bo knows baseball," I joked.

We gave each other a delighted high-five, then I paid for my purchases and followed Cal back to the car.

"Crazy old lady," he muttered, starting the engine.

"She's not, though, is she? I'll bet more than a few people are scared of her."

He smiled. "Bo is what you might call a powerful influence around here." He pulled away from the curb. "Doesn't hurt that she probably has more money stashed away in her sock drawer than the local bank has in its vault. What the hell was all that about corn?"

I shook my head pityingly. "I'll bet you're a football fan, aren't you? Well, 'can of corn' is a baseball term, referring to a pop fly that's easy to catch because a player doesn't have to run for it. The ball just seems to fall straight down into his glove. The phrase originated from the method of retrieving stock in old county stores."

"I get it." Cal shook his head. "You're one strange woman, you know that? Hang on, now. I'm taking a shortcut."

From that announcement, I expected a back road. A foolish notion. We had reached the outskirts of town, and even as he spoke, Cal jerked the steering wheel sharply to the left, hurling us into an open pasture. I hastily fastened my seat belt, but that didn't prevent my teeth from chattering like demented chipmunks as the car jounced across the rutted field. Before I could catch my breath to scream at him, we had left the pasture behind. Cal touched the brake imperceptibly, then swung onto a narrow path, unfortunately coated with loose gravel. We hit a pothole roughly the size of the Grand Canyon, and my teeth caught the edge of my tongue. I yelped, but the sound was drowned out by the rattle of gravel against the hubcaps. Cal grimaced fixedly, probably clamping his own teeth together, but obviously enjoying my terror. I flashed back to grade school and a boy named Jimmy Hollister who had dangled a rubber spider, hoping to hear me squeal, and wondered if males ever outgrew this particular brand of macho insensitivity.

Determined to provide as little entertainment as possible, I pried my eyes from the treacherous road ahead and concentrated on the plastic charm hanging from Cal's key ring. It was bouncing against the steering column with almost clockwork regularity, and I hoped that watching it might send me into a blissful hypnotic state. It might have worked, too, if the picture painted upon the charm had been anything besides a rattlesnake. Honestly, these people were obsessed with reptiles.

With a final squealing of tires, Cal whipped onto a paved surface and brought the patrol car to a stop, grinning Jimmy Hollister's grin, silently daring me to have hysterics.

"More fun than a roller coaster," I said lightly, unbuckling my seat belt and opening the door. "Is there a Ferris wheel, too?"

It was as if I had passed a rite of initiation. Something eased between us. "Matter of fact, there is." He pointed.

And so there was, its brightly colored cars suspended motionless in the morning sunshine. Beyond, a sea of canvas tents billowed, interspersed with more rides: a carousel crammed with newly painted horses, an Octopus, a Whip. It wasn't Astroworld, but it was far more than I had expected of a festival hosted by a county the size of Derrick.

"I told you, it's a big tourist draw," Cal said, as if he'd read my thoughts. "We get folks from as far away as Maine."

"You're kidding." I was still gawking. "What in the world is that?" I indicated an unusual building off to our right. Constructed of rough-hewn stone and timber, it looked like a cross between a fort and a medieval insane asylum.

"We call it our county auditorium, for lack of a better label. Perdue's founder had a town meeting hall in mind when he built it, but now it's used for everything from little theater productions to V.F.W. meetings. I'll take you through it later. Let's go check out the grounds first."

The field that served as the festival site was surrounded by a tall chain-link fence, but the double gate stood open. I could smell cotton candy and something else, unidentifiable, but delectable. People looked up from their various tasks as we passed, a few waving at Cal, most studying me with undisguised curiosity. Cal ducked into one of the larger tents and I followed. As soon as I stepped inside, the elusive aroma that had beckoned surrounded me in tempting waves, reminding me that I had skimped on breakfast.

A stubby man with a prickly gray crew cut stood behind an immense kettle of hot oil. As we watched, he lifted from it a wire basket filled with crisp nuggets of fried chicken, which he dumped into a bowl lined with paper towel. I edged closer, inhaling the ambrosial fragrance. My stomach growled softly.

Cal sniffed appreciatively. "Starting a little early, aren't you, Dave? No tourists until day after tomorrow."

The man chuckled. "Testing out a different recipe. The wife wanted to try some new spices." He wiped his glistening forehead with a wadded handkerchief and peered at me. "Who's your companion? Is that a badge she's wearin'?"

"Sorry. Dave Underwood, this is Taylor Madison. The sheriff hired her to help out during the festival."

"He what?" Underwood roared. "Of all the damn fool notions— beg pardon, miss." He was obviously asking forgiveness for the 'damn,' not for his sentiments. "A woman's got no business in police work. Has Miles flipped his lid?"

Cal remained unperturbed. "We're starting off a brand new century, Dave. If you have any objections, take them up with Sheriff Crawford. In the meantime, I'll volunteer to be your first guinea pig." He grabbed a napkin from a stack and helped himself to a piece of the chicken. "Want some, Taylor?"

My raised consciousness was still reeling from Underwood's outrageous proclamation, but I reached greedily for the food anyway. I could defend my sex later, after demands of the flesh had been satisfied. One bite convinced me that, male chauvinist or not, Dave Underwood could have put Colonel Sanders out of business in a week. Boneless and tender, the chicken had a light aftertaste, not unpleasant, that reminded me of fish. Must have been one of the wife's new spices. I reminded myself that the master chef had referred to his spouse in the same manner he might have mentioned a power saw he owned, and tried to think less kindly of him. But I took another bite of the wonderful chicken anyway.

Cal polished off his piece and reached for another. "Where did you get the meat?"

Underwood was mixing more batter. "Oh, the skinners started early this year."

"Who are the Skinners?" I mumbled to Cal with my mouth full. "Local chicken farmers?"

He frowned at me for a moment, obviously puzzled, then his eyebrows shot up and I was uneasy to glimpse a flicker of Jimmy Hollister's devilment.

"Snake skinners, honey," Underwood informed me before Cal could decide how best to enjoy the revelation. "I usually have to experiment with the meat we have left in the freezer, but what you're eating was fresh-killed this very morning. Better that way."

I muttered something and rushed for the tent flap, one hand pressed hard over my mouth. Cal's laughter and Underwood's surprised exclamation drifted after me.

"That was a dirty trick," I told Cal after a visit to one of the porta-cans. The cup of Coke he handed me was welcome, but I made it clear it wasn't sufficient apology.

"C'mon, Taylor, I really thought you knew. Besides, it's not like I poisoned you."

"It isn't? Last I heard, rattlesnakes were poisonous."

"Venomous," he corrected. "Toadstools are poisonous. The meat you ate wasn't either one. Now, cheer up. Want to check out some of the crafts booths? I'll bet you'd like that."

I clutched the paper cup so hard it crumpled, resisting the urge to fling its contents at him. "I probably would at that," I replied with deceptive calm. "Crafts couldn't possibly offend the little lady's sensibilities, could they?"

"Okay, I had that coming. Don't pay any mind to Underwood, by the way. The sheriff'll set him straight."

Slightly appeased, I allowed him to show me some of the booths. None were yet in actual operation, but the proprietors were more than happy to show off their wares while getting a close-up glimpse of Derrick County's newest novelty: a female deputy.

Shaking offered hands and acknowledging introductions, I browsed through belts, hatbands and boots fashioned from rattlesnake skin. There were also bracelets, earrings, barrettes and chokers. Wallets and bolos, money clips and cigarette cases, dog collars and cufflinks.

One wizened little man—the winner, he informed me proudly, of the "largest snake" trophy for three years running—offered to take me on a hunt.

"I'll show ya all the best hidey-holes," he confided, as Cal smothered a smirk. "You got a snakebite kit yet? Shame on you, Cal. Here ya go, missy. A little present from old Arnold."

I turned the object over in my hand. It was a cylinder made of reddish brown rubber, rounded on both ends.

"Open her up," Arnold urged, and I gave it a twist. It separated into two pieces, and I began to cautiously explore the items crammed into the hollow core: a small razor blade, a length of surgical gauze, a tiny vial of antiseptic, a sterile bandage.

"Hang onto that, little gal," Arnold told me solemnly. "It might save your life someday."

Cal was tugging at my arm, but I ignored him. "I don't understand. What's all this for?"

Arnold dribbled tobacco juice into a Styrofoam cup and squinted at me. "Let's say a rattler up and bites you on the leg. First thing you gotta do is stop the poison from spreading, right? That's what the gauze is for. Tie it above the wound, nice and tight. A turn-ee-kit, see?

"Then, to get the poison out, you use the razor to make an X-shaped cut on top of the fang marks. It's best if you got someone with you to suck out the venom, but if you're alone, you can't always reach the spot yourself. That's where the container comes in handy."

He took half of the rubber cylinder away from me and squeezed it, pressing its mouth against my forearm before releasing the pressure. When he pulled it away, it had left a quarter-sized hickey on my skin. "See there? Pretty good suction, though not as good as a human mouth. It'll get most of the stuff out, though. Splash on a little of this junk," he continued, indicating the vial, "slap on a Band-Aid, and you're good as cured."

"Thanks, Arnold," Cal put in, snatching the kit and stuffing it into his pocket. "I promised to show Taylor the pits, and then we have to get going. See you tomorrow."

"Thank you," I repeated weakly and allowed Cal to drag me away. Once we were out of earshot, he propped me against the side of a vacant booth and, digging the kit from his pocket, tossed it into a nearby litter barrel.

"Hey!" I protested. "I might need that!"

"If a snake bites you, Taylor, what you need is a hospital. As fast as you can get to one. Those stupid kits have caused more permanent injury to people than snakes ever have."

"How?"

"Well, for one thing, slowing down the blood flow is a good idea, but a badly applied tourniquet will stop it, and you don't want to do that. For another, you definitely don't want to cut the wound. It's likely you'll end up damaging a tendon or a nerve. Shit, I wish we could outlaw those hokey kits, but the tourists love them."

I must have still looked skeptical because he grabbed my shoulders and gave me a little shake. "Forget all the western movies, Taylor. People don't fall down and die just because a snake bites them. A rattler never injects all its venom in one bite, but even if you take multiple strikes, you'll have at least an hour to get to a hospital, usually more. Now, would you like to see the snake pits, or not?

I agreed more readily than I would have an hour before, having grown used to the sight of the leathery skin. Besides, I felt the need to dispel my reputation as a naïve city slicker.

The gigantic steel stock tanks were set up in the largest tent, and I heard the noise while we were still some distance away. I shuddered, but kept walking. Cal held the flap open for me, then led the way to the nearest tank. I peered cautiously over the edge.

In case I was beholding a preview of Hell, I sent up a silent vow to lead a better life. The long bodies slithered over and around and under each other, filling my ears with the rasping of rough skin. Cal poked a long stick into the midst of the writhing mass and several snakes coiled defensively, their tails whipping into action. The resulting sound was nothing like a baby's rattle, as I had vaguely expected, but more like the buzzing of an overloaded electrical circuit.

As if from far away, I heard Cal explaining that these were Western Diamondbacks, directing my attention to the diamond-shaped markings that decorated their hides. I pried my fingers from the rim of the tank and turned away, desperately seeking something else on which to focus my attention.

"What are those people doing?" I asked, pointing out a group huddled on one side of the tent, their backs to us.

Cal took my arm. "Come on and see. It's an interesting procedure."

I hung back. "They're not skinning...?"

"No, no. C'mon."

I succeeded in wedging myself into the crowd, and by the time I saw what was going on, I was trapped. As I watched in helpless horror, a man reached his gloved hand into an aquarium and pulled out a writhing snake. I recoiled, bumping into the spectator behind me.

"He's fixin' to milk it," someone whispered in my ear.

"Like a cow?" I squeaked. It made perfect sense, at that. What more appropriate beverage to accompany fried snake than a nice, cold glass of snake's milk?

"Naw, it's not really milk. It's venom. He's takin' the venom."

"Why?" I was whispering, too, as the man hooked the snake's fangs over the rim of a wide-mouthed vial.

Cal had made his way to my side and took over the explanation. "The venom is sent to research facilities, toxicology labs. They use it, among other things, to produce antivenin."

"Oh."

The milker spotted us. "Howdy, Cal. Want a turn?"

Cal chuckled. "Not today, Charlie, thanks. I'll pump a few later on in the week, okay?"

Charlie nodded and began squeezing a point somewhere behind the reptile's head. Translucent fluid dribbled into the container. I closed my eyes.

BY SIX THAT evening, Cal correctly deduced that I'd had enough of snakes for one day, and offered to take me back into town for a harmless hamburger. But the instant he started the engine, a frantic voice began babbling over the radio.

"Unit two. Base to unit two. Aw, c'mon, Les, where are you?"

Cal sighed and keyed the mike. "This is Cal. What's up, Billy?"

"Cal? I thought unit two was Lester's."

"Not today, it isn't. What do you want?"

"I want Lester. No, I mean, the sheriff wants Lester. He's been lookin' for him all over."

"He's not here," Cal replied. "Two, out."

"Aw, Cal, wait a minute. Don't you know where he is? Sheriff

Crawford is mad about something, and if he doesn't find Les, he'll be mad at me instead."

"I'm not Forman's keeper, Billy. Now, I'm turnin' off the radio and goin' to get some dinner. Two, out." He punched a button, cutting Billy off in mid-squawk.

Somehow, I doubted this was recognized radio procedure, but the sarcastic comment died on my lips. Cal was taking a nice, paved road back to town, and the last thing I wanted was to summon up an irritated Jimmy Hollister.

The café was packed. Rita, still on duty, looked exhausted as she cleared a table for us at a recently vacated booth in the rear corner. Merle Haggard, never a favorite of mine, twanged a cheatin' song from the jukebox. I scanned the menu while Rita rested one hip on the table edge in an attempt to give her feet a brief respite. I recognized the pose from my own waitressing days, and was glad I had accepted Crawford's offer instead of pursuing a job here.

"Hey, Cal, have you seen Lester tonight?" Rita asked. It seemed a casual question, but Cal reacted violently.

"Goddammit, no, I haven't!" he roared, slamming the menu card against the tabletop. "Why does everyone seem to think I keep the guy in my back pocket?"

Rita's eyes blazed. "I know you're jealous of him, an' I can't say as I blame you. He's gonna beat the pants off you in the election, and you know it." She snatched up our menus. "Bein' a fancy college boy don't make you better than the rest of us, Cal Arnette. Might do you good to remember that. Lester may not have your schoolin', but I never heard him curse at a lady neither. I'll just bring y'all a coupla burgers, so you can eat 'em quick and make room for someone else to sit." She marched off, quivering with indignation.

"Well," I said, after a moment. "So much for small town life being boring."

Cal's glower faded. "Sorry. I shouldn't have started that. I get so blasted tired of trying to keep track of Lester."

"I don't get it. Why should anyone have to keep track of him?"

"Beats me." Cal sighed, shredding a paper napkin. "All I know is, every time I turn around, Crawford is asking me to check up on the golden boy."

"What election was she talking about?"

"Sheriff's election. Crawford's decided not to run again in November."

I fished out my cigarettes, and he pushed the ashtray toward me.

"So, you and Lester are going to face off, is that it?"

"Maybe. We've both talked about it."

"Oh. Well, good luck, I guess."

Cal grimaced. "Luck won't have much to do with it. Most likely, whoever Crawford decides to back will win. As far as the people around here are concerned, he can do no wrong. Anyone will tell you he's the best sheriff Derrick County has ever had."

Rita stomped up to the booth and practically threw our plates at us. "No dessert? Good." She left.

I picked up a rather soggy french fry and ate it. "So, who's he going to support?"

Cal salted his burger and dumped catsup on his plate. "He says he hasn't decided yet, but that's a lot of crap. He'll choose Lester."

"What makes you so sure of that?"

"For one thing, Crawford and Lester's dad have been friends for years. You'd think they shared custody of Les, the way Crawford looks out for him. More practically, Les has a year's seniority on me, and that would count for something in any department. Besides, Lester is more the clean-cut, all-American-boy type. A Crawford clone."

He took an angry bite of burger. After he'd chewed and swallowed, he swiped his mouth and shook his head. "No, that was unfair. Crawford doesn't care that I'm half Mexican. But Lester was an M.P. in the U.S. Army, and I was a law student. I think the sheriff's idea is that Les has been heading for this profession from the beginning, but he thinks I'm just settling." He smiled tightly. "Copping out, so to speak."

"Are you?" I asked bluntly.

His brown eyes met mine squarely. "No. I wasn't cut out to be a lawyer, and having this job has only confirmed that. I've come to believe that law enforcement is more important on a basic level than the slice of the justice system you experience in a courtroom. I really believe I'd make a better sheriff than Lester, and I don't mean for that to sound as conceited as it does. I also think I might have a chance at winning an unbiased election.

"What I really wish is that Crawford would stay out of it, and let each of us run our own campaign. But that's not going to happen. The people expect him to have a say in his replacement, sort of like a king passing his crown to the favored prince." He sighed, and took a sip of water. "Okay, enough about that. What's your secret?"

"Secret?"

"I haven't asked questions all day, but it's really beginning to bug me. You show up out of nowhere and all of a sudden—bang! You're hired on as a deputy. I'm pretty darn sure you've never been a cop before. Thought at first you were just a tourist who'd had some bad luck, but even Crawford wouldn't hire a total stranger."

I had to smile a little at that, since it was, after all, virtually what he had done.

"I heard it was something to do with Tessa Potter," he went on.

I blinked in surprise.

"C'mon, Taylor, it's a small town, as you've pointed out to me at least a dozen times today." He chuckled. "Besides, I ran into Mabel Donnely this morning while she was setting up her crafts booth."

"And what did she tell you?"

"Not much, but enough to put a good whet on my curiosity. So, spill it. Clear up the mystery."

"Long story. Maybe I'll tell you some other time."

Cal shrugged and polished off the last bite on his plate. "Whatever." He checked his watch and sighed. "I've got to see if Les made it back by the office. He's still got my patrol car, and I want it back, damn it. His stinks like a cesspool."

"So, why did he take yours?"

Cal rolled his eyes. "Because his stinks like a cesspool, why do you think? He 'borrows' mine every chance he gets...easier than cleaning his own. Want me to drop you off somewhere?"

"Thanks, but I can walk. It's a nice night, and I guess I don't have to worry about being mugged in a place like this."

He groaned. "I hope not. I know who'd have to write the report." He tipped an imaginary hat and ambled away. I noticed he'd dropped enough money on the table to pay for both meals plus a generous tip, and thought about telling Rita there was obviously a gentleman lurking somewhere inside the man.

I kept my walk to the hardware store brisk. The night was growing colder, and I supposed I was going to have to break down and buy myself a decent coat. Or, maybe going back to Houston would be an even better idea.

Hank was closing the store when I arrived. He looked up from tallying the day's receipts and gave me a friendly greeting.

"Sheriff dropped these by for you." He lugged my suitcase and my laptop from beneath the counter. "Told me you'd hired on. Good for you!" He handed me a key. "This fits the back door. Don't want you to be locked out if I'm not here. Deputies work some strange hours."

I was touched, not only that he was so concerned with my convenience after I had practically thrust myself into his keeping, but that he would trust someone he barely knew with a key to his store.

"I reckon Tessa must've been tickled pink to see you," he went on, and I heard the subtle question.

I couldn't take offense. Poor man, he had to be confused, since he obviously hadn't yet spoken to Mabel Donnely. I also couldn't think of a way to answer, so instead, I offered to pay rent for the room.

"Shucks, now, don't be silly. It's just a dusty old storeroom, not the Holiday Inn." He looked at his watch. "Well, I'd best be gettin' on home. The missus has dinner on the table by now."

Bless him, he knew how to take a hint.

Hazel was glad to see me, but didn't seem overjoyed. I had a feeling she had spent a delightful day, exploring every piece of junk in the room. She loved squeezing into tight places. I replenished her food and water, then sat on the wide windowsill for a time, stroking her soft fur and looking out over the lights of Perdue. They didn't stretch very far into the distance, and I could sense the miles of uninhabited blackness beyond. I shivered, suddenly feeling lonely and very far from home.

Footsteps sounded out in the hall, and I heard the rattle of a key in the lock. My neighbor was home. A few minutes later, I heard a phone ring, and was struck by an idea. I forced myself to wait a decent interval, not wanting to interrupt the call, then crossed through the bathroom and knocked on the adjoining door.

"Excuse me," I called, "but I wondered if I could borrow..."

The door was yanked open. Cal Arnette looked every bit as startled as I felt.

"What the hell?" we said in unison.

"Don't tell me this is where you're holed up." Cal had already removed his uniform shirt, and seemed to suddenly realize that. He hastily closed the door part way, but not before I had gotten a delicious glimpse of a very nicely tanned and muscled chest.

Dirty old lady, I scolded myself, trying to remember why I had knocked in the first place.

"You wanted to borrow something?" he prompted. "A cup of sugar? Five bucks? My rubber boots? Give me a hint."

"Your phone."

"Oh. In that case, you're in luck. Hang on a second." The door closed, and when it opened again, he had pulled on a Texas A&M T-shirt.

He stepped back and I eased past him into a small living area. Neater than I would have expected of a bachelor, but borderline shabby. The plaid loveseat clashed with a floral-patterned armchair, and one leg of the scarred coffee table was braced with a paperback book.

Cal pointed to the phone. "Help yourself. I've got to go back out for a few minutes." He yawned hugely. "Sorry...I've gotten maybe seven hours of sleep in the last forty-eight, and I have to be at the festival grounds by six a.m. tomorrow. Some men are coming out from Lubbock to finish setting up the rides."

"Oh, should I be ready then, too?"

"Naw, one guy can handle this. Get some rest while you can 'cause things around here'll really be hopping over the next few days."

"Don't you mean slithering?"

He winked, then left.

I retrieved my laptop and got the modem hooked up to the phone jack.

Sitting on the floor with the little computer balanced in my lap, I typed out a three-page e-mail message to my agent, Annie, letting her know what I had gotten myself into. She would probably laugh all the way through it, thinking it served me right, but it felt good to share it with her, just the same. I wasn't quite so alone anymore.

A quick check of my Internet directory showed that the number printed on the phone would allow me to dial a Lubbock access number without incurring long distance charges. "I thank you, and my maxed-out credit card thanks you," I mumbled, keying in the number. Through the laptop's speakers, I heard the rapid beeps of dialing, the whirring of a line ringing somewhere, a click, and the reassuring tone-then-static of a modem finding its soul mate.

Afterward, I even managed to work on chapter fifteen of my latest endeavor for an hour or so, before succumbing to my sagging eyelids and curling up on the lumpy little rollaway next to Hazel.

I didn't sleep well. Either the bed had shrunk, or I had grown a few inches taller. Hazel, who kept trying to dig a nest in my stomach, wasn't any help.

Needless to say, I was cranky as hell by the time I awoke to the shrill ring of a phone. Cal's phone, I realized groggily. It kept ringing, and the pillow I clamped over my ears didn't help at all.

After twenty rings, I staggered through the bathroom and pounded the adjoining door with both fists.

"Damn it, Cal, are you going to answer that?" The phone rang again. And again.

I finally remembered what Cal had said about getting to the festival grounds before six o'clock this morning. The phone was still jangling in that frantic way phones seem to develop when no one will answer them, so I twisted the doorknob, not really surprised to discover Cal hadn't bothered with the lock on his side, and lunged at the noisy beast.

"What?" I shouted into the receiver. Miss Manners would have been highly offended by my complete disregard of telephone etiquette.

"Christ, Cal, what took you so long? You've gotta get over here right away. Oh, God."

A slight lisp clued me in to the identity of the caller.

"Billy, this is Taylor. Cal's not here."

There was a slight gasp at the other end of the line. "Ms. Madison? What are you—?"

I am by no means a morning person, but even in my presently foggy state, I grasped what the boy must be assuming. But Billy was already babbling again, so an explanation would have to wait.

"Whoa," I told him. "Slow down, I can't understand what you're saying. Who's Miss Stenson?"

I heard him take a deep breath, and when he spoke again, it was more slowly, though his tone remained urgent.

"Dorothy Stenson. She's the sheriff's housekeeper. She—she..."

"Spit it out, Billy!"

"She says he's dead! She says Sheriff Crawford is dead!"

Chapter Four

I FELT AS IF someone had given me a hard punch to the stomach. Billy was crying now in great, gasping sobs.

"Billy, wait," I finally managed to say. "Is she sure he's dead? Has she called a doctor?"

"I don't know." He sounded surprised. "I didn't think of that. What should I do now? I can't find Lester or Cal, and I don't know what to do!" His voice was rising in panic, and I stood shivering in my nightshirt, feeling helpless.

"I'll be there as soon as I can, and we'll figure something out. Meanwhile, you get a doctor over to Crawford's house. Fast. Got that?"

"Sure, I'll do it right now." I found myself listening to a dial tone. When that boy said right now, he meant it.

I threw on a sweat suit and hit the door at a dead run. Action was preferable to thinking.

It didn't take me long to cross the street. Billy was waiting outside, hopping from one foot to the other, so pale his pimples stood out like pinpricks of blood.

"Did you find a doctor?" I asked when I could catch my breath.

"I got hold of Doc's wife. She said she'd hunt him down and send him right over. He went to deliver a breech calf."

I sat down on the step. "Billy, I think in this case, a people doctor might've been a better choice than the local vet."

He shot me a disgusted look that shouted 'dumb city woman' as plain as day. "Doc Neil *is* a people doctor, Ms. Madison, but he and Doc Leonard share a building, and Doc Neil helps him out sometimes. More sick animals than sick folks around here." He stuck out his chin. "And if you'll pardon me saying so, ma'am, you'd better get going."

"Going? Where?"

"To the sheriff's house."

I stood up and backed away a little. "Me? What for? I'm not a doctor!"

"No, ma'am," he said patiently, "but you're a deputy, and right now, you're the only one I can find. It's procedure, you know, when there's a death." His lip quivered. "The sheriff would want me to follow procedure."

"I don't have a car." It sounded lame, even to me.

"Neither do I, but you can take that." He pressed a key into my hand and pointed.

That turned out to be a mo-ped of all things, and Billy gave me a little push in its direction, reeling off directions to Sheriff Crawford's house and assuring me that he'd send Cal or Les as soon as he could locate either of them. He sounded a lot steadier suddenly, as if passing the buck was therapeutic. It probably was, at that, but not for the recipient of said buck.

I had never been aboard a mo-ped in my life, but I had ridden a motorcycle, so I felt fairly confident about steering the little bike down the street. I was, however, highly conscious of what I must look like, my knees stuck out at ridiculous angles in order to accommodate my long legs to a machine obviously designed for a midget.

Crawford's house was a small, white wood-frame with a deep front porch and yellow trim. A bosomy woman, with hair that looked as if it had been dyed with black shoe polish, sat on the top step with one hand covering her eyes. She moved the hand when she heard the putter of Billy's mo-ped, and she gaped at me as I pulled into the driveway.

"Miss Stenson?" I called out, still trying to unkink my legs.

She stood and clutched at the front of her green print dress.

"You don't know me. I'm Taylor Madison, the new deputy." I felt my sweatshirt, realizing I had forgotten to pin on my badge. "Uh, you can call Billy to check, if you want."

"I was expecting Lester. Isn't Lester coming?"

"He'll be here any minute, I'm sure. And the doctor is on his way, too."

"No doctor can help him now." She opened the door. "I expect you'd better go on in, since you're here."

I hesitated. "Was it a heart attack?"

She shook her head.

Reluctantly, I climbed the steps.

"He's in the living room." She pointed inside, but stayed on the porch, hugging her elbows.

I stood in the foyer for a moment, feeling disoriented. The room smelled of lemon furniture polish and pipe tobacco, and I saw him as soon as my eyes had adjusted to the dim light that filtered through the front window.

Shivering, I approached the recliner. The chair was fully extended, and Crawford lay with his face turned slightly away from me, his boots dangling over the footrest, one hand curled in his lap, the other arm flung to one side. Beside the chair, a small table held a reading lamp and I tried to switch it on, but the knob clicked twice with no result. I grabbed his wrist, but even as I felt for a pulse point, I knew it was useless. It was like touching a slab of refrigerated meat.

The sun rose another notch, a stray beam trickling through an open door on the east side of the room to illuminate Crawford's cottony hair and, worse, the glistening whites of his eyes. I heard screaming and thought at first that it was me. Very unprofessional behavior from a writer who made her living from dead bodies.

But the sound wasn't a scream after all. It was a siren. It moaned to a halt, and I was still standing frozen in the same spot when Lester pushed past me, almost stepping on the hand that rested on the carpet, its fingers curved upward like the legs of a dead spider.

"Get some light in here!" he bellowed, and almost instantly the lamp came on, directly under my nose.

I closed my eyes briefly, the glare dancing against my eyelids. When I looked again, Lester was kneeling beside the recliner. A choked sob came from the foyer, and I turned in time to see Miss Stenson drop her hand from the light switch, her complexion the color of sour milk.

"Damn it, where's Doc?" Lester was patting Crawford's cheeks as if the sheriff were a swooning Victorian lady and not...

"Dead," I said aloud. "He's dead, Lester, so stop it. Look at his neck."

The only dead person I had actually seen up 'til now was my mother, and she had been laid out in a hospital bed, limbs neatly arranged, pristine sheets pulled up to her chin as the doctor stood by, spouting explanations and tired sympathy. But death had come as a friend to her, erasing the lines of pain, leaving behind a life-sized doll I duly arranged to bury.

The death that took Crawford hadn't paid such a considerate visit. Pale eyes, flat and dull in the lamplight; his head thrown back, exposing the puffy wound that marred the skin of his neck; the smear of blood that had spread to stain the collar of his uniform shirt. I bent closer, feeling a shudder of superstitious fear. Damn Stephen King anyway, along with Bram Stoker. But I couldn't help flashing to all the vampire legends, for a neat pair of puncture marks was clearly defined within the patch of discolored flesh.

Suddenly, Lester was yanking on my arm. "Get out," he ordered through clenched teeth. "Right now, Taylor."

Confused by his harsh tone, I started for the door at the back of the room, through which sunlight was now pouring. He jerked me back, shoving me instead out to the front porch. "You stay here, too, Dorothy!" he shouted as he ran for the squad car. Grabbing a shotgun from beneath the front seat, he sprinted back into the house. Dorothy Stenson and I crept toward the open door to peek inside.

Lester was prowling the room, the shotgun nestled in his arms. He moved in an odd half-crouch, peering under furniture, gingerly lifting a chair cushion with the gun's muzzle. As he approached the oval coffee table that stood in front of the sofa, an angry buzz filled the air. I caught my breath, recognizing the sound. Lester scuttled backward, dropping to his knees, aiming, and firing almost within the same instant. I clamped my hands to my ears as chunks of wood flew everywhere and a large, black hole appeared, as if by magic, in the fabric of the sofa.

"What the hell is going on here?" roared a voice behind us, and Miss Stenson and I were tumbled into each other as a tubby, bald gnome pushed past us and hurried into the house. "Lester? You all right, boy? What in tarnation are you shootin' at?"

I was pretty sure I knew. I followed the little man into the room, trying to hide behind him. This was rather like attempting to conceal a giraffe behind a bulldog, but Lester either didn't notice my presence, or no longer cared. He pointed out the pieces of bloody meat that littered the carpet among splinters of wood and tufts of stuffing. The snake's head rested against one of the table legs.

The gnome barely glanced at the carnage before moving to the recliner and its occupant. I retreated to sit down on the hearth before my knees gave way.

Lester tossed the shotgun onto the sofa and clenched his fists. "Doc?"

"He's dead," the doctor stated grimly. "But I guess y'all had already figured that out."

A keening cry rose from the doorway, and Lester rushed to catch Miss Stenson as she fell. The gnome fixed his piercing eyes on me.

"Don't know who you are, girl, but since Lester has his hands full at the moment, how 'bout you go on into the kitchen and call my office. Tell 'em I need the ambulance."

"Ambulance? But you said he was—"

"He is. But I'm not gonna wrestle his body into my Datsun, and I've got to get him to the clinic."

"What for, Doc?" Lester's question was muffled. Miss Stenson was sobbing into his neck, and her black curls covered his mouth and nose. "Shouldn't we call Luther's?"

Doc shook his head. "Time enough for funeral parlors later. You know I gotta do an autopsy first."

Miss Stenson shrieked. Pushing out of Lester's supportive embrace, she stumbled toward the doctor.

"Don't you dare," she cried. "Hasn't he been hurt enough, without you carving him up like a side of beef? Don't you lay one finger on him, Ted Neil!" She collapsed into tears again.

"I have to agree, Doc," Lester said. "What's the point? It's obvious what happened. I've even apprehended the killer," he added with a touch of macabre humor.

"You know the rules, boy. An autopsy is standard procedure in cases of violent death." Miss Stenson let out another wail. "Les, take Dorothy home, will you? No, missy," he barked as I started to get up. "I'll call the office myself. You stay where you are for a while. Your face is almost as white as Crawford's."

The analogy undid me, and I sat back down without protest. Doc disappeared through the sunlit door while Lester dragged Miss Stenson out the front way, leaving me alone with the sheriff's remains. I tried to keep my eyes off the corpse, but soon determined that even the sight of a dead body was preferable to examining the pink nuggets of snake that seemed to be everywhere else.

Glancing again at Crawford's out flung arm, I noticed the paperback book that rested, its pages splayed, on the floor next to his hand. God, the poor man had been minding his own business, relaxed and reading, when the snake slithered in and... I forced my mind away from the gruesome image. He had been reading? Something about the idea bothered me, but I couldn't quite catch what it was. Biting my lip, I rose from the hearth and tiptoed across the room, avoiding remnants of snake. Squatting carefully, I picked up the book and smoothed its pages, not surprised to find it was an Agatha Christie. The front cover was torn, but I could still read the title: *Sleeping Murder*.

In the next room, Doc barked a final order and banged down the receiver. Stuffing the book into the deep pocket of my sweat pants, I scampered back to my place on the hearth before he could catch me snooping.

He came to sit down beside me, pulling a cigar from his breast pocket and striking a fireplace match. Figuring if he could get away with it, I could, too, I dug out my cigarettes and lit one.

"Poor Miles." He shook his head. "Hell of a way to go."

Something occurred to me as we flicked our ashes into the fireplace.

"Doctor, why didn't he try to get help? Cal told me a snake bite victim can be saved nearly every time, if he gets to a hospital soon enough."

Doc examined the tip of his cigar. "True enough, under most circumstances. A bite to the arm or leg, the most likely places, is usually not fatal, with quick and proper treatment." He sighed. "Miles was unlucky, that's all. The damn critter got him directly on the jugular. I'd say the toxin probably stopped his heart within a minute, two at the outside."

"God." It was more of a prayer than an epithet. "How long do you think he's been—?" I was still having trouble with the "d" word.

"Hard to say. Rigor mortis has set in, but that's not always an accurate indicator. Four to twelve hours."

"That's quite a gap."

He shrugged. "Doesn't matter much for something like this. It was just a nasty accident, not one of those stupid murder mysteries that Miles had his nose poked into every time I saw him."

I thought about volunteering the information that I wrote those "stupid" murder mysteries for a living, but it's hard to carry on a casual conversation with a dead man less than six feet away.

Lester poked his head in the front door. "Ambulance is driving up, Doc."

"Good." He stuck a pudgy hand in my direction. "Sorry we had to meet under these circumstances. Well, actually, I guess we never did really meet, did we?"

"Guess not. See you around." I didn't offer to help load the body. I didn't ask Les if there was anything else he needed me to do. I didn't do any of the things a proper deputy would have done in any mystery novel I had ever read. What I did was slink out the front door and take off down the street, leaving Billy's mo-ped abandoned in the driveway.

I hadn't gone far before it hit me that I had no idea where I was going. Did I still have a job? Did I still want this job? Damn Tessa anyway. If she had given me five minutes of her precious time, answered one simple question, I'd be back in Houston by now instead of being involved with this mess. The shock was wearing off, and I felt tears begin to build behind my eyes. I had liked that man, I really had. What a horrible death for such a truly good person. He had gone out of his way to help me—to help a lot of folks, from what I had been told— and this was his reward?

A car horn startled me out of these thoughts, and I looked up to see Cal pulling close to the curb. He rolled down his window.

"Need a ride?"

"Not really, but I'll take it. Thanks." I got in, noticing immediately that I didn't stick to the seat cover. "This must be your car. You were right. It sure smells better than the other one."

"Yeah. Remember when I had to leave last night, after you came in to borrow the phone? Les had just called, champing at the bit to trade back. Said he'd left some stuff in the trunk, and he needed it." He cruised in silence for a block, then said awkwardly, "I heard you were the first one there."

"News travels fast."

"I got to the house as they were loading the body into the ambulance." He hesitated. "I'm sorry. It must've been pretty hard on you."

I shuddered. "It was horrible, Cal."

"I can't believe he was killed by a damn snake. Peculiar as all get-out."

"Why is it so hard to believe? I get the impression rattlesnakes crawl out of the woodwork around here."

"We've got a lot of them, for sure. And this isn't the first case of one getting into a house—that happens all the time. I guess what makes it strange is where it bit him. Almost like it knew what it was doing."

A chill trailed up my spine. "Don't say that."

He rolled to a stop in front of the sheriff's office. "Are you going to be okay?"

"Yeah." I started to ask him about the status of my job, but his next words answered my question.

"I took Billy on home for the day. He was pretty shaken up. Would you mind handling the radio and the phones for a while? Les is going to contact the funeral home, and I've got to get back out to the festival site."

"Sure, that's fine. You'd better come in for a minute and show me what buttons to push, though. The closest I've ever been to a two-way radio was an old boyfriend's CB."

He nodded. "Same principle. But c'mon, I'll give you the grand tour of our sophisticated communications system."

After about five minutes, I felt confident enough to shoo him out the door. Unless a sudden crime wave swept Perdue, I was pretty sure I could handle two phone lines and a single channel radio. Les checked out at Luther's Funeral Parlor, and I punched the button on the microphone and intoned, "Unit two out," feeling like a crisp, professional dispatcher.

Lester came back on the air. "Taylor? That you? Where's Billy?"

I sighed. So much for procedure. "Cal took him home. He wasn't feeling well."

"You holdin' up all right?"

"Yes, I'm fine, unit two." I groped for a way to end the conversation so I could get on with the important business of brewing a pot of coffee or, better yet, finding out whether the sheriff had stashed a bottle of scotch somewhere. "Uh, bye, unit two."

Lester apparently took the hint because he didn't say anything else. I wrote down the time, as Cal had instructed me, put the coffee on, then leaned back and allowed myself a very brief session of self-pity. The fact that it was brief had nothing to do with my self control. The phone started ringing.

If I had surmised that Billy spent his time whittling or perusing girlie magazines, the next hour convinced me otherwise. Derrick County might be small, but its citizens were every bit as determined to take advantage of the services provided by their tax dollars as were the denizens of Houston. Every third call was someone wanting to know if it was really true about poor Sheriff Crawford. In between, Mrs. Matladge wanted her cat, Puffy, rescued from behind the refrigerator, where the kitty had become wedged while hiding from the postman who had, in the past, squirted Puffy with a water pistol, horrible man.

Mr. Dalton informed me that the stop sign at the corner of Elm and Second had been spray-painted with the letters "FLGH." Now, Mr. Dalton had no idea what the word meant, but at best, it was vandalism, and worst, it could be a gang symbol. Mr. Dalton watched CNN every morning and knew what havoc gangs were capable of wreaking on a community, and thought the sheriff's department ought to nip this right in the bud.

Mrs. Levinworth let me know, in no uncertain terms, she would no longer tolerate that nasty Mr. Formby next door spying on her with his binoculars. She was a decent widow lady, and although she had been told she was still a fine figure of a woman, her figure was her business and not Mr. Formby's, and unless we did something about it, she'd have to take matters into her own hands. Her solution seemed to involve a baseball bat being applied vigorously to Mr. Formby's binoculars and/or his head.

I phoned Les at the funeral parlor and sent him to have a chat with Mr. Formby, then sent Cal, when he checked in, to rescue Puffy. The gang terrorism, I decided, would have to wait.

The phone settled down a bit, and I had managed to pour myself a cup of coffee, when the door opened and a man eased through, his scrawny, hunched frame supported by a cane.

I watched him anxiously, wanting to offer assistance, but afraid of offending the dignity obvious in his determined progress.

He made it to a chair and eased himself into it. Breathing a sigh of relief, I said hello and asked if I could help him.

He looked at me with eyes as gentle as a doe's, strangely out of place in the sagging, weathered face. "Do I smell fresh coffee, honey?"

I nodded. "Would you like a cup?"

"That'd be nice, thanks. I'm glad I finally found you," he continued as I handed him a steaming mug. "Rita told me she saw Cal drop you off here a while back."

"You were looking for me?" I sat down across from him. If I had met him at the festival grounds, I didn't remember. "I'm sorry, Mr.—?"

He laughed softly. "No, I'm the one who's sorry. I can't apologize for Tessa...that's something she'll have to do for herself. But I wish I had been around the other night when she decided to be so rude to her own niece."

Light dawned. "You're Wood Potter."

He looked surprised. "Sure I am. Who'd you think I was?"

I let that one pass. "Did Tessa send you?"

"Hell—sorry, miss—no, she didn't send me. I don't know what's gotten into that woman. I wouldn't have known a thing about it, if Mabel hadn't told me what happened." He sighed and sipped his coffee. "I can't believe I slept through the whole mess, but I was dog-tired that night. I'd spent the afternoon in Lubbock, with a little lady who calls herself a physical therapist." He leaned closer and confided, "I call her Attila, but not when she can hear me."

I smiled, liking him already. "She seems to be doing a good job."

"Oh, sure. If I raised horses instead of sheep, I'd hire her to break them for me." He set his mug aside and reached for my hands. "Little gal, I'd like to do what my wife should have done the other night, and welcome you to Perdue. As far as I'm concerned, you're welcome in our home, too."

"Thank you, Mr. Potter."

"Wood. Even better, how about Uncle Wood?" He beamed at me. "Tessa and I were never blessed with kids, and I sure wouldn't mind adopting a cute little thing like you."

I squeezed his hands, my throat suddenly too tight to allow speech. Was this what I had expected from Tessa? Probably not, but I admitted to myself that it was what I had been hoping for.

"I still don't understand what's gotten into Tess. You'd think after almost thirty years of marriage, we'd be past secrets, wouldn't you? She and Sarah were never close, but for heaven's sake, I'd have expected some mention of a niece. That's another reason I came to visit, little gal. Thought maybe I'd be better off asking you."

I shook my head. "I'm afraid there's not much I can tell you." Releasing his hands, I retrieved my backpack from behind the desk and pulled out the letter. "You might as well read this. Maybe it'll make more sense to you than it did to me."

He pulled a pair of half-glasses from his shirt pocket and balanced them on his nose. I watched his expression carefully as he read, but saw nothing except a reflection of my own confusion.

"Well?" I asked when he had finished.

"Beats the hell—beg pardon, honey—out of me. All this tells me is that Tess knew she had a niece, and that she sent money from time to time."

"What about the part where she told Mom not to come to Perdue? Don't you think that's a little strange?"

"The whole situation is strange," he said. "But that's the one part I might understand. Right after Tess and I got married, I heard her on the phone with Sarah, makin' excuses why it wouldn't be a good idea for her to come visit us. When she hung up, I asked her why she'd done that. Well, she got all flustered like she was embarrassed I'd caught her, and admitted that Sarah tended to get on her nerves. Said it was hard enough learnin' to live with a brand new mother-in-law, without having a big sister fussin' at her, too."

He chuckled. "Can't say I blame her about my mother either. She never had no trouble speakin' her mind. Guess I shoulda pressed it, but to tell you the truth, I waited a long time to make Tess my own, and one less person to share her with was fine with me." He actually blushed.

I patted his thin knee. "I think that's sweet, Uncle Wood. But even if that's part of the reason she didn't want Mom around, it doesn't explain her reaction to me, does it?" I hesitated. "Sheriff Crawford told me..."

He waved a hand. "I can guess what Miles told you, and it's true enough. About them being engaged and all."

I blinked. "Mom and Crawford were engaged?"

"Naw. They dated a while, but then she moved off to Houston. I'm talking about Miles and Tess."

The phone rang. Still thinking about what Wood had said, I rolled the chair a few feet and answered. "Yes," I responded to the most frequent inquiry of the day. "I'm afraid it's true. No, I'm not sure when the funeral will be. Yes, it's awful. I don't know. Thank you, I'll pass that along."

When I replaced the receiver, Wood cocked his head at me. "Someone die?"

"You haven't heard? Sheriff Crawford was found dead at his house this morning."

He sat very still.

I stood and hurried to his side. "I'm sorry. I shouldn't have been so blunt about it. I guess I figured the town grapevine would've it broadcast as far as Amarillo by now. Wood, should I call your doctor? Are you all right?"

He managed a weak laugh. "Don't worry, dear, I'm not gonna pass out on you. Took me by surprise is all. Old Miles. Not so old, though, was he? Younger'n me, and I'm still in my prime, no matter what Doc Neil says. Now, now, don't carry on so. I promise to give you plenty of warning if I'm fixin' to croak. Was it a heart attack?"

"Snakebite." I poured him some fresh coffee, adding sugar. I doubted if sugar would prevent a stroke, but I knew it was a preferred treatment for shock.

"You're pullin' my leg. In his own house?"

"Yes. It bit him on the neck."

"Well, I 'spose I'll hear all about it before sundown." He slurped his coffee and grimaced, but made note of my stern expression and drank it anyway. "Why'd you seem surprised when I told you about Tess and Miles being engaged? I thought you said Miles'd already mentioned it."

"He told me he, um, courted her after Mom left town, but since she married you, I guess I assumed that the relationship didn't work out."

"Well, it did for a while anyway. Dang near broke my heart, I don't mind tellin' you. Thought I'd done waited too long to speak my intentions to her."

I found myself sympathizing with my aunt. I would have hated to have to choose between two such men. On the other hand, I would have given a lot to meet one. Decent men of my generation seemed few and far between.

"But you won her after all."

"Guess I did. But only because of Dorothy Stenson."

"Huh?"

He looked sheepish. "I sent that woman a dozen roses on my

wedding day. No card. Bet she's still wondering about that. It was Dorothy's fault, you see, that Miles and Tess split up."

The phone rang again. Damn. I took another condolence call, checked Cal in from his successful rescue of Mrs. Matladge's cat, then encouraged my newfound uncle to continue his story.

"Dorothy's had her eye on Miles from the time he and his sister and Daddy moved to town. She went wild when it started going around that Tess and Miles were thinking about gettin' married." He winked. "All of a sudden, rumor had it that Miles and Dot had been seen frequenting Simm's Lane. Now, you know what that means."

I thought it over. "I take it that Simm's Lane is Perdue's equivalent of Lover's Leap?"

"You got it. Well, Tess was fit to be tied. Hit her hard, poor kid." I noticed he didn't look all that sorry. "She took off for Houston like a scalded cat. Miles didn't know what to make of it, until the rumor finally made its way back around to him. You know what they say about bein' the last to know."

"Didn't he go after her?"

"Sure he did. Sarah wouldn't let him anywhere near Tess." He paused. "Guess I shoulda sent Sarah some roses, too. Anyhow, Tess stayed gone for more than a year. Folks figured she'd never come back. She might not have either, if it hadn't been for me."

"What did you do?"

He leaned back in the chair. "First thing I did was to bide my time. I'm a fool when it comes to the ways of females, but even I had enough sense to figure out that she needed some time to get Miles out of her system. He is—was—one handsome devil, and a sweet talker to boot. I wasn't either one."

"I think you're very nice looking," I put in.

He smiled. "Bless your little heart. Well, I waited as long as I could stand it, then went to Houston."

"And she fell into your arms." I felt myself blush as the words revealed my romantic streak.

"Not right away. Not 'til I let her in on the rumor that Miles and Dorothy were plannin' their wedding."

"Miss Stenson and the sheriff were married?"

His expression turned sly. "I didn't say the rumor was true, any more than the first one was. But Tess eloped with me that very night. Didn't even tell her sister until after the fact."

I choked on a laugh. "Why, you old scoundrel!"

"Worked, didn't it?" His eyes met mine. "I think I've given her a good life. No one could've loved her more."

"I believe you."

He planted his cane and pushed to his feet. "I'd best be on my way. Don't know why really. Tess is handling all the ranch business now. Sure wish ol' Doc would let me go back to work. I miss my babies."

"Your babies?"

"My sheep. Can't say the same for Tess, though. Town life seems to agree with her. I'm beginning to wonder if she'd be happier if we never moved back to the ranch. She's seemed perkier in the last few months than she's been in years."

"I hope you can be the one to break the news to her. About Sheriff Crawford, I mean. I'm sure it'll be a shock."

He gave me an odd look. "Well, sure, it's always a shock when someone your own age up and dies."

"I meant because they were—friends."

"Friends? Tess and Miles? Heck, they barely said how-do to each other if they met on the street. Still bad feelings between them, I guess."

I tried to conceal my surprise, and thought it better not to inform him that, according to Crawford, he and Tessa had been pals again for quite a while. The woman sure kept a lot of secrets from her husband.

"Wood," I said, "do you think you could persuade Tessa to talk to me?"

The door opened, and Billy crept in. "Hi, Ms. Madison. Thought I'd better get back to work."

"I'll try to reason with her," Wood whispered. He bent to give me a swift peck on the cheek, and then stumped out.

"Do you think you ought to be here?" I asked Billy. "Cal expected you to take the rest of the day off."

The boy straightened his perpetually slumped shoulders. "The sheriff wouldn't have wanted me to wimp out. How can I be a deputy someday if I can't handle bad things happening?" He cleared his throat. "Any calls?"

I filled him in on the gang symbol, the cat, the peeping tom.

He brightened a little, explaining to me that the mailman had indeed fired a water pistol at Puffy, but only after the twenty-pound cat had used his leg for a scratching post for the umpteenth time, and that behind a refrigerator seemed as good a place as any for the crazy feline.

As to Mr. Formby, he had explained a dozen times that he was not watching Mrs. Levinworth, but was instead keeping an eye on the bird population in the woods behind her house. Mr. Formby was an avid bird watcher, but probably wouldn't know what to do with a woman if she stripped naked and threw herself at him. Mrs. Levinworth's baseball bat, incidentally, was of the hollow plastic variety and would be incapable of injuring either Mr. Formby's binoculars or his cranium.

As to the mysterious letters "FLGH" that had been painted on the stop sign, they had also been painted on every flat surface in town, and stood for Fred Landers and Greta Hayes who were sixteen years old, sappy about each other, and thus felt compelled to proclaim their love to the world at large.

By the time he had finished, I was holding my sides with laughter and excused myself, retiring to the bathroom so I could get rid of my morning coffee before I disgraced myself on the office floor.

On my way back to the front room, I noticed that the sheriff's cot had recently been slept in. Strange, I hadn't seen anyone in either of the cells, and hadn't Crawford said that was why he occasionally spent the night here? I mentioned it to Billy.

"Yeah, that was weird. Lester slept here last night. I didn't even know it until he came bustin' out of the back office this morning after you'd left for the sheriff's house. Scared the dickens out of me, let me tell you. And, boy, was he mad when he found out I'd sent you over to the scene! But honest, if I'd known he was here, I never would've made you go, Ms. Madison."

"Billy, you're making me feel elderly. Call me Taylor, okay? So, what was Les doing here? Did you have an overnight prisoner?"

"Nope. I don't know why he was here, but I wish he'd left a note or something. 'Scuse me." He turned to answer the phone, just as Lester walked in.

"What happened with Mrs. Levinworth?" I asked him.

He sighed. "I think it's finally straightened out. This time, I dragged her next door to Formby's house and he let her use the binoculars. When I left, he had found an extra set for her, and they were side by side in the window, counting blue jays or something."

"Another felony averted."

"Case closed," he agreed. "What is it, Billy?"

"Doc Neil wants someone to come by his office." Billy swallowed hard. "He says he's finished the autopsy on Sheriff Crawford."

Chapter Five

I DON'T QUITE KNOW how I ended up back inside the foul-smelling patrol car, on my way to Doctor Neil's office. Les had asked if I wanted to come along, and I'm pretty sure I remember saying no. When he pulled into the parking lot, I noticed that the clinic was directly across the street from Posey's, and I grabbed the opportunity to stall. I told Les I wanted to go buy a candy bar, which was true. I hadn't eaten since the evening before, and I was beginning to get the shakes from too much coffee on an empty stomach. Of course, I was hoping he'd offer to talk to Doc and pick me up when he was finished. No such luck.

"Now that you mention it, I skipped breakfast myself," he said. "I'll come with you."

Bo pounced upon us like a lurking bobcat.

"It's not true, is it?" she asked. "About Miles. It can't be true. Lester?"

"I'm sorry, Bo."

She lit one of her filterless Camels and took a drag so deep that half of it dissolved into ash. "I can't believe it," she muttered. "I remember the day he moved to town. Cute little towheaded rascal, always had a hand in my candy jar." The rest of the Camel disappeared, and she immediately lit another. "Poor thing, no mama to care for him. Just his daddy and a sister not much older than he was. But he did all right for himself, didn't he? Grew up to be a good sheriff."

"The best," Les agreed.

Her eyes pierced him. "No, I wouldn't go that far. Miles had his flaws, one being that he was way too softhearted. Folks knew it, too, and I'd venture to say they took advantage of it on more than one occasion."

I had wolfed down half a Snickers before I got around to digging some change out of my backpack. I went ahead and paid for a Milky Way as well, and as I tucked it into my pocket for later, my fingers brushed against stiff paper. I realized it was the mystery novel that Crawford had been reading. Why had I taken it? What an odd thing to do!

"What I want to know," Bo was mumbling around her third

Camel, "is what Miles did to provoke it."

Les rolled his eyes heavenward.

"Provoke what?" I asked.

"The snake, girl. Lester Forman, stop making faces. You grew up around these parts, and you know as well as I do that rattlers don't clamp their fangs into folks for no good reason."

"Well, this one didn't have a reason." I was surprised at the anger I felt. "The sheriff was minding his own business, reading a book."

"Was he, now?" She spat out a flake of tobacco. "This don't make sense at all. Snakes strike for one of two reasons. Either for food, or because they feel threatened. Now, I doubt something as big as Miles would seem easy enough prey for a quick midnight snack, and I don't see nothing particularly threatening about a man sitting in a chair. Do you, Les?"

"Can't say I do," Lester conceded. "But then, I'm not a snake. You ready, Taylor?"

"Hold it there." Bo grabbed my arm. "Somethin's on your mind, missy. Tell Bo what it is."

I felt a flush rising. "Nothing...it's probably silly. For some reason, the fact that the sheriff was reading when it happened bothers me, but I don't know why."

Bo gave a satisfied nod. "Smart girl."

Lester sighed. "What the hell are you two talking about? It was an accident, for Pete's sake."

I ignored him. "It didn't have anything to do with the snake," I said, more to myself than to Bo.

"Well, something's sure eatin' at you. Keep after it. That's how riddles get solved." She gave me a little push toward the door, where Les was gesturing impatiently. "You'd better go before Deputy Dawg has a hissy fit. We'll talk more later."

"Talk about what?" Les grumbled as we crossed the street to the clinic. "That old woman is as flaky as a box of Post Toasties."

I didn't comment, though I didn't think Bo was crazy at all.

As we entered the clinic, Doctor Neil was escorting a tiny, pigtailed girl into the waiting room. He gave a red balloon a final puff and tied it off. The little girl took it with a shy smile and ran to hide behind her mother.

"She's fine," Doc wheezed. "Keep the bandage clean on that elbow for a couple of days, and she'll be climbing trees again by next week."

After mother and child left, Doc led us back to his office, still panting.

"I'm either gonna have to cut down on cigars or start handing out lollipops again," he gasped, easing into the chair behind his desk. "I think I'll go with the lollipops. After all, I'm not the one who'll have to deal with the kiddies' rotted teeth. Sit, sit." He peered at me. "Lester informed me that you're a newly appointed deputy. I don't imagine you expected anything like this on your first day."

"This is my second day," I corrected. "My first day involved throwing up fried snake meat."

"Snakes," he repeated thoughtfully, his chair squeaking a protest as he leaned back. "Lester, what did you do with that rattler you shot this morning?"

Les frowned. "I put it in a plastic sack and took it to the dump."

"Think you could find it for me?"

"You're kidding. Why?"

Doc shrugged. "I wouldn't mind taking a look at it." He flipped open a folder on his desk. "I've treated quite a few snakebites in my time, you know. Living around here, it's impossible to avoid. So, while my counterparts in the big cities are dedicating their free time to reading medical journals and keeping up on the latest treatment of knife wounds and venereal diseases, I've spent my own evening hours studying toxicology. Aside from venomous snakes, this part of the country is chock full of poisonous plants, so I felt it was important research."

"Commendable," I said, feeling someone should say something.

"Do either of you happen to know how many snakebites are dry? That is to say, the snake strikes out of fear or confusion, but no venom is actually ejected. No? As many as twenty-five percent. As to the remaining three quarters, the majority of those are what I'd term mild bites. By that, I mean that only a trace of venom enters the victim. A rattlesnake never expends all its venom in a single bite." He lowered his bushy eyebrows as if we were planning to contradict him.

Lester shifted in the chair, checked at his watch. "Is there a point to this, Doc?"

"You bet. My autopsy indicates there is entirely too much venom present in the tissue surrounding the bite wound on Crawford's neck. My facilities here are limited, but I would estimate four to five times the amount found in even a severe bite."

Lester's lips set in a tight line. "What are you trying to say?"

Doc shook his head. "I have no idea what I'm trying to say. It doesn't make any sense."

"Couldn't the snake have just, um, spit more into him?" I put in.

"Spit?" Doc almost smiled. "Well, I get what you're asking, deputy, but no. A rattler can certainly strike more than once, injecting venom with each separate bite. As a matter of fact, that happens quite frequently if the snake is provoked in some way."

There was that word again. Unless Crawford had been in the habit of performing calisthenics while reading, I couldn't see what had induced the snake to bite him. Maybe he had been reading aloud, and the rattler hadn't been a Christie fan.

"But the sheriff was only bitten once," Doc went on. "Bitten in a location that would ensure a quick death, and injected with enough venom to kill three men."

Les rubbed his chin. "I'm sorry, Doc, but I still don't see what you're getting at. Are you implying that snake was some kind of mutant or something?"

Doc snorted disgustedly. "You watch too many science fiction movies, Lester. A mutant, indeed. Still, I'd sure like to get my hands on the body of that snake you killed, or whatever's left of it." He stood. "In the meantime, I've sent the sheriff's corpse on to the Medical Examiner's office in Lubbock."

Lester's chair scraped backward as he shot to his feet. "You did what? Are you nuts, Doc? Dorothy's got the funeral scheduled for Sunday."

"She'll have to change her plans. The ME's lab is a lot more sophisticated than mine, and I want their opinion. I think I'm within my rights as Derrick County coroner to request a second opinion."

I was lost. "What do you expect them to find?"

"I don't know. I really don't. Something isn't right, that's all I can tell you. Now, the entire first grade class of Perdue Elementary is due here in about ten minutes for their vaccinations, so unless you want to help hold down twenty screaming six-year-olds, you'll have to excuse me."

Les shuddered visibly. "I'll pass. Come on, Taylor."

"Oh, hold on." Doc slid open a desk drawer and pulled out a plastic bag. "Crawford's personal belongings. Uniform, watch, class ring, lighter, and money clip."

Les took the bag and stuffed it under his arm. "I'll drop it by his house."

"Thanks." Doc put a hand on Lester's shoulder as he walked us out. "How's Paula getting along?"

"Fine. Why do you ask?"

Doc glanced at me. "I'd like to check her over. Tried to talk her into an exam the last time she brought your dad in, but she said she couldn't stay. See what you can do, okay, Les? I'd feel a lot better if I could give her a complete physical."

"Yeah," Les mumbled. "See ya, Doc. And let me know what you find out from Lubbock, will you?"

We got into the car, but Lester didn't start the motor. He sat gazing through the windshield for so long that the upholstery's odor began to get to me, so I rolled down the window and lit a cigarette.

"You okay?" I asked after a few minutes.

"Huh? Oh, sure, just wondering what old Doc's got stuck in his craw this time. I never heard so much horseshit in my life, did you?"

"I really don't know enough about the habits of snakes to be a good judge," I admitted, then decided a subject change was in order. "Has Paula been sick or something?"

He looked at me blankly for a moment. "Oh, all that stuff about a checkup? She had a miscarriage a few months ago."

"God, I'm sorry!"

He sighed. "She was only two months along. I think she's fine now. Guess it wouldn't hurt for her to get a physical, though. I'll mention it to her as soon as she gets back."

"Has she gone somewhere?"

"She took off yesterday afternoon to visit her folks in Dallas."

I smiled in sudden understanding. "I'll bet that's why you slept at the office last night."

"What?" He turned his head. "Who told you that?"

"Billy. I noticed the cot was rumpled and asked him about it. He said you scared him to death when you came running out of the back room this morning."

The tips of Lester's ears reddened.

"Oh, come on, don't be embarrassed. I think it's sort of sweet that you miss your wife so much, you can't sleep without her."

"That's me. Sweet." He turned the key. "Guess we'd better get that stuff over to Crawford's. I'm gonna have to run by Luther's, too, and tell them the funeral has been postponed."

The radio squawked. "Unit two?"

Les groaned and keyed the mike. "What's up, Billy?"

"Puffy's up a tree this time. Miz Matladge says she has a ladder, but she's scared to climb it."

"Shit," Les muttered, but not, thankfully, into the mike. "On my way."

"Tell you what. Why don't you let me out at Crawford's house, and I can drop off this sack. I've got to take Billy's mo-ped back to him anyway."

"Great...that would be a big help. Dorothy Stenson lives in the blue house across the street from Crawford's. Would you mind telling her we're putting the funeral off for a few days? Don't tell her why, though. All we need at this point is to spread a bizarre rumor about mutant snakes."

"Then what reason should I give?"

"Tell her we're waiting to see if he specified any preferences in his will about the type of funeral he wanted. Actually, I've already contacted his lawyer and I know he requested cremation, but Dorothy doesn't have to know that yet. I'll square it with Luther's, in case she asks them."

I nodded agreement as he pulled to a stop in front of the sheriff's little house. I got out, feeling my pocket to make sure I hadn't lost the mo-ped key.

Lester was long gone before it occurred to me that I didn't have a key to the house. Fortunately, when I tried the front door, I found it unlocked. I remembered the sheriff had told me that most people in Perdue didn't bother to lock their doors—and why should they, after all? Apparently, the murderers in these parts slithered through holes in the foundation, or came up through the plumbing.

I stood in the foyer for a minute, flashing back to the first time I had entered this house. Although the living room was well illuminated by the morning sun, I flicked the switch by the door, craving as much light as I could get. The lamp by the recliner came on, and the sight of the now empty chair saddened me. Something else continued to nibble at the edge of my mind. Frowning, I flipped the switch off, then on again, but failed to capture what was nagging me.

Moving into the small dining room, I placed the package on the table and was turning to leave when I heard a rustling sound from the rear of the house. I froze, visions of an entire snake family wriggling through my imagination.

The rustling grew louder, accompanied by a sneeze. A sneeze? Did snakes sneeze?

I looked around for something that would serve as a weapon, finally choosing a heavy, lead crystal vase. Feeling like an utter idiot, I crept down the short hallway, the vase raised above my head like a club.

The first door I came to was partially ajar, and beyond it, the thumping had turned to scrabbling. Using my shoulder to ease the door further open, I peeked into the room.

A four-poster bed filled my immediate line of vision, but I caught a flash of movement out of the corner of my eye and whirled to confront the intruder. The woman caught sight of me at the same instant and we both just stood there, staring at each other.

"Tessa," I said, as soon as I was able to speak. "What in hell are you doing?"

"I could ask you the same thing," she replied, sounding a lot calmer than I felt. She failed, however, in her attempt to appear completely innocent. Every drawer in the room had been pulled out, their contents strewn across the floor.

My heart was still lodged somewhere in the vicinity of my esophagus and I leaned against a bedpost, remembering to lower the vase only when my arms began to ache.

"For that matter," she went on, "I can't imagine what you're still doing in Perdue. I think I made it clear I have nothing to say to you, and you can pass that message along to Sarah. Whatever may have possessed her to send you here, I—"

"Wait a minute. What are you talking about? You think Mom sent me? Mrs. Potter, your sister is dead."

Tessa's eyes widened. She groped behind her for the dresser stool and sank down upon it. "Dead? Sarah?"

"Yes." I couldn't control the sarcasm in my tone. "I'm surprised the fact hasn't come to your attention by now. Perdue's communication system has the Internet beat all to hell." I tossed the vase onto the bed and crossed my arms. "Just as you should be aware the sheriff hired me as a temporary deputy, and it is in that capacity I'm here now. Which is also why I feel within my rights to request that you show me whatever you stuffed into your skirt pocket a few minutes ago."

Tessa's hand dropped guiltily to the pocket in question and she sighed, obviously realizing that denial would be useless. A gold chain dangled in plain view against the dark fabric of her skirt.

I have to give her credit, though. She made one last effort.

"I fail to see that this is any of your business," she said frostily. "I doubt you have any real authority, especially since the man who hired you is—" She faltered, "—no longer with us."

"Oh? In that case, perhaps you'll be more comfortable explaining your actions to, shall we say, Deputy Arnette? Or Deputy Forman? I'll be more than happy to call the SO." It took me two steps to reach the bedside phone and, as I had expected, she relented as soon as I picked up the receiver.

"Wait. I'll show you, all right? Good Lord, you must have inherited that streak of stubbornness from your—" My ears had probably pricked visibly at that, because she broke off. "Here." She held up the object for my inspection. "This is all I took."

I edged closer, and saw that it was a large and rather gaudy locket, an enameled rosebud set into its filigreed case. It looked old, but not particularly valuable; the gold plating had worn away in several spots, and the chain was more green than gilt. I held out my hand, but she snatched it away.

"It's mine," she insisted. "Miles Crawford gave this to me almost thirty years ago, and even though I later returned it to him, it's still my property."

I wasn't sure of the legalities of that, but I let her continue.

"Miles and I have been friends for most of our lives, and I refuse to let this end up in the hands of that horrible Dorothy Stenson. You'll be well advised to keep an eye on that woman. She'll take anything that isn't nailed down."

"Dorothy is not the one ransacking the sheriff's bedroom at the moment," I pointed out.

"You didn't get that cynical tongue from my side of the family either."

I could certainly have disagreed with that statement. But the question now was, what to do about the pendant? Damn it, I was pretty sure this constituted burglary, but I wasn't a real police officer after all. Besides, maybe in Perdue it was acceptable for family friends to invade the deceased's residence and gather souvenirs. And considering what Wood had related about her one-time relationship with Crawford, I really didn't doubt she was telling the truth about his giving it to her.

Still, I should go ahead and call the SO. I couldn't take the responsibility. Could I? And even if I could, why should I? Tessa muttered something under her breath and I looked at her. "What did you say?"

She cleared her throat. "Please," she repeated, and I could tell the word had been wrenched painfully from somewhere deep inside.

Who the hell did she think she was? How could I even consider letting her get away with something like this?

"Okay," I heard someone say. Good grief, it was me. "Take it. But would you please leave now? I'm pretty sure I'm aiding and abetting something."

"Gladly." She huffed, and started out of the room before I could change my mind. She hesitated as she reached the door. "I'm sorry about Sarah," she said, her back to me. Then she left.

I spent a few minutes cramming things back into the drawers. Wonderful, now I was actually concealing the crime. I wondered how many years I'd spend behind bars for this, and decided I didn't care. After the past few days, a little prison time might be restful. As long as they let me take my laptop and Hazel.

As I put the vase back in position on the dining room table, I noticed the house had already begun to acquire a sad, deserted air. My mother's house had felt the same way, as if its owner's death had somehow reduced it from a home to a mere building. Suddenly, I was so anxious to get out of there that I practically ran to the front door.

When the doorknob turned of its own accord beneath my hand, my last remaining nerve snapped and I let out a shriek. It was echoed by a similar shriek from outside.

I found Dorothy Stenson on the front porch, a hand pressed to her massive bosom.

"I thought the house was empty," she gasped. "I saw that woman slink off down the street a good fifteen minutes ago."

"You mean Tessa Potter?"

"What was she doing here anyway?" she asked, pulling a leaflet from her apron pocket and fanning her chin with it. A drift of sour perfume assaulted my nose. "C'mon, let's go inside. It's gettin' a mite warm out here."

"No!" I said, more forcefully than I intended. The last thing I wanted to do was re-enter that house. "Uh, that is, let's sit over there for a while. That corner of the porch looks shady." I indicated a pair of white wicker chairs and, to my relief, she obediently started toward them.

"So." She seated herself without missing a single flutter of the makeshift fan. "Since you're obviously not going to answer my question about that woman, I'll ask what *you're* doing here."

"I dropped off Sheriff Crawford's belongings. Doc sent them."

Her eyes immediately filled with tears and she tried to blink them back. Mascara trickled down her cheeks. "I got in touch with his sister in Chicago. She's not gonna be able to make it here for the funeral because she just got out of the hospital. Some kind of operation on her hip. I told her I'd pack everything up and put it in storage for her."

"That was nice of you." I fired up a cigarette, relaxing a little for the first time that day.

"Well, who else is gonna do it? Not that woman. 'Good friends,' she said they were. But do you think she'll lift a finger, now that he's gone?"

I leaned closer, trying not to choke on her essence of stale perfume and sweat. "Tessa? She and Crawford were good friends?"

Dorothy pursed her brightly painted lips. "That's what she called it."

"What would you call it?"

"Carryin' on, that's what. Or worse, if I wasn't a lady. And practically under poor Wood's nose."

I swallowed smoke and coughed. "Are you sure?"

"I've got eyes, girl. I've kept house for Miles Crawford for years, and I live right across the street. Don't you think I'd notice when he took himself a—"

"Lover?" I suggested weakly.

It was hard to tell for sure, considering her heavy layer of rouge, but I think she blushed.

"I wouldn't use a word that pretty to describe an adulteress, but call it what you will." She peered at me. "I've heard you might be related to her. That true?"

"I'm afraid so." I flicked my cigarette into the bushes and stood up. "About the funeral, Miss Stenson, Les said to tell you that it's been postponed for a few days."

"What? Why? I've got it set up for Sunday afternoon. Do you know how hard it was to talk Brother Young into holdin' a funeral service on Sunday? He don't even like to do weddings on a Sunday! Says he's always too tuckered out from his morning preachin'."

I repeated the explanation Lester had provided, and she scowled.

"Bull puckey. I knew Miles Crawford better than anyone, and I know exactly what he'd want. A proper, Christian burial. Which is exactly what I've already arranged for him." She heaved herself from the chair and hurried toward the door. "I'll get old man Luther on the phone, and we'll see about this. You tell Lester Forman to mind his own business. Lawyers, yet!" Still mumbling, she vanished into the house.

Reluctantly, I wrapped myself around the mo-ped and started it down the street. Had Tessa and Crawford really been having an affair? My aunt had yet to give me a reason to look upon her with the slightest bit of fondness, but I found it hard to believe she would cheat on a husband as adoring as Wood Potter. I shrugged, nearly sending the little bike into a storm drain. Then again, what the hell did I know? I was so tired at this point that my brain was barely capable of remembering the way to the sheriff's office.

I did arrive in one piece, after a rather close encounter with a small boy on a skateboard. He had started laughing so hard at the sight of me that he had nearly run over a plump woman who was out walking her Schnauzer. Looking back, I saw them trying to untangle the dog's leash from the wheels of the skateboard, while the puppy gleefully gnawed upon the boy's denim-clad butt. Billy was probably fielding an irate phone call at this very minute.

When I came in, Lester was sprawled at the rear desk, his feet propped up on a stack of paperwork.

"Working hard, I see." I handed the mo-ped key to Billy, informing him that I'd prefer to walk from now on. "How's Puffy?" I asked.

"Puffy probably needs a man in her life," Lester drawled, easing his feet to the floor. "Guess you don't have that problem, though, do you?"

"What?" I noticed that Billy was studiously avoiding my eye contact.

"Oh, come on, Taylor," Les went on. "You can't keep secrets in a town this small. I ought to warn you that the county commissioners are a little narrow minded about things like that. You might want to watch your step, if you expect to hold onto this job."

"What are you talking about?"

Billy, using a peculiar, sideways crab-walk, managed to get himself into the back office and shut the door. He still hadn't looked at me. My weary brain finally succeeded in adding one plus one.

I trudged over to the coffeepot and poured myself a cup of dregs. "I assume Billy told you about my answering Cal's phone this morning, is that it? Fine. Would you care to hear the explanation, or would you rather continue to concoct your own fantasy? I have to warn you that the fantasy will prove to be much more fun."

I didn't wait for his answer. It didn't matter in the least what reputation the citizens of Perdue might assign to me, but I didn't want Cal fired for lending out his phone. When I had finished, Les had the grace to apologize.

"It was really none of my business anyway, I guess. I almost sounded jealous there for a minute, didn't I?"

"I won't tell Paula if you don't," I offered kindly. "You probably couldn't help it. Men tend to operate in some kind of testosterone haze."

"Thanks heaps. Taylor, this isn't any of my business either, but take a word of warning. Don't get mixed up with the Tex-Mex."

I felt my lips tighten. Idiotic male rivalry is one thing. Out and out bigotry is quite another. "Are we still talking about Cal?"

"Sorry. That sounded sorta crude, didn't it?"

"It did to me." Cal sauntered in. "Care to take another swing at me, Lester? I might just hit back this time."

Lester curled his lip. "Aw, don't get your jockeys in a twist, Cal. I didn't mean anything by it."

"Wait a minute," I put in. "What's all this stuff about swinging and hitting? Have you guys been fighting?"

"I wouldn't call it a fight." Cal found the coffeepot empty and confiscated my cup. He took a swallow, gagged. "No, not a fight," he went on, watching Les. "He got in his punch, and I walked away. How about you, Taylor? Would you call that a fight?"

I could hear Lester's teeth grinding. "Why don't we tell her the whole story, if we're going to tell any of it?" he growled.

"Why don't you?" Cal agreed. "I'm sure you'll put a much better spin on it than I could. Besides, I've got work to do." He brushed by me and stalked out.

I sat down on Billy's desk and looked at Les. "Well?"

"Nothing! Things are a little tense around here right now, what with the election coming up. I'm sure someone has told you that Cal and I are squaring off."

"I've heard."

"Well, shit, that's all it is. We get on each other's nerves once in a while. It's stupid anyway. I'm going to win."

I busied myself putting together a fresh pot of coffee. "Are you that confident?"

"Sure. Crawford is—"

"Crawford was, you mean. Going to back you? Don't you think his death might make things a little different?"

Lester was quiet for a moment. "I guess it might. Cal went to college, I didn't, and people think college makes a man smart." He seemed to relax a little. "But hell, he dropped out his second year of law school, and everyone knows it. Makes him look like a quitter, and these folks won't want a quitter for their sheriff."

I sat down, suddenly so tired I could barely keep my eyes open. "Why did he drop out?"

"Something to do with a rape," Lester said. "I don't know all the details."

"You're telling me that Cal was accused of rape?"

"Like I said, I don't know. I've just heard bits and pieces."

"Oh, good Lord, I've landed in Peyton Place." I stretched, feeling bones in my back pop. "Les, I am totally exhausted. If I don't get a little sleep, I'm not going to be worth a hill of beans for the rest of the day, so I'm going back to my room for a nap."

He nodded. "Good idea. But, Taylor? Lock your door. Better safe than sorry."

Chapter Six

HAZEL GREETED ME as if I had abandoned her for months instead of hours. She dragged her plastic food dish across the room and deposited it gently upon my feet.

"Sorry, baby," I murmured, picking her up and placing her on my shoulder. Her claws dug into my shirt as I filled her dish and gave her fresh water. By the time I had laid out a clean newspaper in her potty corner, I was as weary as if I had single-handedly mucked out the Houston Astrodome after a rodeo.

I didn't lock either door, for the simple reason that neither door possessed a lock. I did, however, drag a large trunk over to block the door to the hallway, and tucked the back of a wooden chair under the bathroom doorknob. For one thing, it was all I could find. For another, I had a mental image of awakening with a pressing need for the porcelain facilities, only to find myself unable to get in. I found what Lester had hinted about Cal hard to believe, but being a city girl, I would always feel more comfortable behind secured doors. At least, that's what I told myself.

I lowered the window shade, placed Hazel on the floor and threw myself into bed. It felt wonderful, except for whatever was pressing itself into my right hip. Cursing, I rolled to one side and dug the offending objects out of my pocket.

The first thing I found was my Milky Way, which was leaking melted chocolate, its wrapper mangled. I tossed it into the trashcan, wiping my fingers on my sweatshirt before delving back into the pocket and coming up with Crawford's book. I kept forgetting I had it.

Sleeping Murder. I had read it, at least twice. Had I picked it up out of some subconscious desire to read it a third time? Somehow, I doubted that. It was all I could do to touch it, considering it had last been handled by a man in the throes of death. I skimmed my hand over the front cover, feeling where it was torn. A neat, horizontal rip ran from the outer edge, as if underlining the second word in the title. The first few pages were badly crumpled, and the book's spine was bent, as if it had been clutched in a tight grip. As it probably had been. Shuddering, I tossed it across the room and turned onto my stomach. I was asleep before I had taken a second breath.

I don't remember my dreams, but they weren't pleasant. I jolted awake, drenched in sweat and in a state of mindless panic. The sun had moved into its afternoon position, leaving my little room dark, and I fumbled for the knob on the floor lamp beside the bed. It clicked twice, but the bulb didn't light. Damn.

Still half asleep, I lurched across the room and felt the wall by the door. When I finally came awake enough to realize that I was groping for a nonexistent switch, I started laughing. But the laughter caught in my throat as the question that had plagued me all day finally answered itself.

I took a long, satisfying shower, closing my eyes against the spray of warm water and concentrating on remembering exactly what I had seen and done that morning. Okay, I had attempted to find a pulse. The room had been dim, so I had reached for the lamp beside the chair. The knob had turned, twice. Click, click. Then Les rushed in, yelling for someone to turn on a light. And the lamp came on, practically blinding me. High wattage, good for reading. Dorothy Stenson was standing in the entranceway, her hand on the switch. The switch by the front door.

Obviously, I had turned the lamp off, then on again, because I had not realized it could also be controlled by the switch on the far side of the room. Yet the sheriff had been reading a book when the snake struck. That's why it had made no sense—it still didn't. The lamp had been off when I arrived, and it had been turned off by using the switch by the door, not the one on the lamp itself.

Unless I could swallow the idea of a fatally injured man staggering across the room to flick the switch and then making it back to his recliner in time to die, someone else would have had to turn off that lamp. Whoever had done it probably hadn't even been conscious of the act. In this age of energy conservation, it was a habit instilled in almost everyone—leave a room, turn off the light.

I dried off, dressed in clean jeans and my least wrinkled shirt, my mind still sifting facts. Locating the book, I carried it to the window and examined it in the weak sunlight.

Bits and pieces of other information melded with what I had already determined, and suddenly, I could no longer ignore the implications.

Sinking down on the edge of the mattress, I watched Hazel stuff her furry face with cat food. A wave of such giddiness swept over me that I thought for a moment I was coming down with something. Hazel let out a soft, satisfied burp and my stomach rumbled enviously. Well, no wonder I was feeling woozy. According to my watch, it had been more than eighteen hours since I had eaten anything more substantial than a candy bar.

When I found myself digging through the wastebasket for the mutilated Milky Way, I decided it was time to head for the café while I was still strong enough to walk. I sneaked down the stairs and out the back door, avoiding Hank and his store full of checker-playing cronies. It was past one o'clock when I arrived, and the lunch crowd had dispersed. Rita was seated on a stool at one end of the counter, sipping a pink milkshake and reading a *National Enquirer*.

I asked her to bring me some of whatever was already cooked, and five minutes later I was tucking into the day's blue plate special. It turned out to be fried catfish, though I didn't stop to analyze it until I had consumed half the meal. A good indication of how hungry I was is that Rita could have informed me I was eating more fried rattlesnake, and it probably wouldn't have interfered with my feeding frenzy.

After delivering my pecan pie and coffee, Rita slid into the seat across from me and made it clear she was in the mood for a good chat. I would have preferred to be alone with my pie and my thoughts, but couldn't come up with a polite way to get rid of her.

"How's the job going?" she asked. "Boy, are you a lucky dog. What I wouldn't give to work with that dreamboat every day."

"I'd have gladly traded places with you this morning," I said dryly, adding cream to my coffee.

She bit her lip. "Wasn't it awful? But I heard Lester was real brave. Did he really go in and shoot the snake?"

"He really did."

Her besotted expression returned. So much for mourning the sheriff. "Isn't he wonderful?"

"I s'pose," I mumbled around a mouthful of pie. "His wife probably likes him, too, don't you think?"

Rita's lips contorted. "Paula doesn't know what she's got, if you ask me. I'll never understand why he married that little creep when he could've had his pick of any girl in Perdue." She leaned across the table, lowering her voice. "It was right out of the blue, you know. Everyone was shocked. For a while, we thought she might have had, you know, a bun in the oven? I mean, for him to up and marry her so quick like that! A city girl, too. From Dallas." Her sneer faded as she caught my eye. "Oh, no offense intended."

I was still goggling over the reference to a "bun in the oven," wondering if I had crossed a time line as well as a county line when I entered Perdue. But no, they had horseless carriages and telephones, so

I hadn't warped back to the nineteenth century.

"Do you know Paula very well?" I asked, more or less for something to say.

"Heck, no. Nobody does. She's stuck up. Hardly ever comes into town, and doesn't go to church even. Can you believe it—Lester himself does the grocery shopping for them! Have you ever heard the like?"

"Astounding," I agreed. The first thing I was going to do when I got back to Houston was send this girl a year's subscription to *Ms.* "She's sort of pretty though, don't you think?"

It was a low blow, but Rita bore it bravely. "I'm really not the one to ask, since I've only laid eyes on her once in the two years they've been married. She sure as heck isn't friendly. Wouldn't even let me sign her cast."

"Her cast?"

Rita shrugged. "Yeah, she had her arm in a sling. Said she'd fallen in the bathtub. Stupid city girl," she added in an undertone, as if country folk never had bathroom accidents.

I opened my mouth to ask for the check, but Rita was looking over my left shoulder, her expression that of a woman who had caught a whiff of skunk. I turned.

Cal nodded a greeting, removing his hat and wiping his forehead with the back of his hand. "Gettin' warm out there for April. How about some iced tea, Rita? Whenever you get the chance."

Her lips tightened, but she slid out of the booth and stomped away.

"No sense wooing that vote," he said. "Mind if I join you?" He seated himself before I had a chance to answer. "Well, you seem more rested. Billy told me you went home for a nap." He sighed. "Wish I could do that, but the tourists are out in full force already. They don't seem to care that the official opening ceremony isn't until tomorrow."

The sight of him brought Lester's warning rushing back into my mind. I had been so exhausted when Les had brought it up that I hadn't considered that, no matter how kind-hearted Crawford might have been, it wouldn't have been legally possible for him to have deputized a convicted rapist. But suppose Cal had been accused and then acquitted? No one who has ever read a newspaper could remain unaware that 'acquitted' doesn't always mean 'innocent.'

Rape is an ugly word to any woman, and no matter how hard I tried to convince myself that I didn't really believe it of this man, I felt my scalp crawl.

He craned his neck, trying to catch my eye. "Hey, you're looking sort of funny. You're not getting sick, are you?"

"Of course not," I told the napkin dispenser. "I'm fine."

"Well, good." He sounded puzzled. "We're sure gonna need your help from now on."

"I'll be there," I assured my coffee cup.

"Okay. Why don't you ride out the grounds with me? I'll walk you through all the events that're on for tomorrow."

I found myself balking at the thought of getting into a car with him. This was how people acted in soap operas, damn it, letting rumors and misunderstandings fester until they destroyed any chance at the truth. "Cal, why did you drop out of law school?" I blurted.

"What?"

"You heard me."

Rita appeared, sloshing tea as she slapped his glass down in front of him.

He watched her walk away. "Wonder if I should have this analyzed before I drink it?"

I watched him squeeze in lemon, add sugar, and stir the brew long enough to churn it into butter. He finally looked at me.

"Why do you want to know?"

"Curiosity." My lips felt frozen; I couldn't manage to soften the lie with a smile.

"I'm a little curious about you, too, but I haven't heard you answering any of my questions." He took a sip of tea and shrugged. "Oh, well, it's no secret, just not very pretty. I guess you could say I dropped out because of a rape."

Oh, God. I went numb to the bone.

"There was this girl in my class," he went on. "Smart as a whip, but really shy. She was on the verge of failing her litigation course because she couldn't bring herself to get up in front of sixty plus people and present a case. A bunch of us tried to help her. We'd hold practice sessions at the dorm and feed her hints like the old standby of picturing everyone in his underwear, or focusing on one person in the crowd and pretending she was holding a private conversation instead of addressing a crowd. Nothing helped, poor kid." He sighed. "I finally suggested she contact the professor and see what he recommended. So, she made an appointment to meet with him one evening."

Rita brought my check, and I rudely gestured for her to get lost without ever taking my eyes off Cal.

"I should never have volunteered to drive her over there," he said.

"Somehow, I should've known what would happen."

I had a horrible vision of Cal pulling his car off the road, lunging at the frightened girl, ripping her clothes. The blue plate special rolled uneasily in my stomach.

"I had to get a book from the library before it closed, so I dropped her off at his house and said I'd pick her up in half an hour. I'd driven about a block when I noticed that she'd left her briefcase in the seat. I figured she might need it, so I turned around and went back." His eyes darkened. "I lifted my hand to knock and that's when I heard her scream. I don't even remember how I got in there. The cops told me later that I had busted the lock, and I had probably kicked the door in, but I really don't remember." His eyes squeezed shut. "I do remember what I saw. I'll never forget that."

A breath I hadn't realized I was holding whooshed out. "He was—?"

Cal nodded grimly. "Oh, yeah. He was all right. I got him off her and called the cops."

"Oh." I was so relieved it took a moment for the logical question to occur to me. "But that doesn't explain why you left school."

"The case went to trial, and it took every one of her friends to convince her to testify against him, but she did. So did I, of course. And you know what happened?" He curled one hand into a fist. "Not a damned thing. The esteemed jury was so dazzled by his defense attorney, so appalled such an accusation could even be made against a fine, upstanding, tenured professor that they found the bastard not guilty." His jaw clenched. "That man is still teaching to this day. Pure as the driven snow."

I shook my head in disbelief. "And the girl?"

"I don't know. She dropped out, moved away. We never heard from her again. Don't get me wrong. I still believe in the law, but I'm not so sure I believe in justice anymore. Not the kind you find in a courtroom anyway." He laughed bitterly. "I was going to be a defense attorney. Can you believe it?"

"You could've become a prosecutor instead," I pointed out.

"Right. The prosecutor on that case was good, one of the best. But he didn't win, did he? Maybe it's people in general, Taylor. Maybe we've all been brainwashed by talk shows and TV shrinks to accept that there are no bad people, that criminals are the way they are because they ate Twinkies as a kid, or watched violent movies, or didn't get that shiny, red bike for Christmas. Bullshit. Some people are born bad." He took a deep breath. "Sorry, didn't mean to climb up on a soapbox."

"It's okay, and sounds like you're entitled. But I still hate to think of your leaving school. I mean, it's almost as if that horrible man ruined your life along with the girl's."

"Oh, I dropped law school, but I finished college. After I came to work for Crawford, I took night school courses at Texas Tech until I had earned my degree in Criminal Justice. Might go back later and try for my Masters, but I'll wait and see how the election turns out. If I lose, I'll probably find another place to live. I don't have family here anymore, and there's really nothing to hold me here."

He stirred ice cubes with his forefinger. "Aside from the fact I really like this town, of course. Guess I'll find out come November how much it likes me." He looked up, frowning. "Okay, now, how about the truth? What on earth made you bring all this up?"

I hesitated, then told him.

He sighed. "So that's the new game plan, is it? A little mud-slinging ought to sew the election up even tighter."

"No. Honestly, Cal, I'm the one who jumped to conclusions. I was exhausted, and I just overreacted. Les told me straight out he didn't know the whole story."

"He probably doesn't. I didn't exactly broadcast it when I moved back to town. Okay, you're right. Les and I don't always see eye to eye, but I sure don't feel like getting into another fight. Too many other things to take care of right now. Speaking of which, are you ready to go?"

"You bet." I welcomed back the trust like a long-lost friend.

Something occurred to me as I threw some money on the table to pay for my lunch. "Hey, Cal, is being a cop really any better than being a lawyer? You still have rules to follow, and I would imagine sometimes those rules can be every bit as frustrating."

He smiled. "At least cops get to carry guns."

A trace of my former uncertainty returned, but I shook it off. He hadn't meant that the way it sounded. Had he?

My mind veered to even darker speculations. I took advantage of the drive out to the festival grounds to mull things over, hoping I would find the holes in my budding theory, hoping I was as wrong about this as Lester had been about Cal. But missing pieces were not the same as holes, and though I had a few of the former, I couldn't come up with any of the latter. I studied Cal's profile as he drove, wondering if it was time yet to share my suspicions, but decided to wait until I could gather at least a few more facts. I needed to be standing on a solid foundation if and when I dropped this particular bombshell. With any luck, something would happen to make me change my mind.

As many times as I had been told that tourists flocked to this event, I was amazed at the number of people swarming the site. Cal and I were swallowed up the moment we walked through the gate, forced apart by the mass of sweaty bodies. Country music blared from overhead speakers, mingling badly with the tinny tune screeching from the carousel. A nauseating blend of smells assailed me from every direction: cotton candy, corn dogs, caramel apples, and the now recognizable aroma of fried snake.

Having no idea what I was supposed to be doing, I wandered over to the craft booths, surprised by how many of the locals greeted me by name. I fielded a few questions about the sheriff's death, developing a 'no comment' type of answer that left no one satisfied, but didn't hurt anyone's feelings either.

After declining to purchase a pair of earrings fashioned from snake rattles, I ended up buying two key rings. One was a plastic disk with a picture of a German Shepherd painted on it. A tiny, electronic chip inside activated when the disk was pressed, making the key ring bark. Loudly, too. My agent, Annie, raised German Shepherds, and I knew she'd love it. I also, rather wickedly, suspected that the first time she pressed it, it would set off a chain reaction among her brood of dogs, and that she'd spend hours trying to make them all shut up.

The second one I bought, strictly on impulse, for Wood. This one depicted a sheep, and baaed quite nicely. Perhaps it would keep him from missing his "babies" so much.

The booth operator, a plump matron who looked out of place in her jeans and scuffed boots, wrapped my purchases in tissue paper as carefully as if they had been made of gold. "Too bad we don't have the snakes this year," she complained. "These are cute, but they're not selling very well."

"Pardon me?" I had been digging for an elusive penny in the bottom of my backpack.

"The key chains with snakes on 'em were our biggest sellers last year, but we had a mix-up in the shipment and didn't get any this time." She sighed. "Heard tell they ended up at some county fair in Minnesota. Hell, I doubt if those Yankees have ever even seen a rattler."

"Probably not," I agreed. *Lucky Yankees*, I added to myself as I thanked her and wandered back into the crowd.

When I finally located Cal, I almost wished I hadn't. He was in the process of milking a rattler, cheered on by an awed group of tourists. I had thought he was joking about knowing how, but he handled the creature with the ease of an expert. Backing away, I plowed into someone behind me.

"*Ooof!* Sorry. Oh, Doctor Neil. Are you all right?"

"Fine," he assured me. "Cal's good at that, isn't he?"

"Seems to be." I bit my lip, my theory rearing its ugly head. Hell, I might as well start with Doc, if I was determined to start at all. "Doc, have you found anything out from the lab in Lubbock yet?"

He snorted. "I'll be lucky if I hear back by the end of next week. They're understaffed and overworked. Why the interest?"

I hesitated, unwilling to say too much, too soon. "Just wondering. What you said about the autopsy struck me as odd."

"Damned odd," he agreed.

I focused on Cal for a moment, watching as he forced the deadly fluid into a container. "You said that a snake only ejects part of its venom in a single bite."

He nodded. "Right. Rattlers have a gland that produces the venom, and that gland is made up of thousands of tiny tubes capable of storing unused venom."

"So, if a snake bites someone several times, it would be possible for it to inject the victim with venom each time."

"Sure." He peered at me. "Have you decided to take up herpetology as a hobby?"

"Good God, no." I shuddered. "But I'm a writer, in case no one told you, and I tend to gather trivia whenever I can. You never know when it might come in handy."

He seemed to accept that. "I see what you're getting at, and it's true a snake can store quite a lot of venom. It's also true that it will eject whatever amount of venom it instinctively feels is necessary to subdue its intended victim. But as far as Crawford is concerned, that was still too much venom to be found for a single bite. I wouldn't have been so surprised to find that amount spread out over several bites, you understand."

"I think so. But, Doc," I tried to choose my words carefully. "Suppose a snake was forced to keep pumping venom into a single location?"

He lifted an eyebrow. "Forced?"

I pointed at Cal. "That's what he's doing, isn't it?"

"Well, in a manner of speaking, yes. Young lady, I hope you're not saying what I think I'm hearing."

"I have rounds to make, Doc," I put in hastily. "Nice talking to you."

It wasn't hard to merge into the crowd, and I breathed a sigh of relief when I realized he wasn't attempting to follow me. I only hoped he'd write me off as a nut, and not go running to Les or Cal. I needed a little more time to think, but felt convinced I had picked up another puzzle piece.

I wandered for a couple of hours, keeping my eyes peeled for any kind of trouble, though I wasn't sure what I would do if, for instance, a fight broke out. Fortunately, the few problems I ran across, I was able to handle on my own. The most frightening was the five-year-old boy whom I had caught, literally, as he was attempting to climb over the side of one of the snake tanks. All he had wanted was a chance to see inside, and his father, mooning over an expensive display of snakeskin boots, had ignored the child's repeated requests for a lift. I plucked him off the tank's rim, carried him to his father along with a stern admonition, and spent the next twenty minutes trembling at the thought of that baby tumbling into the midst of all those squirming, buzzing, biting creatures.

Cal finally caught up with me while I was taking a rest. The west Texas sun had decided to flaunt its full strength rays, and patches of shade were few and far between. I had located one such patch, about three feet square, lodged between a wall of the auditorium building and a stunted mesquite tree, and was crunching the ice left over from a hastily consumed cup of Dr. Pepper.

He nudged me, so I reluctantly moved over half an inch to let him share the cool spot. I did point out that it didn't seem fair, since he possessed a nice, wide-brimmed straw hat and so was able to create his own shade wherever he went.

"Buy one of your own," he suggested unsympathetically. "Are you ready to take a break?"

"That's what I'm trying to do, but it was much nicer before someone started crowding me."

He laughed. "I meant, away from here. There's something else we need to take care of before it gets dark."

"Hey, I'm with you." I was all for any opportunity to get away from that noisy, smelly place.

Or so I thought.

Fifteen minutes later, I found myself facing a mound of dirt, upon which had been secured a large paper target that featured the life-sized silhouette of a man's head and torso.

"*Ow!*" I hollered as Cal tried to screw a wad of rubber into my left ear. "What is that thing?"

"What does it look like? An earplug. Unless you prefer to have your ears ring for a day or two after we finish here. Guns make a lot of noise, Taylor."

"I don't remember expressing a desire to shoot one," I grumbled. "Here, let me do that myself. Good grief, you've got it all tangled up in my hair. Would you mind telling me exactly why we're doing this?"

"It was the last promise I made to Sheriff Crawford," he said quietly, and I shut right up.

While I was positioning the plugs to a more comfortable position within my ear canals, Cal examined a couple of handguns and a shotgun.

"We'll start with the .357," he said, after examining my hands. "Your fingers are long, so you shouldn't have any trouble with the grip size. Now, we're going to use .38 ammunition in this to start. It's a less powerful load and won't give as much of a kick. Are you ready?"

"Do I have a choice?" I retorted, and held out my hand for the gun. But, no. First, I stood for thirty minutes in the blazing hot afternoon sun and listened to a lecture on aiming at the target and nothing else, never pointing the weapon at anyone unless I was willing to shoot, never shooting unless I intended to kill. Never assuming that a weapon was unloaded, and how to check.

That done, I next got a lesson on how to locate a "sight picture" (this had to do with how to use the little raised sights on the end of the barrel), the proper way to grip a handgun (which always involved the use of both hands, unless I someday found myself in a situation where one hand had been injured and rendered useless), where to aim (always central body mass, never at the head or at an extremity), and to squeeze the trigger instead of pulling it. The sun, by this time, was beginning a distinctly downward dip.

He finally shut up and looked at me. "Well?"

"What?" I asked, still trying to keep everything straight in my head.

He gestured at the target. "Go ahead."

"Oh." I raised the gun, surprised at how heavy it was, and took careful aim. *Squeeze the trigger,* I reminded myself. *Keep your sight picture, firm up your grip and...BLAM!*

"Holy shit," I whispered. This had been a mild load? The palms of my hands tingled from the shock, and my ears were ringing like chapel bells, plugs or not.

Cal took the gun and carried it with him, muzzle pointed at the ground, as he walked over to check my target. "Want to come see how you did?" he called.

I crept forward until I could see the dime-sized hole in the target. It was slightly above and slightly to the right of the exact center of the target, which is where I had been aiming.

"Nice shot."

"What do you mean, nice? I wanted to hit it here." I touched the middle of the three-inch white circle that was marked with an X.

Cal guffawed. "Oh, God, a perfectionist! Taylor, most people would be happy to even hit the target with their first-ever shot. Give yourself a break. You weren't expecting the recoil, which is why it's a little high, and you're not used to the grips, which is why you pulled a bit to the right. With a little practice, you'll be really good."

I hadn't expected to like shooting, but by the time dusk arrived, Cal had to practically drag me back to the car. We had never gotten around to the shotgun, but in addition to the .357, I had tried out a .45 semi-automatic and an adorable little two-shot derringer. The .357 was still my favorite. The .45 bucked like a wild bronco every time I fired it, no matter how I adjusted my grip, and the derringer was almost useless if I shot it from more than a three-foot range. Cal agreed that it made a good "boot gun," but that was about the only use he had for it.

As we drove back to town, Billy informed us by radio that Dorothy had lost her fight with Luther's regarding Crawford's funeral, but had arranged to hold a memorial service at his house tomorrow morning. We were all invited.

Cal acknowledged the message, then looked at me. "Les told me about Doc's insistence on sending the body to Lubbock. I'm not sure I understand all this, Taylor."

I opened my mouth to fill him in on my private theory, then closed it again as he pulled to a stop in front of the hardware store, presenting me with the perfect excuse to keep my thoughts to myself for a little while longer. I was well aware of how foolish I was going to sound when I finally shared the conclusion I had reached. Unfortunately, I also knew beyond a doubt that I would, indeed, share it.

Heaven help me, I had no choice.

Chapter Seven

I WAS AT THE café early. The official opening ceremony for the festival would take place at eleven o'clock that morning, and Billy told us that Dorothy had scheduled the memorial service for nine because she didn't want to give anyone an excuse for not attending. I was determined to eat a decent breakfast, since I had once again skipped dinner the night before.

I had spent the remainder of the evening hunched over my laptop, making notes on my speculations about Crawford's death and muttering to myself. It hadn't been much use. The time had come for me to share my idea with someone else.

A young farmer whistled at me as I stepped into the café. Politically incorrect as all get-out, but it made me feel good anyway. I hadn't packed anything fancy for this trip, and the best I could come up with for Crawford's memorial was a denim skirt and plain white blouse, with leather flats replacing my sneakers.

I'd just ordered a huge stack of pancakes with bacon on the side when Billy ambled in, looking spiffy in tight jeans, a fancy western-cut shirt, and elaborate boots. I gestured for him to join me in the booth. He did, but he didn't seem too happy about it.

"Wow, great outfit," I told him.

"Les said I could help out at the festival today," he mumbled, picking an imaginary piece of lint from the front of his shirt. "He got old man Perkins, the janitor, to handle the phones."

I raised an eyebrow. "What's wrong? Don't you want to?"

"Sure, I want to. It's the closest I've come to being a real deputy, and that's what I want to be more than anything."

"Then what's the matter with you?"

He finally looked at me, his cheeks bright red. "I owe you an apology, Miss Madison. It was wrong of me to spread gossip about you the way I did. I really didn't mean it that way."

I laughed. "Billy, I can understand why you must've thought what you did. I might have jumped to the same conclusion, in your place. Now, I'll agree that it wasn't such a great idea to tell someone else about it before talking to me, but that was an upsetting morning for everyone. I'm sure you were chatting with Les, and it came out before you realized it."

He nodded eagerly. "That's just exactly the way it happened. You mean, you're not mad at me?"

"Nope, not a bit."

"Oh." He beamed. "Gee, thanks. I didn't think you'd ever talk to me again."

"Is this a private party, or can anyone join?" Cal slid into the booth beside Billy. "Hey, Bill, did you remember your badge?"

"Got it right here." Billy patted his pocket.

"You're supposed to wear it on the outside, you know."

"Right now? I mean, I didn't think it would be okay until I actually got out to the grounds."

"Right now," Cal assured him, and the boy pinned the star to his shirt, preening like a rooster. "And how are you this morning?" Cal asked me. "You certainly look like a million."

"Thanks, you're not so bad yourself." Cal was decked out in black jeans and a black shirt with pearl buttons.

"Yep, I'm dandy. Considering."

"Considering what?"

"Considering that when I got home around midnight, someone had removed the only light bulb from the bathroom, and I had to feel my way to the, er, necessity."

I flushed and Billy burst out laughing.

"Oh, jeez, I'm sorry. My lamp burned out."

"No problem. I replaced it before I left."

It finally hit me what was wrong with this picture. "Why aren't you in uniform?" I asked Cal.

He shrugged. "It's sort of traditional for opening day. Everyone dresses in western clothes, including the law. Doesn't matter, really, as long as we still wear our badges and gun belts."

My breakfast arrived, and both men eyed it, askance.

"How can you eat like that and stay so skinny?" Les inquired as he sat down beside me. He was decked out, too, in dark blue jeans and a flaming red shirt, a red-and-white bandanna knotted about his neck.

"You guys are determined to make me feel like a spinster school marm, aren't you?" I grumbled, then took a huge bite of my pancakes. "Yum. At least I don't have to worry about fitting into tight jeans."

All three of them examined me critically.

"You look fine," Les finally said. "It's not a matter of what you're wearing, but what you're not wearing."

"Exactly," Cal agreed. "This is an important annual event in

Derrick County, and you have done nothing to commemorate it."

"Like what?" I asked suspiciously.

"Honey, you're not wearin' any snake," Les informed me. "Men? Show her."

The three of them stood up, posing for me like fashion models and pointing to their various accouterments. Les's hatband, Cal's gun belt, and Billy's boots were all, I realized, made of snakeskin.

Rita came by with the coffee pot. "Oooh, wish I had my camera!"

"I saved up for three years to buy these boots," Billy told me proudly. "'Course, you don't need to go that far, Miss Taylor. Maybe some earrings?"

"No, thanks. I saw those earrings, and I can live without them."

"A barrette?" Cal suggested.

"Or a headband," Les put in.

"No and no. I refuse to wear snake on any part of my body. Forget it."

"By the way, Les—" Cal took a sip of coffee. "—I hate to bring this up, but with the sheriff, well, not here, we have a few things to decide. For instance, someone has to take his place this evening to hand out the awards. I figured you'd do that, as senior deputy."

I felt Les stiffen beside me, and when I looked at him, his face was the color of chalk.

"You handle it," he snapped. "Excuse me." He got up and headed for the bathroom, almost running.

"What was that all about?"

Cal sighed. "Shit, I shouldn't have asked him. I plumb didn't think it through."

"He's gonna be mad all day now," Billy said.

"We hand out awards to the snake hunters," Cal went on, when he saw that I was still confused. "A trophy for the biggest snake, the most snakes, things like that. Crawford always did it before."

I shook my head. "So? What's the big deal?"

"Part of the presentation on the largest snake is to use a snake hook to lift it out of the tank so the crowd can see it. And Les..."

"Lester don't like snakes," Billy put in.

"Well, I'm with him."

"It's more than that, Taylor. He's almost phobic about them," Cal said. "Poor guy. He fainted dead away last year when one got loose. Now, don't let on that I told you about this. No reason to shame him."

"I won't." Remembering how Lester had rushed into Crawford's house with that shotgun, knowing what was in there waiting for him, I was even more impressed than I had been at the time. It had taken something beyond courage for a man who was so terrified of snakes to do that.

When Les returned, I decided to change the subject. Unfortunately, the subject I had in mind wasn't going to be any more pleasant than the one I was trying to avoid. I pushed my plate away.

"Guys, there's something I have to tell you." I took a deep breath and watched Cal steal a bite of my pancakes. "I think Sheriff Crawford was murdered."

Les jumped, Cal choked, and Billy's jaw dropped. Not bad for an initial reaction.

"You think what?" Les roared. Cal continued to choke, and Billy, his mouth still hanging open, reached over to slap him on the back.

"*Shhh!*" Trying to sound calm and rational, I reminded them what Doc had said about the amount of venom he'd found at the autopsy. I also shared my thoughts concerning the sheriff's reading lamp. Then, I paused for a beat, wondering how best to work in the book. Finally, I pulled it out of my backpack where I'd been keeping it, and showed them the cover.

Lester squinted at it. "So?"

"Don't you see where it's torn?" I insisted. "It's as if he deliberately ripped it right under that word. I think he intended to tear the word out, if he'd only had a little more time."

Cal started laughing, and after a moment, both Lester and Billy joined him. "Oh, Taylor, you've got to be putting us on, right? I mean, how hokey can you get? You really believe he was trying to tear the word "murder" from that cover?"

"He was sending a message." I was straining to maintain my dignity. It wasn't easy, with all of them hooting like insane owls. "You know what a fan Crawford was of mystery novels. Don't you see that he'd have tried to leave a clue? He wouldn't have wanted his murder to be written off as an accident. Laugh all you want to. I know it's the truth."

"Hey, Cal, she does write those mystery books, you know," Les said. "She's used to clues and such."

"Yeah, that's right. Maybe we should pay attention." They both regarded me solemnly for about thirty seconds before breaking into hilarity again.

"Stop it, both of you. I'm not joking." I gritted my teeth. "Okay, forget the book cover if you think it's so absurd, but what about the venom? And the lamp?"

Cal swallowed a laugh and wiped his eyes. "Doc may be wrong about the venom, Taylor. Besides, how do you think someone would go about using a snake as a murder weapon? Think hard. You're suggesting that the killer held that snake and forced it to bite Crawford? Sure thing. Better look for a suspect with a few bites of his own."

"As for the lamp," Les put in, "how do you know Dorothy didn't flip that switch off when she went into the house that morning? You said yourself that people do things like that from habit."

"Why would she turn a light off when she came into a house?"

"Maybe she called the SO and then hit the switch when she walked out the front door to wait for a deputy." Cal touched my hand, and I pulled it sharply away. "Taylor, think about what you're saying. Who would want to kill Sheriff Crawford anyway? Everyone loved him."

A gasp. Rita stood frozen, one hand pressed against her mouth. "Someone killed the sheriff?" she asked. "Oh, my God!" She turned away and stumbled back toward the counter.

Cal groaned. "Billy, she's your sister. Go talk to her. Tell her to keep her mouth shut, will ya?"

Billy stood up, shaking his head. "I'll try, Cal, but you might as well tell a rooster not to crow."

I found myself as startled by Cal's last statement as Rita had been. It came as a shock to realize I had spent so much time convincing myself that Crawford had been murdered, I hadn't even thought about who might have wanted him dead. Lord, how stupid could I get?

Cal smacked the table with an open palm. "Great, Taylor, now it'll be all over town by noon. What in hell is wrong with you?"

"Cal—" Les began, but Cal continued hotly.

"You know, I wasn't sure it was such a great idea for Crawford to hire you in the first place, but this takes the cake. You're going to get everyone stirred up for no reason."

"I don't think that's your decision to make, Cal Arnette," said a disembodied voice from somewhere behind him. "Election hasn't been held yet." Bonita Posey appeared next to the booth.

"But, Bo, did you hear what she was saying?"

"I've got ears, Cal. Question is, why are both of you so all-fired certain she's wrong?"

Les gave an impolite snort, and Bo toddled around to sit beside him.

"You too, Forman? Tsk. Thought you'd have learned by now to keep an open mind."

"It's open, Bo, but it's not vacant," Les drawled. "This doesn't make any sense."

"Why? Because neither of you thought of it first? I'd say this little gal has been pretty observant."

Cal lost his grin. "You mean you believe this bullshit?"

"I didn't say that. Don't know yet that there's anything to believe. I'm sayin', what's the harm in checkin' it out? Y'all are deputies, which makes it your job to investigate things like this. So, investigate."

"Is that an order?" Les grumbled.

"It is."

Order? I looked at him. Where did a storekeeper get off giving orders to a deputy?

Bo seemed to read my mind. "Guess no one's told you that I'm one of the county commissioners. The other one is Dave Underwood, but he hardly counts for much. This time of year, he's too busy sellin' his fried snake nuggets and rakin' in the dough. I believe you've made his acquaintance, Taylor. And," she added, with a significant glare at Les and Cal, "Dave wouldn't want to cross one of my decisions, so nobody ought to take it into his head to go see him behind old Bo's back. I'm holdin' him by the—"

"—short hairs," Lester and Cal concluded in unison.

"Got it in one." Bo stood up. "See y'all at the festival. Let me know what turns up about Miles. I'll be waitin' to hear."

Lester looked at the ceiling and Cal at the floor. I didn't know whether to laugh or cry.

"I'm sorry," I told them finally. "It wasn't my intention to stir up a hornet's nest."

I heard someone chuckling, and was surprised to see that it was Lester.

"Hell, Cal," he said. "Looks like we've got us a murder case, whether we want it or not. I hereby appoint Deputy Taylor Madison to investigate to her heart's content. As long as it doesn't interfere with her other duties that is. Taylor, have at it. Maybe you'll get another novel out of it anyway."

"Me? What about the two of you?"

"You thought we'd help you? You thought the entire staff of the sheriff's office would pitch in and solve this so-called murder? I don't have time, and neither does Cal." He pointed a finger at me. "Just be careful where you go pokin' your pretty little nose in this town, Deputy. Folks in these parts don't much care for snoopers." He stood, offering a gallant arm to help me out of the booth. "I believe we have a memorial service to attend."

I had expected angry silence during the ride to Crawford's house, but all three men talked the whole way, discussing the festival and dividing up various duties. They included me easily, as if Cal hadn't been yelling at me minutes earlier—as if, in fact, the word murder had never been uttered.

I was relieved, but skeptical, wondering what they had up their respective sleeves. They assigned me the dubious honor of presiding over the Miss Snakeskin beauty contest. I was amazed to think anyone would vie for such a title, which sounded as derogatory as all get-out to me. Did the contestants have to swear off moisturizing lotion for a year prior to the competition?

Billy, beside me in the back seat, pouted a little, no doubt wishing he had been chosen as the judge. I whispered to him that I was going to need a man's opinion, and was hereby appointing him my assistant. He brightened.

"By the way, Billy..." I was still whispering. "Whose car is this?" I had grown accustomed to the beige squad cars Cal and Les both drove, but this one was a deep chocolate brown and had been recently waxed to gleaming perfection. Inside, it was even more immaculate than Cal's, and no cage separated the front seat from the back.

"It was the sheriff's," Billy told me. "Roger brought it back from the shop this mornin'. I guess Les has decided to drive it now." He didn't sound entirely approving, and I couldn't say I blamed him. It seemed disrespectful, somehow.

On the other hand, I could understand Lester being anxious to escape his rolling cesspool. I had to wonder how long it would be before this car began to take on the same neglected odor.

"I don't suppose Roger said anything about my Volkswagen, did he?"

"Oh, yeah. Said to tell you he should be gettin' the parts in today, and he'd let you know."

"Okay." I didn't know why I was in such a hurry anyway. No one had handed me a paycheck yet, and I wasn't sure how I was going to get my car out of hock.

Mourners had filled Crawford's house with so many flowers that their combined fragrances made it hard to breathe. Dorothy met us at the door, dressed in black from head to toe as befitted a grieving widow rather than a housekeeper. Even her hair had been given a fresh soak of black dye, and a Jackie Kennedy style pillbox hat perched atop the stiff curls. I was surprised she wasn't wearing a veil.

The turnout couldn't have been a disappointment to her. The tiny house was overflowing with people, all of whom were murmuring to each other and looking sad. I saw Tessa hunched in one corner of the room, her eyes rimmed in red.

Dorothy clapped her hands to get our attention. "I've asked Brother Young to say a few words." She gestured toward a short, thin man with a beaky nose and a protuberant Adam's apple that even his high collar failed to hide. He looked like an anorexic buzzard.

His speaking voice, however, was beautiful. Rich and mellow, it filled every corner of the room, though he never raised it above a conversational level. He was full of praise and admiration for Crawford the man and for Crawford the sheriff, and spoke eloquently if briefly. By the time he concluded with a short prayer, there wasn't a dry eye in the house, mine included.

Dorothy thanked him, then proceeded to pass around heaping platters of food. Forced by my heavy breakfast to decline, I escaped to the front porch for a smoke. Eventually, I needed to get Dorothy alone for a few minutes so I could ask her a question or two, but now was obviously not the time.

The porch was as crowded as the house, so I walked around to the back door and sat on the lowest of the three concrete steps. The backyard was pleasant and cool, a large maple tree spreading its budding branches above a well-tended tomato garden that was only now beginning to green up. A bird feeder was positioned as far from the tomatoes as the small yard would allow, and I smiled to myself, thinking that Crawford had been trying a bit of bribery here. Okay, birds, I'll keep your bellies full of seed if you'll leave my tomatoes alone. That would have been so like Crawford, always making sure that the little folk got a fair shake. A couple of sparrows, apparently having accepted his offer, were pecking busily at the feeder

A loud argument from inside broke my reverie. Flicking my cigarette stub into the grass, I crept to the kitchen window and peered through.

Dorothy was blocking the door that led into the living room, arms firmly crossed over her huge chest.

"I didn't invite you," she was saying, "and I have every right to ask you to leave."

"And I have every right to be here," the other woman insisted. She turned slightly, and I saw it was Tessa. "Damn it, Dorothy, I'm only paying my respects along with everyone else."

"Don't you curse in this house," Dorothy growled. "As for

respect, Tessa Potter, you don't know the meaning of the word. If you had any respect for your husband, you wouldn't have been messing around with Miles. And if you'd had any respect for Miles, you wouldn't have taken a chance on ruining his reputation, not to mention his career. Don't you think I know why he wasn't planning on running for sheriff again?"

"You don't know half as much as you think you do," Tessa retorted angrily. "And if I were you, I wouldn't throw stones, Dorothy. What about the lives you've ruined with your vicious gossip and lying rumors?"

"At least I've never committed adultery."

"No, just fornication."

Dorothy started for her, hands curled into claws. "You nasty little—"

"Hold it!" I ordered.

Both women spun around, and while they were still intent upon the open window, I made it up the steps and through the door.

"Ladies, unless you want everyone in the house to know your business, I'd suggest you postpone this discussion until later."

Dorothy paled. Tessa wrinkled her nose at me as if I was a still-warm pile of cow manure.

"Now, go away, Tessa," I said bluntly. "I want to have a little chat with Miss Stenson."

"You can't tell me to go away!"

"Sure, I can. Granted, this isn't my house, but seems to me that Dorothy's in charge of it for now, and I distinctly heard her ask you to leave. What's the matter, Tessa?" I added, when her eyes glinted with anger. "You were quick enough when it came to tossing me out of your house. This is the same principle. It's just that you're on the receiving end this time around."

She left, her cheeks as red as Crawford's tomatoes would soon be.

Dorothy burst into nervous giggles. "Oh, my, you certainly told her!"

I sat on the edge of the kitchen table, my knees suddenly weak. "Yeah, I guess I did. Miss Stenson, before you go back to your guests, I wonder if I could talk to you for a minute."

"You bet you can, honey. After the way you told off that hussy, you can talk to me about anything you want." She pulled out a kitchen chair and sat, easing off her shoes.

"I know this isn't a pleasant memory for you, but it's important. Would you think back to the morning you found the sheriff...er, deceased, and try to tell me exactly what happened? From the time you arrived."

Her lip trembled, but she straightened her spine and nodded. "All right, since you say it's important, but I can't imagine why it would be. I don't have any trouble remembering, that's for sure. That day will be burned into my memory for the rest of my life."

I kept quiet, waiting.

"I got here early, like I always do. The sun hadn't been up for long, and there was still dew on the grass. I tracked some mud in—I remember cleaning it up with a paper towel." She pointed to an area of the tiled floor.

"Then you came in the back door?" A-ha. So much for Les's idea.

"Certainly. I always did. 'Round these parts, the front door's for company. Besides, the first thing I did every morning was to put on pot of coffee, so it only made sense."

"Okay. Go on."

She sighed. "Well, I started the coffee, then laid the table for his breakfast. Cold cereal and coffee, that's all the man would ever eat in the morning. Lord knows, I'd have fixed him bacon and eggs or waffles or anything else."

"I'm sure you would have. Please, go on."

"Oh. Well, then I went into the living room to start my dusting and I saw him." She shivered. "Do you know, it occurred to me last night that I was in the room with that snake for a good five minutes? Oh, land, I thought I'd never stop shaking. I could tell Miles was dead the minute I laid eyes on him, but I figured it was his heart give out. I never got close enough to see the marks."

"Then how were you so sure he was dead?"

"'Cause, missy, his eyes were wide open and staring at nothin'. And 'cause he was so pale and stiff. I've seen dead folk before—too many of 'em."

"It was light enough in there to see him pretty clearly then?" I was trying not to sound too eager. I didn't want to put words in her mouth.

"Sure it was. I had the light on in the kitchen, and it was shinin' through the door. That chair was lit up like it was in a spotlight. It was awful."

"Yes, it was," I agreed. "Was the lamp by his chair on?"

"No."

"Are you sure?"

She nodded. "I'm sure. I turned it on later when Lester hollered for me to, but it was off when I got here. I thought at first that he'd fallen asleep in the recliner again. I swear, he slept in that chair more often than he did in his own bed. I'll bet I found him there two or three mornings a week." She snorted. "Typical old bachelor."

I tried to choose my words carefully, but I had to know. "Miss Stenson, the switch in the entranceway that controls the lamp. You couldn't have accidentally flipped it off on your way out the front door, could you?"

"I don't see how I could have, since I didn't go out the front door."

"You didn't?"

"No, I came in the kitchen and called the sheriff's office, then went outside to wait, but I used the back door." She twisted her hands. "You may think it's silly, but I couldn't bring myself to go back into that room. Looking back, I guess it's best I didn't, considering that snake was still loose in there." She shivered.

And there went your second idea, Les, I thought, torn between satisfaction and the first glimmer of real fear. If my theory was still holding water, it only meant there really was a murderer out there somewhere. And I didn't like being the only one who really believed it. I didn't like it at all.

"Why?" Dorothy asked so suddenly that I jumped.

"Sorry?"

"Why are you asking questions about the lamp and such?"

I had to tell her something. "Uh, well, since I was the first one here, I have to write a report." I had no idea whether that was true, but it sounded plausible. "Les likes lots of detail in a report."

"Oh." She nodded, apparently satisfied, then sighed and slid one foot back into a black shoe.

I had opened my mouth to ask her one more question, when all hell broke loose out front. A woman's scream was followed by a tremendous crash, and the entire house seemed to shift on its foundation. There were no earthquakes in west Texas, were there? There was a moment of shocked silence, and then an excited babble. I rushed out of the kitchen with Dorothy right on my heels.

Squirming my way through the crush of bodies, I made it out to the front porch, or what was left of it. An ancient pick-up, more rust than paint, had plowed into one of the wooden uprights that supported the overhang of the roof. Half of the porch had collapsed; the other half leaned crookedly into the lawn.

A dozen people had been flung out on to the grass by the force of the impact, but they all seemed to be unharmed. They had helped each

other to their feet, and were brushing off their clothing. Cal had pulled
an elderly woman from beneath the debris and was trying to ascertain
whether she was injured. The woman, apparently mistaking his motives
for groping her, was steadily whacking him about the ears with a
skinny black parasol. Cruelly leaving him to his own devices, I inched
my way out and caught sight of Lester, who was extricating the truck's
driver from the crumpled cab.

"Should I call an ambulance?" I shouted over the ruckus.

"No, I think he's okay," Les called out.

I hardly saw how that could be possible, but I nodded. Cal, who
had freed himself from the indignant crone, came to stand beside me.

"Oh, shit," he murmured when he saw the driver.

A scrawny older man pushed his way out of Lester's grip and
staggered toward the house. He peered up at me for a moment, rubbing
at the salt-and-pepper stubble covering his chin, his eyes unfocused.
His lip was split and dribbling blood, but he didn't seem to notice. The
crowd behind me had gone silent.

"Well, whaddaya know?" The words were slow and slurred. "A
party, and nobody invited me."

Lester had caught up with him by this time and put a hand on his
shoulder, but the gray-haired man paid no attention. He took another
wobbly step.

"Poor Miles," he said. "That's why you're all here, ain't it—for
poor ol' Miles? Well, ya wanna know the truth?" He was shouting now.
"I'm glad he's dead!"

Everyone gasped. Lester stepped forward and made another grab,
but the man eluded him once more.

"It's better this way. It really is," he appealed to us. "Miles was
my friend for a long time, but he changed. He changed and he betrayed
me. He would've betrayed all of you, don't you see?" Tears coursed
down his grizzled cheeks. "Don't any of you see?"

"That's enough." Lester grasped the older man's upper arm and
held on. "Come on, let's get out of here." He looked up at Cal. "I'll
take him on home. Might take me a while to get him settled, so y'all
hitch a ride to the SO and pick up another car."

I gaped at him. "You're taking him home?" A wave of sheer fury
washed over me. "For God's sake, Lester, he's drunk on his ass, and he
could've killed somebody here! What's wrong with you? Don't you
lock up drunks in this town?"

Lester met my eyes steadily. "Turn me in to your good pal Bo if
you want to, Taylor," he said. "But I'm taking my father home."

Chapter Eight

I WATCHED AS LESTER helped his drunken father into the patrol car, then turned away. Still shaking with anger, I clambered off the wrecked porch and started around back. Behind me, I heard Cal telling folks he thought it best if they all went on home now, thank you for coming, yes, it was a beautiful service. Resuming my previous seat on the back steps, I fired up another cigarette and listened to the departing murmur, the gunning of car motors and, finally, quiet. A shadow fell over me.

Cal sat down beside me. "Billy's helping Dorothy clean up a little. We'll leave in a few minutes. Are you okay?"

I took a deep drag of smoke. "Why wouldn't I be? I was in the kitchen when it happened."

"I'm not talking about that."

"I know." The sparrows at the feeder had been eyeing us warily. Apparently deciding we posed no threat, they continued eating. "Yes, I'm okay now. I'd like to say I don't know what came over me, but that would be a lie. I know perfectly well what came over me. I guess I'm only a little surprised it hit me so hard."

Tossing away the cigarette, I lit another. Great, so much for quitting. "My mother was killed by a drunk driver, Cal. She was walking home from the drugstore, and he veered up onto the sidewalk. She didn't have a chance."

"I'm sorry."

"Me, too. It wasn't a pleasant way to go, if there is a pleasant way." I looked at him. "I was sorry it happened to her, sorry to see a life snuffed out for no good reason, sorry as hell that the courts gave the bastard a slap on the wrist and let him go, probably to run over somebody else. I still think it stinks."

His eyes were unreadable behind dark glasses, but he nodded. "It does stink."

"I wanted to see him punished, you know? Yeah, you know exactly what I'm talking about. It's like that law professor you told me about. But my motives aren't as pure as yours."

"Motives?"

I barked a painful laugh. "If he had gone to jail, I could've felt my mother's death had been avenged. It would've given me something to feel besides anger."

"And grief," he added.

"No!" I stood up, my back to him. "You don't get it. There *is* no grief, and there never was. I watched them lower her coffin into the ground, and it was as if they were burying a mannequin." The shame hit me again, and I cowered as if warding off a physical blow. "Damn it, I tried. I really did. I tried to remember the good times, to summon a few tears for what I'd lost, but the truth is that there were damn few good times, and I didn't lose much of anything."

I heard the clinking of Cal's gun belt as he rose, felt his hands on my shoulders, and turned awkwardly into his arms, my eyes hot with tears I had never been able to shed.

"It's hard to love someone when they don't, or can't, love you," I whispered into his shirt. "I don't think she actually hated me, but she spent her life pushing me away. Nothing I did was good enough for her. Every word out of my mouth was proclaimed silly, ridiculous, or vulgar. I might as well have been a doll stuffed with sawdust, for all the attention she paid to my feelings. Hell, I don't think she believed I *had* feelings.

"Do you know what I felt when she died, Cal? Relief. God help me, I was relieved I wouldn't have to play the game anymore, trying so hard to love someone who thought every decision I made was stupid, who ridiculed every hope or dream I shared with her. Someone who never even liked me." I backed out of his embrace, rubbing my burning eyes and trying to summon a smile. "Whew, what a speech. Sorry, next time I'll tell it to a shrink."

"You don't need a shrink," he said. "A friend couldn't hurt, though."

The tears still wouldn't come, but it felt good to let him hold me, so I did.

"Uh, 'scuse me."

We broke apart like guilty lovers. Billy was standing at the back door.

"You all finished, Billy? Okay, we'll be right with you."

Billy vanished back inside, and Cal cleared his throat, gazing at the sparrows.

"Thanks," I said.

"Right. So, you ready to go battle crime?"

"Sure thing."

Dorothy offered to drive us back to the SO, where we piled into

Cal's patrol car. I insisted on sitting in the back seat, more embarrassed than I'd ever been in my life. I didn't often lose control, and wasn't accustomed to having an audience on the rare occasions that I did.

Then Cal made an announcement that made me feel even worse.

"By the way, Taylor, Jack Forman wasn't drunk."

"What?"

"He's a diabetic. I've seen him like that before, once or twice, when his insulin level gets out of whack. He really can't help it."

I closed my eyes. "My God, Les must think I'm a real bitch."

"Les will understand, so don't worry about it. Okay, folks, here we are."

The grand opening didn't strike me as all that grand. There was no parade, no fireworks, no brass band. There were, however, even more people than there had been the day before, and Cal paused at the gate. "I'll hold her left hand, Billy, and you hold her right. No doubt we'll end up separated sometime today, but let's at least try to make it in together. Ready?" We marched through the gate and managed, barely, to stay together all the way to the first refreshment stand.

Cal bought us each a soft drink, then pulled me over to a tent I hadn't yet visited.

"Thought you might like to learn a little of the county history," he told me as we ducked inside. "Here it is, in a nutshell."

The first thing I saw was a model of an oil derrick, the whole contraption about three feet tall. A miniature oil pump stood next to it and, apparently powered by batteries, it was pumping away. I had seen dozens of the real things during my drive west, scattered across otherwise empty stretches of flat, dry land. They reminded me of gigantic metal crickets, back legs splayed as their noses dipped again and again to the earth, drinking the precious fluid beneath the soil.

"Once upon a time," Cal intoned, "a man named Samuel Perdue discovered oil, not too far from where we're standing right now. He had already decided to start a town and to name it after himself, so he named the county after his first derrick. His only derrick, as it turned out. He almost went broke looking for more oil, but never found any. A fluke of nature, I guess. So he moved on to a new business." He pointed to the other side of the tent.

A highly polished wooden plaque, about four feet square, held an assortment of barbed wire. Eight-inch sections of the wicked-looking stuff were mounted in neat rows, the metal ranging from shiny to dull, the barbs of varied sizes and shapes. Cal touched the rusty wire that occupied a place of honor in the exact center of the plaque.

"This is rumored to be an actual piece cut from the first fence Samuel Perdue stretched across his property."

"Rather like a splinter from the True Cross, I take it?" I muttered.

Cal quirked an eyebrow. "No sarcasm allowed. It was the first and only barbed wire fence in Derrick County, but it didn't stay up for very long."

"Why not?"

"Perdue discovered that dry, dusty country like this wasn't a prime location in which to raise cattle, so he switched to sheep. You can't have barbed wire fences when you raise sheep, Taylor. Their wool gets caught in the barbs, and they're too dumb to work themselves loose. They'd be more likely to stand there and starve to death."

"Poor things!"

"Yeah." Cal gave a disgusted snort, and I suspected he would have been squarely on the cattle side of the cattleman/sheepman wars that had once rocked the west.

"So, where did the rest of this wire come from?" I asked.

"Oh. This is old man Huffmeister's prized collection. He ordered the rest as samples from a bunch of ranch supply catalogs." I must have looked incredulous, because Cal snickered. "What can I say? Everyone has a hobby. Besides, it's earned him a place in the county museum that, by the way, occupies the back room of the library. You ought to visit it sometime."

"What's on display?"

He gestured to the barbed wire and the derrick. "This."

I rolled my eyes and escaped the tent. "See ya later, cowboy." His laughter trailed me as I pushed my way through the crowd.

Sick to death of snake milking and fried snake and snake paraphernalia and snakes in general, I ambled over to the rides, pausing to lean against a low wooden railing and watch as squealing children rode the carousel horses. The simple music and the swirling colors had lulled me into a nearly oblivious fugue, but I was jerked back into awareness by a stinging slap on the shoulder. I turned to find Tessa snarling up at me. Behind her, I could see Wood trying to reach us, his progress slowed by the crowd and by his limping gait.

"You have no business in this town," Tessa informed me without preamble.

"Come off it, Tessa." I felt tired to my soul. "You can kick me out of your house, but not out of an entire town. All I want is the answer to one simple question. Why are you acting as if I'm a threat to you?"

"I don't know what you're talking about."

"Don't you? Your reaction to me is all wrong. Even if you and my mother had some major fight years ago, even if you had disowned each other, it doesn't explain why you're treating me the way you are." I moved closer to her, and her eyes widened. I could actually smell the sharp odor of fear beneath her delicate cologne. "What is it about me that frightens you so? What could I possibly do to hurt you?"

She stood speechless for so long that Wood made it to her side by the time she finally spoke. "Damn you. Damn you to hell." She pushed past her husband and walked away.

Wood watched her leave, then turned to me. "I'm sure sorry. For the life of me, I can't figure out what's gotten into that woman."

I shrugged. "Me neither, but I'm beginning to get used to it. Come on, Wood, don't worry. It's okay."

"There's nothin' okay about it." He frowned. "I'm gonna get to the bottom of this, gal, I swear I am."

"Well, let me know when you do." My mood lifted as I remembered something I had in my pack. "Meanwhile, I've got a present for you." I pulled out the key ring and handed it to him, feeling a little foolish.

He unwrapped the tissue paper and goggled at the trinket as if I had given him the Hope diamond. I showed him where to press it, and he gave a delighted laugh when the little painted sheep baaed.

"Well, I swan," he said, a Texanism I'd heard all my life, but one that still made me shake my head because I had no idea what it meant. "It sounds sorta like Nell."

I smiled at him. "Nell?"

"My favorite ewe. Her mama died birthin' her, and I had to feed her from a bottle to keep her alive." He smiled. "She still thinks I'm her daddy. Used to follow me everywhere, even into the house. You shoulda heard Tessa holler when that happened! Lord, was that woman mad."

I didn't remind him that I'd seen Tessa mad often enough to last me for years. "I'm glad you like it. Now, I think you'd better go find your wife, don't you?"

"Guess I'd better at that."

He stumped away, his cane raising little puffs of red dust. I watched the carousel for a few more minutes, but its spell had been broken.

My breakfast was wearing off, so I decided to search out a bite of lunch. I found a small table near the hot dog stand and sat down gratefully, scooting my chair under a corner of the booth's awning. I spotted Lester well before he noticed me, and was still trying to decide how best to approach him when the vendor tossed my paper-wrapped corn dog down to me. By the time I had thrown a couple of quarters back to him, Les was in the chair beside me.

"How about another one of those, Pete?" he called out, and the proprietor nodded. Les turned to me.

I spoke before he could. "I owe you an apology, Les. Cal told me about your father's illness, and I'm sorry I jumped to conclusions." I went on to tell him how my mother had been killed, though I didn't go into the sordid detail I had dumped on Cal.

When I had finished, Les's shoulders slumped. "Jesus, Taylor, that's awful. No wonder you lost it."

"Well, but I'm still sorry I yelled at you."

"Forget it."

"Is he all right?"

"He's fine now. He hates giving himself those injections of insulin, so sometimes he forgets. Accidentally on purpose, if you know what I mean. I try to make sure I'm around to give him the shot when it's time, but with the festival and all, I've been so busy I didn't get to it this morning. Paula does it sometimes, too, but she's—"

"She's not back yet?"

"No." He fielded his own lunch, and asked Pete for a couple of sodas as well. "But don't throw them," he pleaded in mock terror. "I'll come fetch 'em myself."

Billy appeared, and I gestured for him to join us. He sidled closer, one hand behind his back. "I bought you somethin'," he said shyly, and placed a brown paper sack on the table between us.

"For me? How nice, Billy, but you shouldn't have..." The words died on my lips as I pulled the item from its wrapping. It was a heavy glass globe, sort of like a crystal ball, and embedded within was the severed head of a rattlesnake, its mouth opened wide to display a pair of sharp fangs. Its cold, dead eyes peered into mine, and I couldn't control a shiver of revulsion.

"Oh, my. It's just, just—" I failed to come up with a proper adjective. The tiny hairs at the back of my neck were standing at attention.

"It's a paperweight." He looked very proud of himself. "I figured with you being a writer and all, it would come in handy."

"Billy, this was very thoughtful of you. Thank you."

"Well, you said you didn't want to wear snake, but you had to have somethin'."

"Right," Lester concurred, munching his corndog. "Now you're an honorary citizen."

"I'm overwhelmed." Hastily, I rewrapped the grisly item and tucked it into my backpack.

"By the way, Les," the boy went on, "Cal's got me checkin' in by radio every half hour, and old Perkins had a message for you. You're s'posed to call some guy in Lubbock about a class you missed Wednesday night. Perkins says he's got the number."

Lester's jaw tightened. "Next time you talk to Perkins, you can tell him to toss that message, Billy."

"But Perkins said it sounded real important, Les."

"I don't care what he said. I'm finished with that stupid class, and I don't need to be hounded about it." He tossed his napkin into a trash bin and stood up. "See y'all later."

"Well," I said, watching him merge into the crowd. "What was that all about?"

Billy shrugged. "You remember the day you got hired, when the sheriff was yellin' at Les?"

"Yeah."

"Well, that's what it was all about. Sheriff Crawford set him up with a class in Lubbock, and Les kept skipping. He don't like goin' to school, I guess."

"What kind of class was it?"

"I don't know. But Sheriff Crawford, he was real hot on self-improvement and education. He said the world was changin' fast, and if we didn't keep up with it, it'd pass us on by."

"True enough."

"Now, me, I'm goin' through the police academy as soon as I can. They won't take me 'til I'm twenty-one, though, so I got about a few more months to wait out. Well, the sheriff, he said why not work on other things until the time came?" He checked around us as if making sure no one would overhear, and leaned close to me. "See, I lisp."

I feigned surprise. "You do?"

Billy looked smug. "Can't hardly tell no more, can you? I've been goin' to this speech therapy, and it's gettin' better all the time. Sheriff said next he'd send me to a school that'd learn me better grammar. He said it didn't seem to take too good when I was in high school."

I smothered a smile. "Good for you, Billy. So, what kind of school was Lester attending?"

His brow wrinkled. "I don't rightly know. Can't remember Les ever talkin' about it. But it was sure somethin' the sheriff wanted him to go to regular. Whooee, did they have a spat about that!" He thought for a minute. "Well, you remember, don't you? Wednesday night, when I called Cal on the radio and told him the sheriff was huntin' for Les? I don't know how he found out Les didn't go that night, but he was callin' me from his house every fifteen minutes, askin' if I'd found Les yet. I don't think I ever heard him that mad before."

I did remember. "Did you ever find Les?"

"Oh, yeah, he showed up right after I talked to Cal. I sent him on over to the sheriff's house. Good thing Les is too old to take to the wood shed, 'cause that's what the sheriff sounded like he was fixin' to do." He looked at his wristwatch and jumped to his feet. "Holy cow, you should be at the auditorium by now. C'mon!"

"For what?" I protested as he dragged me to my feet and away from my precious bit of shade.

"The contest, Miss Madison, did you forget? I still get to help you with the judgin', don't I?"

"Uh, sure."

"We need to help 'em set up. Let's go."

The moment we stepped inside the auditorium, I decided this wasn't going to be such a bad assignment after all. The ancient air conditioning unit wheezed and gasped and rattled like a chronic asthmatic, but the building's thick stone walls kept the cooled air locked within. Compared to the sweltering heat outside, it was heavenly.

Billy led me into a cavernous room where a dozen or so people were busily hanging streamers and blowing up balloons. He told me this was in preparation for the dance that evening. I followed him to the back of the room and up wooden steps to a stage. Giggles and squeals issued from behind the crimson velvet curtain, and Billy came to an abrupt halt, his ears growing pink.

"Maybe I'd better stay out here," he stammered.

When I ducked through the curtain to a small backstage room, it was immediately clear that he had made the right decision. Several half-dressed teenage girls were engaged in trying on clothes, fussing with each other's hairdos, and trading items of makeup. I stood there, wondering what was expected of me.

A raven-haired beauty paused in the act of adding what must have been a seventh layer of mascara to already gummy lashes. She met my eyes in the mirror and her lips curved into a fake smile.

"Aren't you a little old for this, honey?" she purred. "The age limit is eighteen, not eighty, and that bad bleach job isn't going to fool anyone."

A few of the girls tittered nervously, but most ignored her.

I returned her smile. "I'm not a contestant, sweetie. I'm the judge."

The brunette choked as if she had swallowed her mascara tube, and the titters were loud and sustained this time.

"Dropped in to see if you girls needed anything," I told them. "No? Okay. Oh, and remember—" I looked pointedly at the brunette. "—I deduct points for lipstick smears on the teeth." When I left, she was frantically scrubbing her pearly whites with a tissue.

I wandered out onto the stage, my footsteps echoing across the old boards, and spent a moment recalling, with no fondness whatsoever, my one attempt at acting. It had been a high school production of *Hamlet* and I played a lady-in-waiting. The audience wound up doing all the waiting. Waiting, that is, for me to emerge from my hiding place in the backstage broom closet. My drama class, troopers that they were, eventually ad-libbed their way through my absence and continued the play. Much to everyone's relief, I dropped drama and signed up for woodworking the very next day.

A woman with a blue-rinsed beehive and thick glasses burst through the curtain, scaring me all the way from eleven years past into next week. I pressed a hand to my heart; she pressed a clipboard to hers.

"I'm Mrs. Davis," she said. "May I help you?"

I introduced myself and admitted I didn't have the slightest idea what I was supposed to be doing.

"Oh, your job is easy," she assured me. "You'll sit over there—" She pointed to a folding table at the far side of stage right. "—and watch the pageant. You might want to take a few notes as the girls perform, so's to reassure the parents that you're really paying attention, you know." She tipped me a sly wink.

"Then, at the end, pick a winner. Believe me, I'd trade with you. I've got to make sure the little dears are dressed and onstage at the proper times. Sounds simple, doesn't it? But it usually involves breaking up cat fights, mopping up vomit from a nervous stomach or two, and reviving the occasional fainter."

"You can have it," I told her. "And bless you."

She sighed and took off in the direction of the giggles.

I located another folding chair for Billy, and placed it beside mine at the table. A promise was a promise, as long as I retained the deciding vote. Impartiality be damned; little Miss Raven-hair would not win this contest, even if her talent segment included standing on her head and juggling eggs with her toes while singing the national anthem.

I went out front and filled Billy in on our judging duties, then spent an hour helping the decorating committee set up folding chairs for the audience. The chairs would have to be moved immediately following the contest so the dance could begin. I hastily volunteered to assist with that procedure as well, feeling only a smidgen of guilt at the cries of gratitude. No need to share my ulterior motive, which was to remain in this blessedly cool building for as long as possible.

Billy and I took our places as folks began drifting in for the contest. I gave him a sheet of paper and a pencil, and passed along Mrs. Davis's advice regarding the watchful parents. He nodded seriously.

Lester passed by our table on his way to the microphone and slipped me a note. *First dance is mine*, it read, and I was pleasantly surprised. It hadn't occurred to me that I would be able to actually attend the dance. Good thing the memorial service had forced me to wear a skirt today. Every other woman in the room was dressed to the nines.

Les tapped the microphone, and everyone grew quiet. He gave a general welcome-to-the-festival speech, read off the license plate numbers of two cars whose owners had left their headlights on, and then proceeded to floor me with the final item on his agenda.

"And now, allow me to introduce Derrick County's first ever Miss Snakeskin. I won't tell how long ago that was if she won't, but I think you'll all agree she's grown even more lovely. You gals backstage had better be glad she's not competing this year, 'cause she'd be sure to walk off with the crown again. Ladies and gentlemen, here she is— Tessa Ross Potter!"

I swear, my chin hit the table with an audible thump as my aunt took her place on the stage.

She looked elegant, every highlighted brown hair in place, a burgundy silk dress clinging to her petite curves. She smiled out at the audience, and I realized with a start that she was really beautiful when she smiled.

"Thanks, Lester. You should be a professional flatterer," she said into the mike, and the audience laughed. "I don't mind telling you that it has been thirty years since I stood on this stage as a contestant. The girls today have it a lot easier than we did.

"Back when this competition was first devised, it was much more than a beauty pageant. We were all expected to take part in the hunt, and we each had to skin a snake in order to qualify. We even learned to milk them, which, as you know, is a real skill. No one then gave a thought to the danger involved, but in these days of lawsuits and liability insurance, such requirements can no longer apply."

She cupped a hand to her ear. "Did I hear a sigh of relief from backstage?" There was laughter and applause as she wished the girls luck and made her exit.

It's really a good thing Billy was watching every move the contestants made, and scribbling detailed notes whenever he was able to pry his eyes from the multitude of legs and breasts on display. I couldn't stop thinking about Tessa, and wondering if I would ever manage to get past the stiff, angry shell I had come to know, in order to reach the charming, funny woman inside. Before I knew it, the time had come to select the winner. Billy, not surprisingly, had fallen for Miss Raven-hair, but I crossed her off and accepted his second choice instead.

A tiny girl with mouse brown hair and a myopic squint almost became the fainter of the year when her name was announced. Tessa was supposed to preside over the crowning, but after a few awkward minutes of backstage scrabbling and curious whispers from the audience, Mrs. Davis approached me with the news that no one could locate my aunt. Reluctantly, I ventured out on stage to present the crown and wrap the new queen in a velveteen cape with (shudder) snakeskin trim. Billy fell over his own feet as he hastened forward with a bouquet of roses.

As I settled the cape around the girl's shoulders and reached to adjust the rhinestone crown, someone screamed. I felt a rush of wind as something brushed my shoulder and crashed to the floor beside me.

Chapter Nine

I COULDN'T FIGURE OUT what had happened. Everyone seemed to be looking up, so I looked up, too. All I saw was a wooden catwalk stretching overhead, rigged with ropes and pulleys and other equipment designed to assist in the manipulation of background scenery. I sure saw something when I decided to look down, though. The new Miss Snakeskin lay sprawled across my feet in a dead faint.

As if her fall had broken a spell of silence, the crowd burst into immediate sound and action, and I was amazed to witness pudgy little Doc Neil climbing over the steep front of the stage. I tried to move out of his way, assuming he was coming to assist the unconscious beauty queen, but he ignored her, wrapping a sturdy arm about my waist and leading me back to my chair.

"Are you all right?" he asked gruffly, patting me down as if searching for concealed weapons.

"I'm fine." I was actually more than a little bewildered. "Miss Snakeskin is the one who's out cold, Doc, not me." I peeked over his shoulder, relieved to see Mrs. Davis bending over the prone girl. As she swept aside the swirl of cape, I caught sight of what the fabric had been concealing. "Oh, shit," I whispered.

The sandbag had burst a seam upon impact with the floor, and its contents were trickling steadily through a crack between the boards. I wasn't good at judging weights, but even so, it didn't escape me that something roughly the size of a baby goat would be pretty darn heavy.

"It barely missed you," Doc informed me.

I found myself incapable of uttering a word.

Les had made it to the stage by that time, and was shooing people away. Doc and I watched him examine the section of rope attached to the bag. Cal and Billy joined him, and the three of them huddled together, muttering to each other. Mrs. Davis had succeeded in reviving the fallen girl and was helping her into the wings, Miss Snakeskin clutching her crown to keep it atop her disheveled head. Someone brought me a cup of fruit punch, and I sipped it gratefully.

"Well?" Doc demanded as Lester approached us. "How the hell did this happen?"

"Looks to us like the rope had rotted," Lester said, and Cal nodded. "It just picked a bad time to give way."

"A bad time to give way," Doc repeated slowly, a vein in his forehead throbbing. "A bad time. Who's in charge of this godforsaken place, Lester?" he roared, the vein threatening to pop from his flesh and land in my lap. "Another inch and we'd be scraping this girl's brains off the floor. Do you understand that? They'd still be finding shards of her skull ten years from now. It would have crushed her skull like a melon."

I laid a hand on his arm, feeling a little green. "I get the picture, Doc. Thank you so much for the vivid description." Taking a deep breath, I willed myself to remain calm. "Now, it was only an accident, and no one was hurt, so let's try to get everybody back on course, okay? I don't see any reason for the dance to be ruined over this."

Doc considered me for a moment. "That's probably a good idea. But," he added to Lester and Cal, "I want this stage blocked off. No one comes back up here until all of that rigging has been completely checked out."

"We'll take care of it," Cal said grimly.

I got to my feet slowly and made my way down the steps, complete strangers reaching out to assist me along the way. "I'm okay, really," I kept assuring them, but no one was satisfied until I had been settled into a chair and plied with a cup of punch and an assortment of cookies. Wood appeared out of nowhere, sinking down beside me and clutching my arm.

"You're not hurt?" he asked, his doe eyes intent upon me. "Hell, gal, I thought you were a goner for sure."

"Nope, still here," I told him, and it wasn't such a lie this time. The dizziness of delayed shock was passing, replaced by a feeling of near euphoria, an overwhelming surge of joy at being alive. "I'm sorry if you were frightened, Wood." And I was, but at the same time, it felt awfully good to know someone cared that much about my well-being. Several people in the crowd were still keeping a wary eye on me.

"Where's Tessa?" I asked him.

"That's what I was wondering," he said. "When the time came for her to crown the winner and she didn't show up, it worried me. I scooted backstage to look for her, but then all hell broke loose and I came out front to see what was going on."

"Did you ever find her?"

"Mrs. Davis located her for me a few minutes ago. She'd gotten a run in one of her stockings, so she went to the dressing room to borrow a pair of pantyhose. She had 'em halfway on when they started calling her name." He laughed. "Sorry, but every time I watch my wife wriggle into pantyhose, I thank God I was born a man."

"I'm pretty sure men invented the damned things," I said. "Along with spike heels." I excused myself and headed outside for a much-needed cigarette.

Leaning against a warm stone wall, I watched the sun sink into the western hills. A bank of low clouds burst into color as if God had spilled His entire paint box into them, and I found myself trying to remember if I had ever taken the time to enjoy a Houston sunset. Probably not. Anyway, I doubted it would have been this spectacular.

"'Scuse me."

I started. "Jeez, Billy, you don't have to sneak up on me."

"So'y." He shuffled his feet in the dust, looking everywhere but at me.

"What's wrong?"

He chewed on his lower lip, reluctantly meeting my eyes. "Miss Taylor, I think I oughta tell you something, but I'm not sure."

I hated it when people said things like that. It was almost as bad as someone actually beginning a revelation, and then saying, "Never mind." I took a drag off my cigarette and gazed at the Ferris wheel, now outlined by twinkling, multi-colored lights. "Well, I'm sure you'll make the right decision," I told him, feigning indifference. That tactic had always worked on the insufferable big brothers of friends while I was growing up.

It worked on Billy, too.

"Lester and Cal will kill me if they find out I did this." He moved closer. "But I have to tell you. I'd never forgive myself if I don't. Taylor, that rope wasn't rotten at all. It'd been cut."

"Cut?" My knees weakened and I braced myself against the wall. "You're telling me someone deliberately cut that rope? And that Cal and Lester know?"

He nodded. "Lester said it was a clean cut. Must've been a real sharp knife."

"But why didn't they tell me?"

"They agreed there was no need to scare you any worse." He looked miserable. "I promised I wouldn't tell you either."

I was torn between anger at the two deputies and the first flicker of genuine fear. Why would anyone try to hurt me? I squeezed my eyes shut. Not only was that a dumb question, it was evasive as hell. Whoever had dropped that sandbag hadn't merely intended to hurt me, but to kill me. Worse, both Wood and Tessa had been backstage at the fateful moment.

"Taylor?"

I opened my eyes to find Billy peering at me anxiously.

"Maybe I shouldn't have said anything."

"I'm glad you did. Tell me, what are the two of them planning to do about this?"

He shrugged. "I don't know. They said they'd take care of it."

"I see." I looked at him. "Billy, you're a lot smarter than people give you credit for. I'm sure you've figured out what this means."

His jaw tightened. "Yes'm. It means you're makin' someone mighty nervous. I reckon it's because of what you said about the sheriff bein' murdered."

"That's what I think, too. Now, Les and Cal don't believe me. At least, they didn't. If they have a single brain between them, this little incident will make them reconsider. But until they agree to help me, I'm going to have to rely on you."

"Sure thing." He squared his thin shoulders. "What do you want me to do? Name it."

"Thanks. I'll have to do some thinking, but I'll let you know." I tossed the glowing butt into the twilight and took his arm. "Right now, we'd better get back inside. Looks like the whole town has gathered for this shindig, and there's one lady in particular I'd like to talk to."

As we entered, the last of the chairs were being moved back against the walls and the band, denied access to the stage, had set up instead just in front of it. I apologized to the nearest member of the decorating committee for reneging on my promise to help, but he patted my hand kindly and told me they wouldn't have allowed it anyway, after what I had been through.

I wandered through the throng as the band began warming up, searching for a certain someone. I finally spotted her by the buffet table, and was heading that way when a hand closed around my wrist. Les smiled at me and I did my best to smile back, though I had to fight the inclination to spit in his eye. For the time being, however, I planned to go on pretending ignorance. There was no reason to get Billy into trouble.

"I know I requested the first dance," he murmured, "but would you mind if I took the second instead?"

"Not at all."

He gave my wrist a light squeeze and moved away. I watched him out of the corner of my eye as I started again toward the long table, but what I saw stopped me dead in my tracks.

The massive Dora Gleason was seated in a corner, her bulk filling two of the small chairs. She remained where she was as the band launched into their first tune and everyone began drifting out onto the dance floor. If the infamous Mr. Gleason was present, he certainly wasn't keeping his wife company, and she looked as forlorn as an abandoned puppy. As I watched, Les approached her, lifted one of her hands, and bowed to kiss it. Dora giggled like a young girl as he helped her to her feet and escorted her into the whirling crowd. Over his shoulder, I caught a glint of tears in her eyes, and felt my own sting as well. Until this moment, I had forgotten the promise that the late sheriff had made to the woman, but apparently Lester had not.

Sniffling a little, I turned away and walked directly into someone's arms.

"Well," Cal said. "As long as you're already in position." He swung me into a lively Texas two-step before I could catch my breath to refuse. I hadn't danced in years, and country-western style had never been one of my strong suits anyway, but I managed to hang on and stay on my feet.

"Thank you," I panted when the number was over, and made my escape through the applauding celebrants.

Dorothy Stenson was still ladling punch when I reached her, and I quietly asked if I could talk to her privately.

"Sure, honey." She handed the ladle over to a silver-haired lady. "Are you okay?" she asked as I led her over to a couple of chairs in the middle of an empty row.

"Yes, thanks."

"Horrible." She shuddered. "Good contest, though, except for that. You picked a fine little girl to win. I've known her family for years. Cotton farmers for generations, but that gal is going to be different. Straight-A student, smart as all get-out." She frowned. "Only thing that bothered me was Tessa Potter standing up there, preenin' like a movie star. Did you ever hear such bragging in your life? I'll have you know that I'd have won that contest thirty years ago if she hadn't cheated."

This revelation made me forget what I'd come to ask her. "Tessa cheated?"

Dorothy snorted. "I don't know what else you'd call it. All that stuff about us having to learn to milk snakes. Hogwash. Now, we did have to go on a hunt, that was true enough, and we each had to skin a snake. All that simply to qualify for the contest, mind you—some idiot on the Chamber of Commerce came up with that notion. But once we were in, it was supposed to be a straight beauty pageant."

She leaned back in the chair, dabbing her sweaty makeup with a tissue. "Not to sound immodest, but I was a stunner in those days. Ask anyone who knew me then. I was head cheerleader and homecoming queen my senior year. And talent? Why, I sang "Love Me Tender" in the competition and got a standing ovation, soon as folks could dry their eyes." Her dreamy expression hardened. "Then, along came little Miss Tessa, and ruined everything. Do you know what she did? She milked a damn rattlesnake, right there on the stage. Two ladies in the front row passed clean out."

I had to hide a smile. "You're kidding."

"I am not. In those days, it simply wasn't done—not by young ladies, at any rate. But Wood Potter was so besotted with her that he would've sat naked atop a flagpole if she'd asked him to, so he taught her the procedure. And whether the audience was impressed or not, the judge was. So she won."

Two points for initiative, Auntie T, I thought. "Well, I'm sorry, Dorothy. Would you mind if I asked you a couple of things?"

"Of course not, sweetie. Guess that's why you dragged me over here in the first place, isn't it? Sometimes I get to flappin' my gums, and don't pay attention. Now, what is it?"

I bit my lip, wondering how best to go about it, and ended up deciding to cut to the chase. "Did you see Sheriff Crawford on Wednesday night?"

Her painted mouth curved downward. "Why, yes. I cooked his dinner that evening. I wish now it had been something fancier than fried chicken, but that's what he wanted."

"I'm sure he enjoyed it. Dorothy, I'd appreciate it if you'd tell me anything you remember about that night."

She opened her mouth to reply, then shut it again, shooting me a sly smile. "You know, you keep asking me questions about the sheriff, and I think it's time you told me why." She held up a hand. "And don't give me that stuff about some report you have to write either. I asked Lester about that, and he said you didn't."

I sighed. Why did I keep forgetting what a small town this was? People here actually talked to each other. Quite frequently, it seemed.

"Never mind," she continued, her eyes gleaming. "I just wondered if you were still trying to keep it a secret, and I can see that you are. Won't do you any good, missy. The word's out."

"What word?"

"Murder," she said softly. "Don't look so surprised. Did you really think Rita would keep something like that to herself? I also know Cal got real angry at you for saying it, and that Bonita Posey stepped in to shut him up."

"Terrific," I mumbled. "So, what does the poll say so far? About my theory, that is."

"Most folks think you're a little crazy, but they forgive you. For one thing, you're a writer, and it only figures that your imagination is a lot more active than it should be, and then, too, you're a city girl. You're probably used to murders happening all the time."

I didn't know whether to laugh or scream. "And what's your opinion?"

"Well..." She bent to whisper in my ear. "If you spread this around, I'll deny it, but I think you might be right."

She couldn't have amazed me more if she'd jumped up on the buffet table and danced the hootchie-coo. "I know I shouldn't look a gift horse in the mouth," I said, "but why?"

"Rita told me everything, honey, and your reasoning sounds pretty sturdy to me. That lamp, for instance. It never occurred to me at the time, but you're right in saying that poor Miles couldn't very well have turned it off himself. Now, why don't you go ahead and ask your questions, and maybe I can even help solve the crime. Always wanted to play detective."

She was entirely too eager for my liking, but at least I now had another person in my corner besides Billy. I waved off a young man in overalls who had paused to ask me for a dance, then started over with Dorothy.

"Maybe it would be better if you tell me everything you remember about that evening. I'm looking for something you might consider unusual, out of the ordinary."

"Oh, there was plenty unusual that night," she said, to my surprise. "The first thing happened while I was carryin' the supper dishes into the kitchen. The phone rang, so I answered." Her brow wrinkled in thought. "Now, Miles got calls at home all the time. Wasn't all that long ago this county made do with the sheriff and an occasional part-time deputy, so folks sorta got used to calling him at his house. Miles tried to break 'em, but old habits die hard."

I nodded.

"This call was pretty odd. It was a woman, and I could tell she was cryin'."

"Did you recognize the voice?"

"No, she was chokin' up too bad. Anyway, she asked to speak to the sheriff, so I put him on and went on into the kitchen. That's all I know."

I lifted an eyebrow.

"Well," she confessed, "maybe I did overhear part of what he said. Not that I was eavesdropping, mind, but the kitchen door was open."

"Gotcha. What did you hear?"

She shut her eyes, concentrating. "As best I can remember, he said, 'Calm down. What's the matter?' Then he said, 'This can't go on,' or somethin' like that. And he said, 'I know you love him, you don't have to keep telling me that, but I have to do it.' Then, just before he hung up, he said, 'I've tried it your way, God help me, but this can't be covered up anymore.' And that's all."

I wished I could pull out my notebook, but I had a feeling Dorothy and I were attracting enough attention already, our heads together while we ignored the dance.

"Good, Dorothy. Then what happened?"

"He picked up the phone again, like he was going to dial it, then put it back down when he saw me watching. He told me to scoot on home. I reminded him that I still had dishes to wash, but he insisted he'd do 'em himself, and practically pushed me out the door."

"Oh." I was disappointed. "So, that's all you can tell me."

She flushed. "Well, not quite. He was acting so funny, you know? And I worried about leaving him all alone. So, I kept an eye on the house for a while after I went home." When she saw I wasn't going to accuse her of nosiness, she relaxed and went on. "About an hour later, I saw a woman ring his doorbell."

"A woman?" Now we were getting somewhere. "You couldn't see who it was?"

"No. His porch light had been burned out for weeks. I kept reminding him, but he never got around to putting a new bulb in. The only good glimpse I got of her was when he opened the door and the foyer light spilled out. She was wearing one of those coats with a hood, and had the hood pulled up over her head, so I can't even tell you what color her hair was."

Something niggled at the back of my mind. "Are you sure it was a woman?"

Dorothy started to nod, then paused. "Well, that was my impression." She thought about it. "I guess it could've been a man. She—or he—was all hunched over, and looked to be real skinny. That was easy to see, even with that big coat flappin' around. But, heck, there are lots of scrawny men in the world."

Scrawny, hunched over. Damn. "I don't suppose you can tell me how long she—or he—stayed?"

Dorothy lifted her sagging chin. "Say, I'm not one of them peepin' Toms, you know. Do you think I sit in that window for hours at a time?"

I decided tact was overrated. "Probably."

She chortled. "The visitor stayed for about forty-five minutes. I wondered if it might've been the same lady who called on the phone, but if it was a man, that changes things." Dorothy grunted as she rose. "Wish I could think of something else, but that's about it. I've got to get back to that table before Wilma Needham has my head." She hesitated, pursing her lips. "Don't bite off more than you can chew, honey. I've read a few mystery books myself, and what happened to you tonight sure looked like a warning to me. You be careful."

"I intend to," I assured her. "One more thing, Dorothy. How certain are you that the sheriff and Tessa Potter were having an affair?"

"Certain enough to have told her husband about it. And I wouldn't hurt a sweet man like Wood Potter for the fun of it."

This was getting worse. "You told him? When?"

"I don't remember. A few days ago. Does it matter?"

"Probably not." But it did matter because it meant Wood knew a lot more than he had told me.

I had gained a lot of new information to mull over, but it wasn't long before I determined that a county dance isn't the best place to put one's thoughts in order. Dorothy's chair was still warm when Lester pulled me to my feet and out on the floor.

"This one's mine." He drew me close for a nice, slow number. Now, this was much better. Unlike the boys I remembered from high school, Les didn't seem to mind that we were almost the same height. His palm felt hot against my back, and I had to admit that being held by a man was something I had missed.

"I saw you ask Mrs. Gleason to dance," I whispered. "That was very nice of you."

He laughed. "I'm glad you think so, since I nearly got de-jeweled over it."

"Huh?"

He pointed to Dora, who was now dancing with a cadaverous little man one-tenth her size. If she tripped and fell on him, he'd be crushed like a spider under a boot. "That's Mr. Gleason, and he didn't take too kindly to me dancing with his wife. But, if you'll notice, he's dancing with her now, every song. And that was the whole point after all."

I patted his back, forgetting for a moment that I was still mad at him for lying about the rope. "You're okay, Lester Forman. Sometimes."

"You're not so bad yourself," he murmured, his green eyes glinting as he pulled me still closer.

Uh, oh. Warning signs flashed. He was damned good looking and I was a human female with normal urges. Not a good combination. I pushed against his chest, easing his hold on me a little, as a litany of why-nots galloped through my head. I scolded myself that this was merely a biological reaction, brought about by two years of celibacy. Not that I didn't enjoy sex, but I wasn't fond of one-night-stands, and it seemed that all the men I had met lately were.

While I'd been busy with mental gymnastics, Les had guided us into a shadowy area near the stage. "Taylor," he murmured, then cupped my chin in his hand and kissed me.

He was apologizing even before I'd managed to struggle out of his embrace. "I'm sorry. God, I'm sorry. I don't know why I did that."

"You're married!" I reminded him in a low whisper. We were still hidden in the shadows, and I didn't want anyone overhearing.

"Damn it, don't you think I know that? I said I was sorry."

I didn't know what else to say, so I simply left him standing there. Shoving my way through the dancing crowd, I reached the lobby and stood trying to catch my breath.

I stayed there watching the watching the next number. It was the Cotton-eyed Joe, a dance that had always boggled my mind. It looked like a hell of a lot of fun, though I had never mastered the intricate hop-skip-and-jump steps involved. At intervals, everyone would stop, shout "Bullshit!" then resume dancing. Only in Texas.

To allow recovery from the fast-paced dance, the band eased into a soft Mickey Gilley ballad, and again I felt someone pull me into his arms. I was more than a little relieved when it turned out to be Cal.

Without a word, he tilted my head so it rested on his shoulder and rocked me into the rhythm of the song. He was a little taller than Les, and I fit into his embrace easily, no adjustments required. I noticed he hadn't moved us back out onto the main floor, but had stayed in the deserted entryway as if deliberately isolating us from the masses.

The tingle that had barely touched me while I was dancing with Les returned, and this time it blossomed unchecked into an electric current that made me feel a little dizzy. I tried to lift my head, to look into his eyes so I could determine whether he felt it, too, but he wouldn't allow it. The song ended on a mournful note and Cal was gone, so suddenly I wondered if I had imagined the entire episode. Good grief, what was wrong with me? If this was what celibacy did to a person, I was going to have to rethink my lifestyle.

I didn't see Cal again at all that evening. Les tipped me a wink as he was dancing with a drooling Miss Raven-hair. Dorothy, still enslaved behind the punchbowl, kept sending me odd little signals as if we were engaging in a game of spy/counterspy. Billy, bless his heart, watched me from the shadows as if afraid another sandbag would materialize from thin air and finish me off. Wood waved at me now and again, but Tessa, who had reappeared sometime during the dance, had him practically chained to her side. All I really wanted to do was go back to my room and think, minus the distraction of blaring music and friendly guys who seemed intent upon dancing my feet into bloody stumps.

Billy ended up being the one to drive me home, even escorting me to my door and checking out the room (presumably for lurking sandbags). I invited him in and he stammered, almost declining until he caught a glimpse of Hazel. It was love at first sight for both of them, and I graciously allowed him to fill her dishes and change her potty paper.

I sat on the wide windowsill, watching him dangle a piece of string for her to swat. Ferrets can be very cat-like in their play habits.

"Billy, when was last time you talked to Sheriff Crawford?" I asked.

"Wednesday night."

"I know that," I reminded him gently. "But about what time?"

"Let's see—I think it was about seven or so. No, wait." He dropped the string and Hazel chattered angrily. "He called so many times. I think the last time was about eight-thirty. Yeah. Cal had walked over from the diner, and he was mad 'cause Lester hadn't brought his car back. Then he went on home, and he'd only been gone for about five minutes when Les showed up. Les called Cal at home, then went out front to wait for him so they could trade cars. The sheriff called about then, looking for Cal that time."

He scratched his head. "I remember that the sheriff still sounded upset, but not as mad as he'd been earlier while he was lookin' all over for Les. Anyway, he said if I could get hold of Cal, to send him by the house. So I stuck my head out the door and hollered to catch Cal before he could drive off. But Cal was actin' real funny."

"Funny? In what way?"

"He said if the sheriff called again, to say I hadn't been able to locate him." He looked puzzled. "Cal never asked me to lie for him before. I sure didn't like it much either."

"So, did you?"

"Didn't have to. The sheriff never called back after that."

"Did Cal say why he wanted you to cover for him?"

"Not really. Said something about being plumb tired of playing nursemaid to a grown man, and that he couldn't take any more for a while. That make any sense to you?"

"Maybe a little." I was remembering a few things Cal had told me.

After Billy left, I plugged in my laptop and started making notes on what I had learned while it was still fresh in my mind. I always think better on paper or, in this case, a computer screen. Somehow, being able to see my thoughts written out makes them more coherent. I would rather have talked it all over with another person, but at this point, I wasn't sure who I could trust.

Hazel crawled up to nestle on my shoulder as I typed, and I talked to her as I had so many times before when I was battling my way through an attack of writer's block.

"Who would've wanted Crawford dead?" I asked her, and she chuckled into my ear. I didn't blame her. If someone had asked me that same question a few days earlier, I would have laughed too. I had come to Perdue a total stranger, and within twenty-four hours of my arrival, I would have argued that Miles Crawford didn't have an enemy in the world. The people of this county had more than liked him, they had idolized him.

Or so it had seemed.

"But small towns can hide some pretty nasty secrets," I informed Hazel. "Or so I've always heard. And I've sure learned a few since Crawford died." The cursor flashed, waiting.

Who, I typed again, would have wanted Crawford dead? This time I added, Why?

The first name I put down twisted my heart. Wood Potter. Hazel snorted, as if agreeing that the thought was ludicrous. "But he loves his wife," I told her. "He fought for her once before, you know, and actually won her through a sort of subterfuge. What makes you think he wouldn't commit murder if he thought his marriage was in danger?"

Remembering his gentle eyes, I almost deleted his name, but I was forced to leave it. Not only had he been keeping things from me, he had been the one to teach Tessa how to milk snakes, which meant he knew how to handle them. Besides, the person Dorothy saw enter Crawford's house—hunched and scrawny—could easily have been Wood and not a woman.

The addendum was even harder to bear. I had to concede that whoever murdered Crawford had also tried to kill me, when they felt I was getting too close to the truth for comfort. Somehow, I found it easier to accept that Wood could kill a rival in love than to take it the necessary step further, and believe he would have tried to murder me as well. But that was wishful thinking on my part, and I knew it.

"Okay, what about Tessa?" I asked. Hazel scratched her neck. "When Dorothy accused her of having an affair with Crawford, she denied it, true. But Dorothy seemed pretty sure Crawford was resigning as sheriff so he could run away with Tessa. Suppose he had changed his mind? You know the old saying about a woman scorned. How badly scorned would she have to be in order to resort to murder? And Tessa knows how to handle snakes, too. I found that out this evening." My fingers flew across the keyboard, keeping track of my thoughts.

The second part of this one was easy. "You bet she'd try to kill me," I muttered. "And she was nowhere to be found right before the sandbag dropped."

Lester?

"Could be," I said aloud, although Hazel had dozed off and was snoring softly. "According to Billy, he had an angry exchange with the sheriff on Wednesday evening, something about a missed class. But come on. It's hard to believe a man would kill his boss over a school he didn't want to attend." Besides, Lester had everything to lose and nothing to gain by Crawford's death. Crawford had, after all, planned to actively support him for sheriff in the upcoming election. And, too, of all the people I had listed, Lester Forman seemed the least likely to pull off this particular type of murder. The man was snake-phobic.

As to my near miss, I had to put down in all fairness that I didn't know where he had been at the time. But if I couldn't come up with a case against him for the sheriff's murder, what reason would he have to want me dead?

Unless...

I sat up straighter, waking Hazel who gave an angry squeak. "Jack Forman." Hazel yawned. "He's Lester's father," I explained to her. "Diabetic reaction or not, he stated very clearly that he was glad Crawford was dead. I don't know the reason behind that yet, but suppose he really did kill the sheriff? And suppose Lester found out?

How far would he go to protect his own father? Under the circumstances, maybe he believed he had no choice but to get rid of me."

Hazel crawled down my arm and clawed at my wrist, trying to make me stop typing and pet her. I pushed her aside gently, trying to concentrate. "Cal?" She looked up at me. "Well, he's certainly as adept as anyone else in this town at handling snakes, but why would he want to kill Crawford?" It was a stupid question with an obvious answer. "Because he wants to be sheriff, too, and it's a cinch he wouldn't win as long as the beloved Sheriff Crawford was backing his opponent.

"Maybe he was counting on the memory of the great Crawford fading sufficiently by November so the people would give him an even chance. After all, out of sight, out of mind. If Crawford wasn't right up there on the platform, so to speak, actively campaigning for Lester, Cal might have a real shot at winning."

And where had he been during the sandbag attack? I had no idea. I hadn't seen him until he joined Lester on the stage to examine the rope.

"Speaking of that, why did the two of them keep me in the dark about the rope being cut?"

But Hazel had gone back to sleep and didn't answer.

My head was beginning to spin, so I saved the information to my hard drive and had reached to turn off the laptop when I was struck by a surge of paranoia. Did I really want this information where anyone who was semi-computer literate could access it? No, I didn't.

I crept through the bathroom and knocked gently at Cal's door. When there was no answer, I turned the knob, not surprised when the door swung open.

I plugged in the machine and called up the file, adding a brief note that read, cryptically, *Keep this in a safe place for me*, then hooked up the modem and sent the whole thing off to Annie.

I felt a lot better after I deleted the file, but it sure didn't improve my dreams. In the most vivid nightmare of my life, the paperweight Billy had given me cracked open, and the snake's head flew across the room to sink its fangs into my neck.

I screamed myself awake.

Chapter Ten

SOMETHING GRIPPED MY hand and I struggled to pull away, certain in my groggy state of panic that it was the snake.

"Taylor, for God's sake, what is it? Are you all right?" Cal bent over the bed, his long, dark hair wild about his bare shoulders.

"What?" I sat up, shivering, surprised to find dawn creeping through the window. "Am I awake?"

"I think so, unless I'm the one dreaming this. You were screaming."

"I was?" Images from the nightmare came back to me. Bolting out of bed, I grabbed my backpack and pulled out the gruesome paperweight, still wrapped in brown paper. "Here." I tossed it to Cal. "Flush this down the toilet for me, will you?"

He peeked inside the sack. "Where did this come from?"

"Billy gave it to me. He and Les agreed it would make me an honorary citizen, or some such nonsense. But after the dream I just had, I'd rather not ever lay eyes on it again, if you don't mind. Would you please get it away from me? Keep it, if you want to, or use it for target practice. I don't care, but get it out of here."

"Must've been some dream."

"A doozy." I suddenly realized I was standing around in a sleep shirt that too many sessions in the dryer had rendered far shorter than it had started out to be. Not exactly suitable dress for entertaining. Well, maybe for a certain type of entertaining. What a horrifying thought. "Um, Cal, not to be rude, but get out of here."

He pushed a strand of hair out of his eyes. "Excuse me?"

"I'd like to get dressed."

He surveyed my attire with a slow smile. "If you insist, but it's still pretty early. Wouldn't you rather grab a little more sleep?"

"I have too much to do." I pointed at the bathroom. "Out. Oh, dang it, Cal," I relented as he shrugged and slipped by me. "Hand over that awful paperweight. Billy would be crushed if I didn't keep it."

"Sometimes you're too nice for your own good, Taylor." Cal gave the parcel back to me. "Breakfast in fifteen minutes, my place."

"Why?"

"Why what?"

"Why are you inviting me to breakfast?"

He tilted his head. "What an odd question. Let's see how many answers I can come up with. Because I'm being neighborly? Because I don't like to eat alone? Because I accidentally cracked too many eggs?"

I raised a hand, laughing. "Okay, okay. Now, can you really cook, or should I bring my own Alka Seltzer?"

"You'll have to find out for yourself." He disappeared through the connecting door.

I stuffed the crystal globe into an inside pocket of my suitcase, reminding myself that I'd have to dig it out and display it in a prominent place if Billy decided to visit me again.

Hazel crept out from beneath the bed where she'd been hiding. "What's wrong, girl? Too much noise for you?" I scooped her up, stroking her head. "Are you hungry? Well, let me shower and dress, because we've been invited to a home-cooked breakfast. At least, I have, and I don't think Cal would mind an extra mouth to feed."

He didn't. Once his initial surprise had passed, he allowed Hazel to perch on his shoulder while he turned sausages in the pan and scrambled eggs.

"I think she likes me," he said as she nuzzled his cheek, and I refrained from telling him that she was probably using his morning growth of stubble as a convenient head scratcher. "But why does she smell so, um, funny?"

I laughed, popping bread into the toaster. "If you think that's bad, you ought to get a whiff of a male ferret. It's a natural musk they have, much stronger in males than in females."

"Oh. Should I feed her some of this?"

"She wouldn't mind a spoonful of scrambled egg."

When we had finished eating, we leaned back to enjoy a second cup of his really excellent coffee.

"Hey, I've tasted the coffee you make at the SO," I said, pouring myself a third cup. "It tastes like used dishwater. How come this is so good?"

"Because the county buys its coffee wholesale from Juan Valdez's black sheep brother, Pedro," he said wryly. "And I'm not generous or well-paid enough to donate my special blend to my place of employment."

"Can't say I blame you." I looked at my watch. "Well, thanks for a terrific breakfast, really, but I have to be going."

"Where?"

"Huh?"

"Where do you have to be going?" He enunciated slowly and carefully.

"I do have a job, you know."

"I'm aware of that. But the festival doesn't open today until noon."

"I know."

He propped his elbows on the table. "So, where?"

"Stop asking me that. It's none of your business."

A spark of lightning flashed in his dark eyes. "Suppose I'm making it my business? Shit, Taylor, I didn't mean to say it like that. Wait, okay? I'll be right back." He dashed into another room and, true to his word, was back again before I could make up my mind to sneak out.

"Here. If you're going to keep on stirring things up, at least take this with you." He handed me the derringer.

I sat back down, balancing the little gun on my palm. "Gee, how thoughtful of you, Calvin." My voice dripped false sweetness. "But why would I have need of a deadly weapon?"

"My name isn't Calvin," he growled. "And you know perfectly well why."

"Yes, I do. But I thought you and Lester had decided to keep that a big secret."

"We had. But I'm not stupid enough to believe Billy didn't spill the beans. The kid's halfway besotted with you."

"It's a teenage crush, and he'll have one on somebody else by next week. What I'd like you to tell me is, what made you and Sheriff Junior think you had any right to try to keep something like that from me in the first place?"

His scowl faded. "I don't know. Trying to protect you, I guess."

He looked so gloomy that I eased up a bit. "Don't get me wrong. I'm not exactly a helpless female, but I'm not so much of an idiot I'd turn down a little added protection. However, you've got to see that hiding the truth from me isn't protecting me. If anything, it's the opposite. Haven't you ever heard the old adage about forewarned being forearmed?"

"Which is why I want you to carry that." He indicated the derringer. "You haven't said anything I didn't spend last night telling myself."

"Glad to hear it."

"Okay." He pushed the dirty dishes out of the way and placed a saucer in the middle of the table. "Now, let me bum a cigarette so we can talk this over."

I goggled at him. "I didn't think you smoked."

"You've driven me to it," he mumbled, lighting up and coughing a little. "All right, for the third time. What do you intend to do today?"

"Ask some more questions."

"Then let me go with you."

"Why?" I tapped ashes into the saucer. "Have you decided I'm right about the sheriff's murder?"

"I haven't decided anything except that you're pissing someone off. For all I know, it might not have anything to do with Crawford or how he died. You might have just stuck your foot in your mouth somewhere along the line. In case you didn't realize it, Taylor, you're capable of being an extreme smart ass."

"Why, thank you so much."

"So, I'll go along and make sure you stay out of trouble."

"No. I promise I'll tread gently, okay? But I don't want Mr. Macho Cop scaring the crap out of whoever I'm trying to question. Speaking of questions, can I ask you one?"

He lifted an eyebrow. "I guess so."

"Where were you last night when that sandbag fell?"

His mouth dropped open. "What the hell are you implying?"

"I'm not accusing you of anything. I'm trying to get my facts straight. I know where everyone else was, but I didn't see you until afterward."

"Who do you mean by everyone else? Building a list of suspects, are you?"

"You might call it that."

"Who's on it?"

"I'd rather not say at this time." I was trying to sound like Joe Friday. "Are you going to answer my question?"

He sighed. "I'd been handing out trophies to the snake hunters, over in the big tent where the tanks are. If you'll remember, Lester declined to preside over that particular event, and it coincided with the beauty pageant. I had barely walked through the door when all the commotion started up on the stage."

"Did anyone see you come in?"

"I don't know." He was beginning to sound irritated. "I didn't realize at the time that I'd need an alibi, so I didn't bother to set one up. Sorry."

"Is there a back door to the auditorium? One that leads to the backstage area? I wanted to check that out last night, but Doc had people guarding the stage like military sentries, and I couldn't sneak past them."

Cal rolled his eyes. "Yes, Miss Marple, there is a back door, but no one has used it since the festival began. They had to back one of the tents up against the building, and it's blocking that particular door."

I considered. "Which tent?"

"The one we went into yesterday—the museum exhibit."

"A really popular attraction," I said sarcastically. "It would've been easy as pie for someone to duck into that tent and access the door."

"Me, for instance?"

I waved a hand. "You, or anyone else who might have been outside at the proper moment. Or someone who was already inside the auditorium could've slipped back out by that door, and then re-entered the building later from another direction to divert suspicion."

He shook his head. "You have an amazing brain. I only hope you're planning to leave it to science. Now, can I ask you a question?"

"Sure."

"Why are you pursuing this? Why haven't you high-tailed it back to Houston by now?" He leaned across the table, studying me. "You know, if I was in your shoes, and someone had tried to cream me with a heavy object, I'm pretty sure the idea would've occurred to me by now."

I had to admit, it was a damn good question. I only wished I could give him a sensible answer. I had liked the sheriff, and it upset me that someone could murder him, and everyone so willingly chalked it up to being an accident. Maybe I was tired of seeing the bad guys, like the drunk who had killed my mother, walk away without qualm or consequence.

But I couldn't shake the feeling there was more to my meddling than an overdeveloped longing for justice. One thing for sure, though. The near catastrophe with the sandbag had made the whole thing a lot more personal and, if anything, had made me even more determined to get to the bottom of this mess.

Cal was still waiting for an answer, so I shrugged and said, quite honestly, "Beats me."

"That's sorta what I thought you'd say. Would it make any difference if I promised you that I'd take over the investigation? Would that make you go back home?"

"Are you that anxious to get rid of me?" I spoke teasingly, but I couldn't deny a real pang at the thought of leaving.

"No, but it sure seems as if someone is."

I stood up. "I've got to be going. Any further words of encouragement?"

"Please be careful. Taylor!"

Halfway out the door, I turned back.

"Take the gun," he reminded me.

An idea had come to me during my morning shower; one I hoped would save me a lot of walking. My poor feet were still swollen from hours of dancing the night before, and even the soft sneakers felt like I had my toes caught in steel traps.

I was relieved to find Billy alone at the SO. Cal had hassled me enough for one morning; I didn't feel up to a repeat performance with Lester.

"Sure, I guess it'd be all right," Billy said in answer to my request. "Les is still driving the sheriff's car, so his is just sitting around."

"Great. Do you have the keys?"

"Keys are in it."

I couldn't believe there was a place left on earth where people would leave their car keys in the ignition, but sure enough, there they were. I rolled down all the windows, trying to lessen the ever-present odor, and started the engine. I only hoped I hadn't forgotten how to drive.

My first order of business, I had decided, was going to be to have a little chat with Lester's father. It only made sense to begin with a man who had, in so many words, expressed satisfaction at Crawford's demise.

According to Billy, Jack Forman ran the old gas station where I had made a brief and frustrating stop during my cold walk into town that first evening. It was still closed when I parked the patrol car next to the first rusty gas pump. I had been told the house Lester shared with his wife and father was around back, so I started that way, my sneakers crunching through knee-high weeds.

The two-story house was in better shape than the old filling station, but not by much. Its white paint was peeling in so many places that the entire front of the structure reminded me of an enormous Rorschach test. I blinked away the impression of two pelicans mating and continued up the dirt path.

I had put a tentative foot on the first sagging porch step when someone behind me called out.

The man who had wrecked his pickup, along with Crawford's

memorial service, was standing at the entrance to small pre-fab building that had been erected directly behind the crumbling gas station. He showed me a gap-toothed smile as I headed in his direction.

"Don't get many visitors these days," he said, obviously not recognizing me from the morning before. "Did ya come to have a peek at the zoo?"

"I didn't know the town had a zoo," I told him.

"Not the town," he scoffed. "Me. It's my zoo, all mine. But I don't mind showin' it off." He looked me up and down. "You're right pretty. Tell ya what, I won't even charge any admission. How about it?"

"Sure." I would much rather have gone to fetch Doc Neil. I didn't need medical training to see there was something dreadfully wrong with the old man. His eyes, probably once the same clear green as Lester's, were as murky as pond algae and seemed unfocused. As I followed him into the shed, I noticed that his gait was halting and he kept reaching to touch a wall in order to retain his balance. "Mr. Forman, are you feeling all right?"

He addressed a point somewhere above my left shoulder. "Jack, call me Jack. Jack Sprat, I used to be fat." He cackled, and a trickle of drool slid down his chin. "C'mon in, young 'un, the weather's fine."

It was, indeed, quite a bit cooler inside the little building than it was outside, and I saw that a boxy air conditioner, intended as a window unit, had been mounted in a hole cut into the shed's metal siding. This made the second of the only two air conditioners I had yet seen in all of Perdue, the first being the huge, cranky monster that served the auditorium. From what I had observed, most folks opened all their windows and turned on the oscillating fan. If we tried that during a Houston summer, the humidity would drown us all within an hour.

"Have to be careful with the temperature," he was telling me, one hand groping for, I hoped, a light switch. The sun was in the wrong position to sufficiently illuminate much of the interior, and I was uneasily reminded of caves and cellars. "Got to keep it at around seventy-five all the time. Too cold, and they'll try to hibernate. Too hot, and they'll up and die. Gotta have special lighting, too, so they'll shed when they're s'posed to."

A horrible suspicion dawned. "Sh-shed?" Oh, no.

The lights came on and I hastily backed as far away as the small room would allow. I would have been out the door already, had the old man not been blocking it.

One long wall of the building was taken up by a row of sturdy cages, constructed of wood with thick glass fronts. Air holes had been drilled into the sides and backs, and through them I could hear the occupants begin to move, blunt noses seeking the source of the sudden light. Forman stumbled against the cage nearest him and one of the smaller snakes coiled protectively, its horn-tipped tail whipping into noisy action.

"How're my little honeys today?" he cooed, tapping the glass with his finger. The coiled snake sprang at the glass in a motion so fast I couldn't follow it. One moment it was curled, the next it was a blur.

Forman picked up a long stick with a hook at one end and made as if he was going to open the hinged top of the first cage.

"No!" I shouted, and he dropped the stick with a clatter, his eyes making another attempt to focus on me. "I'm sorry, I didn't mean to shout. Your zoo is very nice, Mr. Forman, but to tell you the truth, I don't like being around snakes. Could we go outside, do you think?"

He looked puzzled. "Jack. Name's Jack, like jackrabbits. Not many jackrabbits left, you know. Cars, that's what done it. Cars run over snakes, too, but not my snakes. They're safe here."

I pushed past him and made it outside, welcoming the sunlight as if it were my best friend. He followed slowly, weaving like the drunk I had once thought him to be.

"Mr. Forman—Jack," I corrected myself hastily, trying to avoid a reference to a Jack-in-the-box or a Jack-of-all-trades, or whatever he might come up with next, "I wanted to ask you about something you said yesterday morning at Sheriff Crawford's house."

He dripped a little more drool. "Old Miles, that son of a gun. How's he doin'? Ain't seen the old fart in a coon's age."

I bit my lip. "Uh, Jack?"

He shook a gnarled finger in my general direction. "Mind you, I'm still mad at him, but not too mad to share a pitcher of iced tea. You tell him to get his sorry ass on over here, and we'll have us a game of gin rummy like we used to."

Clearly, I would need to approach this from a different angle. "Why are you mad at him?" I asked.

"Aw, Miles gets a little squirrelly now and again. Last time I saw him, he was after me about gettin' rid of my snakes, said they were too dangerous to keep around. He was afraid some kid would sneak in there and get bit. But I fixed that, you can tell him. Got a lock on the door, and good padlocks on all the cages, too." He mumbled something else, but his speech had become so slurred I couldn't catch it.

"Jack, is it time for your medicine?"

He looked blank. "Medicine? Am I sick?"

"Your insulin," I suggested. "Don't you take insulin?"

"Shots," he agreed, wrinkling his nose. "I hate shots. They hurt. Wasn't as bad when I was fat, but now it's as if that durn needle sticks clear into the bone."

"I know it must hurt," I sympathized, "but I'll bet the shots make you feel better, don't they?" I swallowed. "I think I could give you one if you'd show me where your insulin is."

"Why, what a sweet gal you are. Sometimes Paula gives me my shots, and she doesn't hurt me as bad as Lester does." He tried to wink, but ended up blinking both eyes like a sleepy lizard. "Could be 'cause she gives me somethin' pretty to look at. You know Paula? Cutest little button you ever did see. Sickly, though."

"Paula is sick?"

"All the time. Got somethin' wrong with her skin. I keep tellin' her she oughta just shed it like one of my snakes, and start all over."

I remembered the one time I had met her, and the heavy makeup she had worn.

"Can't get out in the sun much, that's why she stays around the house all the time. Poor thing has to wear long sleeves, even in the summer. You a friend of hers? She's away for a while, gone to visit her folks."

I remembered wondering about the heavy makeup, and now I felt bad about my catty thoughts. Obviously, it had been applied to conceal some sort of rash.

"Jack, maybe we should find your insulin now." I started toward the house, hoping he'd follow, but when I looked back, he hadn't moved.

"I thought you were gonna give me my shot," he whined. "You said I needed one, and Lester forgot. He forgets all the time."

"We have to find your insulin," I reminded him patiently.

He shook his head. "Paula, you know my insulin isn't in the house. Lester doesn't like keepin' it in the kitchen refrigerator."

I sighed. So I was Paula now. He wasn't only sick, he was obviously blind. "You're right. I knew that. Why don't you go get it for me?"

"Okay." He ducked back inside the portable building and, a minute later, brought out a tiny bottle and a syringe.

I took the little vial and held it up to the light, looking for a label that might tell me how much I was supposed to give him. I was more than a little apprehensive about taking on this kind of responsibility.

What if there was something else wrong with him, something unrelated to his diabetes? Maybe insulin wasn't what he needed. Besides, wasn't insulin clear? Though it was still chilly from refrigeration, this stuff looked cloudy, as if it had gone bad.

"Jack, I really think I'd better call someone else to do this, like Doc Neil. Can I use the phone?"

"I don't want Doc Neil to do it, Paula. Why can't you do it?" He rubbed his eyes like a fretful child. "You're not the same since you fell down and lost that baby. You never talk to me anymore. You just stay in your room. It's so noisy all the time now. I don't like the noise." He slumped against the wall.

"What the hell do you think you're doing?" Lester bore down on us like an avenging angel, rushing to put a supportive arm around his father.

"He's not feeling well," I stammered.

"No shit." He bent close to the old man. "Dad? Can you hear me?"

I held out the bottle. "I was going to give him some of this, but—"

Les snatched it from my hand. "Are you nuts?"

"I decided I'd better not," I continued. "I thought I'd call Doc Neil."

"He's my father, and I'll take care of him," Les informed me through clenched teeth. "You still haven't told me what you're doing here."

"I, um, heard about his snakes."

"Yeah. I know how much you love snakes. I'm sure you couldn't wait to see them, huh? Try again, Taylor."

His tone was beginning to get on my nerves. "Okay, you want the truth? I came to ask him why he'd said he was glad Crawford was dead."

"Really? And did you get an answer?"

"Well, he doesn't seem to remember saying it. In fact, Les, he doesn't seem to remember that Crawford *is* dead. This isn't normal behavior."

"It's pretty normal for him lately, and I could've told you, if you'd asked me, that he had no idea what he was saying."

Jack stirred, looking up at his son. "Lester? Have you set those traps in the attic yet? I'm still hearing rats up there." The old man gazed imploringly at me. "Paula, make him set the traps. I can't stand all that shuffling and scratching. Can't hardly get to sleep anymore. I'd do it myself, but Doc told me I shouldn't be climbing stairs."

"Speaking of Doc," I put in, "I think we ought to take him on to the clinic, don't you?

Les leaned down and scooped up his father as if old Jack was a rag doll. "I'll take him to Doc's."

I trailed in his wake, watching him help his father into the front seat of the shiny patrol car, then climb in himself and drive away.

Leaning against my borrowed car, I tried to calm my jangled nerves. I couldn't blame him for being angry with me. He'd caught me in the act of grilling his poor, sick father like a cheese sandwich, after all. I felt like I'd caused nothing but trouble since first setting foot in this friendly little town, but I reminded myself, the situation with my aunt was beyond my control. It was her attitude, not mine, causing the friction there. And as to the sheriff's murder—

Death, Taylor. You're the one who's calling it murder, the only one who really believes it. This was ridiculous. Even in the novels I wrote, my characters had clear-cut motivations for involving themselves in investigations. Where was mine?

Shaking my head, I got into the car and reached for the ignition. The keys weren't there. What the hell? Instinctively, I patted the front pocket of my jeans, and immediately felt the reassuring bump. Once a city girl, always a city girl. It simply wasn't within my genetic makeup to leave a key in the ignition. I dug them out and started the car, heading back to the SO. I needed to do some heavy thinking about whether or not I had outstayed my welcome in Perdue.

Billy greeted me with a fresh cup of coffee. He sat at his desk, watching me drink it, his eyes roaming now and then to a quick inspection of my proportions. I tried not to let him know I noticed. Besotted, Cal had called it. Teenage hormones sounded more accurate to me. Still, he was someone to talk to. Someone, he had proven last night, who would at least tell me the truth if I asked for it. I decided to take a chance.

"I'm thinking about going home to Houston," I told him flat out.

His eyes widened. "You can't leave now—we're still working on the case."

"There is no case, Billy," I told him gently. "Not as far as the real law in this town is concerned anyway. I can't keep bucking the system like this. I don't have the authority."

"But you're a great deputy!"

"I'm not a deputy. I'm a writer who's been playing cop for a few days, and pissing people off left and right." I put down the cup and rubbed at my temples, where a headache was beginning to eat through my skull. "Cal and Lester would both be happier if I went back to my real life, and I can't blame them. I think it's time I go home."

The phone rang, cutting off Billy's response. He picked up the receiver, said half a word, then just sat and listened. I could hear the screeching from halfway across the room, though I couldn't make out the words. After a couple of minutes, he pulled the receiver from his ear and mutely held it out to me.

"Hello?" That was all I had the chance to say for quite a while. Dorothy Stenson was fit to be tied.

Chapter Eleven

DOROTHY WAS SO upset that I wondered for a moment if she had discovered another dead body. It was a relief when I finally caught the operative word.

"Whoa, Dorothy. What robbery?"

"She means burglary," Billy scoffed into my unoccupied ear. "It's not robbery unless the victim gets held up. Even I know that."

I waved a hand to shush him. "When did it happen?" I asked Dorothy.

"How am I supposed to know? What difference does it make? This is what comes of the local police going out to play with snakes, instead of watching for criminals like they're paid to do."

I refrained from pointing out that in a town where no one locked their doors, a theft shouldn't come as a major surprise. "Okay, Dorothy, calm down a little, will you? Tell me what all was taken."

"Only one thing that I know of. I'm not a snoop, Taylor. You could hardly expect me to be able to make a list of everything Miles owned."

"Hold it. I thought we were talking about your house."

"Of course not! I told that little bean brain it was the sheriff's house—didn't he say so? Miles' sister called me this morning and asked if I would pack up a few mementos and ship them to her. Well, the minute I started searching the bedroom, I knew something was wrong. It's as plain as sin someone's been pawing through the drawers in there. Everything was stuffed back into them, any which way. Socks in with his dress shirts, the handkerchiefs I always ironed for him wadded up and crammed into the underwear drawer."

My heart had sunk to somewhere around my knees. "Um, Dorothy? What exactly did you find missing?" I asked, hoping against hope she wouldn't say a locket.

"A locket," she said. So much for hope. "Kathleen had paid Miles a visit late last year, and she told me where he kept it. She says it's not really valuable, but her father gave it to her mother on their wedding day, and there's a lot of sentiment attached. It was passed along to Miles for him to give to his own bride which, of course, never happened, and Kathleen would like to have it now."

I sat down heavily. "Yes, I'm sure she would. Don't worry, Dorothy, I'll find it."

"Are you going to come over and lift fingerprints like they do on TV?"

"Believe me, that won't be necessary." I shut my eyes as she started in on another tirade, and handed the phone back to Billy. He took it gingerly between finger and thumb, wrinkling his nose as if I had given him a used diaper.

"Let her yell for a while, then make an excuse and hang up," I instructed him. "I have to go recover some stolen property."

Crawford, Lester, and Cal had all made it plain that I was only a temporary deputy with limited authority. One of the things I wasn't supposed to do was respond to criminal complaint calls by myself, but this was a situation I'd brought about through my own stupidity. It's not possible to kick yourself while driving a car, but if it had been, I would have kicked myself black and blue on the way to Tessa's house. I settled for calling myself every name I could think of, beginning with idiot and ending, as I pulled into her driveway, with numbskull.

Folks in Perdue don't cotton to peepholes any more than they do to locks, so Tessa had opened the door before becoming aware that her visitor was an unwelcome one. She tried, of course, to close it again, but one of my past part-time jobs had been selling encyclopedias, and I had the foot-in-the-door maneuver down pat.

"We have to talk," I told her, without preamble. I brushed past her and took a seat on the couch.

"How dare you barge into my house? This is beyond rude, and I'm going to call Lester Forman right now."

I smiled. "Go ahead and call him. While you're at it, tell him to bring his handcuffs. Nobody thought to give me a set, and we'll need them when we arrest you."

Her hand hovered above the phone. "Arrest me? For what?"

I relayed Dorothy's frantic phone call. "It's as much my fault as anyone's," I conceded. "I had no right to let you take that locket."

Tessa had grown very pale. "But it's mine. I told you that Miles gave it to me."

"I'm sorry, but even you have to admit that a blood relative has more right to it than does a former fiancée. You have to give it back, Tessa."

"I can't. I—I lost it."

"Oh, good grief." I got to my feet. "Okay, I was trying to be nice about this, though I have no idea why I'd bother. Now, I'm not really up on police procedure, but I guess I'd better call Lester and tell him to get a search warrant."

"That's ridiculous!"

"What's ridiculous is that I'm handing you a way out of this mess on a silver platter, and you're not taking it. Unless, of course, you have some weird yen to get hauled off to jail."

She pursed her lips, one hand fumbling with the collar of her knit blouse. "You can't prove a thing. I told you, I lost it, so you won't find it even if you do search the house. Go ahead and take me to jail, if you don't mind looking foolish."

"Maybe we should stop off at Doc Neil's office on the way, auntie," I said softly. "That's a nasty lump on your chest." I pointed to the oval outline, clearly visible beneath the thin fabric.

The fidgeting hand froze, then fluttered like a dying bird to her side. Defeated, she finally reached behind her neck to unfasten the clasp. Her fingers couldn't seem to manage it, so I stepped behind her and did it myself, feeling her shudder as my hand brushed against her skin.

"I'm sorry. It obviously means a lot to you."

She turned, hard lines bracketing her mouth. "It doesn't mean a damn thing to me, not anymore."

I shook my head, confused. "Then why were you so determined to keep it?"

"Open it." She sat on the arm of the couch, folding her arms across her chest as if straining to keep herself from shattering into tiny pieces. "You might as well. Once Dorothy gets her hands on it, everyone in the county will know."

"Know what?" But I was already prying at the catch. I could hear Tessa's heavy breathing as I eased the locket apart.

Each half held an old black-and-white portrait. On the left, a nice-looking young man with center-parted dark hair and a curly mustache gazed solemnly back at me. I gasped when I saw the picture on the right.

It was like looking into a tiny mirror. Even without benefit of color, I could see that her hair, though longer than mine and swept up into a knot atop her head, was the same pale blonde as my own. Her nose, her eyes, the shape of her face—all belonged to me.

"Who?" It was all I could manage to say.

"Henry and Fiona Crawford," she said, so low I could barely hear.

The cool, quiet room revolved around me, and I reached out for something, anything, to grab hold of. Nothing was there, so I sat down where I was, right in the middle of the floor, trying to absorb too many implications at once.

"My father," I murmured. "Miles Crawford was my father." I cradled the old locket in my hands, gazing into my grandmother's face. My face. "Did he know?"

"Not until you showed up in Perdue." Tessa's voice grated like a rusty hinge.

I remembered Crawford's reaction that first night, when he walked into the hardware store and saw me.

"The resemblance would be a little difficult to overlook," I agreed sourly. Why hadn't he told me? If not at that moment, then later, when I showed him the letter and ranted about finding my father? I thought back to the story he had told about my mother and what I had later learned from Wood. A few more puzzle pieces clicked into place.

"My mother left because she was pregnant. I'm right, aren't I? Odd as it may seem now, with single mothers all over the place, that was the sixties and Perdue is a small town with more than its share of self-righteous snobs. I'll bet the free love movement never made it past the Derrick County line, did it? She knew she'd be ostracized, or worse, if she stayed." I pulled my knees up, wrapping my arms around them. "It must've been horrible for her."

Tessa blanched.

"She didn't even tell you, did she? Of course, she didn't. After all, Crawford had broken up with her because he fell for you. He told me that you blamed him for her moving away. Said it took him almost a year to convince you to go out with him. My God." Another piece settled into its niche. "When you went to visit her in Houston, she'd already given birth to me, hadn't she? That's why you stayed there. And she probably made you promise not to tell Crawford."

Tessa shook her head. "I was so sure you knew," she whispered.

"You thought I knew who my father was? I told you I didn't."

She was still shaking her head. "Sarah swore she was going to tell you. I begged her not to, I sent money, I tried to make her understand my position, but she was a hard woman. She hated me. She'd have taken such pleasure in telling you, just to hurt me."

I got to my feet, my joints feeling as stiff and sore as if I had taken a few punches. "Wait, I don't get it. You didn't want her to tell me who my father was?"

Tessa's eyes snapped back into focus. "I didn't want her to tell you who your mother was."

My carefully assembled puzzle fell apart.

I don't recall how I ended up on the couch, a snifter of brandy clutched in my hand. Tessa was beside me, the new lines of strain etched around her mouth making her resemble my mother more than ever. No, that wasn't right, was it? She didn't look like my mother, she looked like Sarah Madison. And Sarah had looked like this woman, who was my—

I took a mouthful of brandy and choked it down, welcoming the warmth that traced its way along my frozen limbs. "This is a little hard to swallow," I muttered, and I wasn't talking about the liquor.

"I can imagine." The words were devoid of sympathy or apology. "I don't expect you to understand, but I did what I had to do. I was young and very foolish, as the young so often are. I loved Miles Crawford with all my heart, and he loved me. Sarah did leave because of him, because of how he felt about me, and I did tell him that I blamed him for it. I shouldn't have, of course.

"He never loved Sarah, and she knew that, but she did love him. I doubt if she ever loved anyone else in her life the way she loved him. And for a long time, I pushed him away out of my own sense of guilt." She laughed harshly. "Sarah had a talent for inflicting guilt."

"Tell me about it," I muttered.

She ignored me. "Miles and I became engaged, and youthful hormones were the same then as they are now, believe it or not. I had been raised, like all the girls of my generation, to believe premarital sex was sinful, but we were only weeks away from our wedding and it didn't seem wrong. Then, all at once, I was hearing rumors about Miles and Dorothy." She winced at the memory. "I had missed a period, and it didn't take a genius to figure out what that meant. I was so hurt and so confused. I couldn't tell my father, and Mother had been dead for two years by then. I took the next bus to Houston without even thinking it through."

I was still too numb to be angry, but I could feel a tiny knot of fury in the pit of my stomach, waiting for the proper time to explode. "I understand you were scared. I even understand you couldn't have been thinking very clearly at the time. But you had nine months to get used to the idea. None of this explains how you could've just left me there like an old suitcase. Even if you didn't want me, it should've been obvious that she didn't either. She resented the hell out of me. I've known that all my life, and now I'm beginning to see why. You just dumped me in her lap and took off."

"I had no choice."

"Don't give me that! Of course you had a choice." I hated

sounding so calm, but my emotions couldn't seem to crash through the wall I had constructed around them so long ago. "You could've had an abortion. You could've put me up for adoption. Trust me, I'd have had a better life with any stranger you picked off the street than I had with your sister." I felt a twinge of guilt as the brutal words left my mouth. Knowing what I knew now, I was surprised Sarah had treated me as well as she had.

"We're talking about the sixties," Tessa reminded me. "Abortion was illegal. Sarah offered to find one of those back-alley butchers for me, but the prospect was too terrifying. And I didn't put you up for adoption because, by the time you were born, I had made up my mind to come back to Perdue and try to patch things up with Miles. I found out he had been trying for months to contact me, but Sarah had fended him off. I was furious with her, and had decided to tell him everything." She drew a shuddering breath. "Then Wood came to Houston."

"Oh." Wood, armed with his lifelong crush on Tessa and the latest rumor about Dorothy and Miles.

"It broke my heart when he told me Miles was marrying that awful woman. The next thing I knew, he was down on one knee, begging me to be his wife. I don't even remember saying yes. God forgive me, I think I was lashing out at Miles, punishing him. It never occurred to me how unfair I was being to Wood. Suddenly, I found myself on a plane to Vegas because Wood didn't want to wait around for a Texas marriage license, said he didn't plan to give me time to reconsider. I left a note for Sarah, and asked Wood to leave her some money."

"Where was I?"

"You were back in the hospital. You had developed some sort of digestive disorder, and the doctor wanted to monitor your condition for a few days."

"Very convenient," I murmured. "Wood might not have been as quick to propose if you'd had a baby in your arms."

"I had every intention of telling him about you. I was waiting for the right time."

"Gosh, it's been twenty-eight years and, let's see, four months. When do you suppose the right time will present itself?"

"It wasn't that simple. Don't you see that this type of thing would have been a major scandal in a town the size of Perdue? It didn't take me long to realize that the story about Dorothy and Miles had been vicious gossip, probably started by Dorothy herself. How do you think

I felt when I came back here and learned that my baby's father still loved me? Still wanted me?

"But I was already married to a kind, gentle man who loved me more than his own life. Was I supposed to leave him for Miles? Or was I supposed to saddle him with the bastard child of a man he knew I still had feelings for? And what about Miles? He was only beginning his career and something like this would've ruined him. I didn't know what to do."

I shrugged.

"My solution was cowardly. You don't have to tell me that. But I swear to you, I never meant for it to be permanent. I thought I could figure out how to fix things, if only I had some time to think. Sarah kept pushing to bring you here, and I kept stalling. No one in Perdue had ever met Miles' mother—his father didn't move here until after her death. But I had been given that locket, remember? I knew what she looked like, and I had no doubt Miles would take one look at you and guess everything. You came out of the womb with that strange, pale hair."

She squeezed her eyes shut for a moment. "I sent Sarah money, of course, but after a while she started sending it back. Then she stopped answering my letters. The years passed, Taylor. I don't know where they went."

I got up and poured myself another shot of brandy. "It must've been quite a shock when I showed up on your doorstep the other night."

"A shock? I thought for a minute that my heart had frozen. After all that time, all the lies. Everything caught up with me in one huge rush."

"And you thought I'd found out about my parentage."

She shivered. "I was certain Sarah had sent you. She always said she'd tell you the truth one day."

"Well, she never did. If I hadn't discovered that letter, I wouldn't have even known you existed."

"I'm sure that's why she kept it," Tessa said wearily. "Evidence."

"Maybe." My mind had begun working in another direction. "Tessa, I've heard a rumor myself lately. Is it true you've been having an affair with Miles since you and Wood moved back into town?"

Her lips twisted. "Dorothy told you that, I'm sure. No, it's not true. Miles and I barely spoke during all the years since my marriage to Wood. We lived out on the ranch, you know, and rarely even came into town. Thank God for that. It probably saved my sanity."

"But Dorothy says you've been seen together a lot since you

moved back to town after Wood's stroke."

Tessa sighed. "Miles was a lonely man. We'd become friends again, that's all."

"That's all?" I shook my head. "I don't buy it, Tessa. I think he was still in love with you. Dorothy implied he was trying to convince you to leave Wood for him. Were you planning to? Is that why he decided not to run for sheriff again?"

She looked away. "All right. Yes, he was still in love with me. And yes, he had asked me to leave Wood. But I refused. I love my husband, Taylor. I'm not sure I realized it until six months ago, but when you come that close to losing someone, you find out in a hurry what they really mean to you. Wood has been the best thing in my life. I wouldn't give him up for anything, certainly not for a thirty-year-old failed romance. I think I almost had Miles convinced of that, until you came to town."

"I'll bet he was pissed."

She nodded. "He was, at first. But then he seemed to take it as a sign that we were meant to be together. I was terrified he would go to Wood and tell him everything."

Crawford hadn't done that, as far as I knew, but Dorothy had told Wood things he shouldn't have known.

Tessa clasped her hands, leaning toward me. "Taylor, God knows you don't owe me a damn thing. I wouldn't blame you if you hated me. But I'm begging you. Don't tell Wood that you're my daughter. He's still not well, and I don't know what this would do to him. Please. I'll—I'll pay you anything you want."

I gaped at her. "You're offering to let me blackmail you? Tessa, get real. I won't tell Wood if you don't want him to know. Whatever you might believe, I didn't come here to cause you pain."

She raised a trembling hand to her throat. "No, of course you didn't. I'm sorry." She stood up. "I'm really sorry for everything. I never meant for you to be hurt, for anyone to be hurt. Please, could you leave now? Wood will be home any minute, and I'd rather he didn't find you here. I need some time to get myself together."

"I'll leave, but not quite yet." I was remembering something I had been told about the final evening of the sheriff's life. "Tessa, a woman made a phone call to Miles Crawford early Wednesday evening. Dorothy says she was crying. Was that you?"

She looked surprised. "No."

"Dorothy also saw a woman ring his doorbell later that evening. I suppose that wasn't you either."

This time she blushed, so I had my answer before she gave it. "I did stop by for a few minutes."

"To talk about me? To find out what he might have told me?"

Her chin lifted. "I needed to know." She sighed. "But it turned out to be a wasted effort on my part. He was in no mood to discuss it."

"So what did you talk about?"

"Well, he did most of the talking. He was upset with Lester. No, really, he was more than upset. I don't think I've ever seen Miles in such a state."

Billy had said practically the same thing about the sheriff's fit of temper. "Did he tell you why he was mad at Les?"

"Something Lester should've done, but didn't." She peered at the clock on the mantel and twisted her hands together. "Please, Taylor."

"What was it that Lester was supposed to do?" I persisted.

"I really shouldn't talk about it. Miles told me a lot of things in confidence, Taylor. There weren't many people he could confide in...certainly not that nosy Dorothy." When she saw I still wasn't making any effort to rise, she made an exasperated gesture. "Oh, very well, just don't spread it around, all right? I'm sure you know Miles was planning to back Lester in the sheriff's election. Well, he felt there were a few things Lester needed to resolve first. One being his marital relationship."

I blinked. "You mean Lester and Paula were having problems?"

"From what I understood, yes. Miles had them going to some sort of marriage counselor in Lubbock two nights a week, and he found out Lester had been skipping sessions."

I wanted a chance to mull that one over, but it was obvious she was becoming frantic to get me out of there. I finally stood up. "I need to ask one more question."

She tapped an impatient foot. "About Miles?"

"No, about me. Where in hell did the name Madison come from? Mom—I mean Sarah—never married, did she? And your maiden name was Ross."

The tension broke for a moment, and she almost smiled. "We had to come up with a name for the birth certificate, and Sarah lived on Madison Street in Houston."

"Oh, fine," I grumbled. "I won't even ask where you got Taylor. Probably her neighbor's cat."

"No, Taylor was our grandfather's name." She hesitated. "I have to ask something. You don't really think that Miles was murdered, do you?"

"Yes. And if I didn't have a reason to prove it before, I sure do now." I picked up the locket from the coffee table. "Tell you what, Tessa. I'll mail this off to Miles' sister myself. That way, Dorothy will never even see it."

She regarded me suspiciously. "You'd do that for me? Why?"

I didn't have an answer for that one.

Halfway to the car, I reached into my pocket for the keys, only to discover they had worked themselves through a hole in the pocket's lining. As I stood in the driveway, tugging on the key chain, a horribly familiar buzzing noise froze me to the spot. It was a sound I had hoped never to hear again, especially not in such close proximity. Cal's derringer was in my backpack, but I was afraid to shift my position in order to get at it.

Someone had told me that, if a rattler was in position to strike, the best thing to do is remain absolutely still, and I was more than aware that if it was rattling, it was already in position to strike. Wondering if a snake, like an angry dog, could sense fear, I made an effort to relax my muscles, though feigning nonchalance while sweat flowed freely from every pore seemed ludicrous.

The sound ceased as suddenly as if I had been struck deaf. Moving only my eyes, I searched the ground around me as well as I could, but I couldn't see it anywhere. My heart was pounding so hard I was afraid it would rip its way out of my chest. What to do now? I couldn't stand in Tessa's driveway for the rest of my life, playing an eternal game of Statues.

Mentally measuring the distance between myself and the car, I took a deep breath and leaped, landing squarely in the center of the battered hood. I spent a good two minutes examining myself for fang marks, then another five scanning every visible inch of the landscape around me. I still couldn't see it. Climbing atop the roof of the car, I eased my way feet-first in through the open driver's window, then cranked the window shut. Better asphyxiated by a foul odor than poisoned by a snake.

When my nerves had steadied a bit, I shifted onto one hip and renewed my struggle to free the keys from my pocket. This time I succeeded, though an audible rip told me I'd have to do some work with a needle and thread before I wore these jeans again.

As I shoved the ignition key home, I noticed the disk that dangled from the key chain and, after a moment of stunned silence, I started laughing. Painted on the disk was the picture of a coiled rattlesnake. I pressed the center, and the terrible buzzing filled the car. Hardly as cute as Wood's baaing sheep or Annie's barking dog, but still a gimmick. A toy.

As my terror died away, my laughter died with it and I leaned my head against the steering wheel and sobbed. I cried for Tessa, for Sarah, for Wood. I cried for Miles and for the relationship we might have had. I cried for the unloved little girl I had been, and the disoriented adult I had become. I cried until there were no tears left.

I drove back to the Sheriff's Office, but my image in the rearview mirror convinced me not to go in. Abandoning the car, I walked across the street to the hardware store. Unfortunately, Hank was working in the storeroom when I attempted to sneak in through the rear door, and I had to spend some time reassuring him that I hadn't been attacked by a swarm of African killer bees before he would let me continue on up the stairs.

That was one of many reasons I avoided tears whenever possible; my face always puffed up like an angry toad. The crying jag on the day of Crawford's memorial had been a brief shower, sparing me the usual consequences, but today's had been a Texas gully-washer.

Stretching out on the bed, I draped a cold washcloth over my face and tried to relax. It had been a hell of a day already, and it was barely past noon. I told myself a sensible person would stay right here for the rest of the night, then pack her bags and catch the next bus, plane, or camel caravan back to Houston. A sensible person would never have set foot in this bizarre little town in the first place.

Hazel crawled across my neck, nosing the damp cloth until I pulled it aside, letting her see it really was me underneath. She regarded me uncertainly, but finally curled up next to my pillow. I was struck by the unpleasant realization that if anything were to happen to me, Hazel would probably be the only living creature on earth who would really miss me. I sat up in bed. Who would take care of her? Should I make a will? At the ripe old age of twenty-eight, I had never even considered the need for a will. Could Annie arrange for my royalties to go to my beneficiary? Not that they amounted to much yet, but they'd keep Hazel in cat food and litter for a few years. Which still left the problem of choosing a beneficiary from my limited supply of acquaintances.

Flinging the washcloth away, I got out of bed and started pacing, which isn't an easy thing to do in a cluttered eight-by-ten room. I decided it might be safer to lean against the windowsill and seek inspiration in the view of the distant hills. Someone knocked at the connecting door, then opened it without waiting for a response.

"What are you up to?" Cal inquired.

"Oh, nothing much, just contemplating my own mortality."

"Sounds cheerful. Thought I'd better come check on you. Hank told me you were in bad shape."

I turned around and he got a good look.

"Whoa, he wasn't exaggerating either. You look like you have golf balls stuffed into your cheeks. What the hell happened?"

I didn't mean to tell him, I really didn't. I had even formed a halfway plausible lie involving an allergic reaction, but when my mouth opened, that wasn't what came out. I started by showing him the locket and ended with the false snake alarm, then collapsed atop the bed, wrung dry. "How the hell do you do that?"

He had crossed the room midway through my story and was sitting beside me on the bed, looking more than a little shell-shocked. "Huh? How do I do what?"

"You're in the wrong profession, you know. If you affect everyone the way you do me, you could make a fortune as a shrink. There wouldn't be a hidden complex or a buried trauma left in North America."

"I think I'll pass up that particular opportunity," he said wryly. "Shit, gal, you've had quite a morning. Are you okay?"

I shrugged. "I guess so. At least, I accomplished my original purpose for coming to Perdue."

"And then some. So, what now?"

"What do you think?"

He sighed. "You're going to snoop some more, right?"

"He was my father, Cal. Someone murdered him. If I wasn't willing to give up before, you can't seriously believe I would now?" The multiple shocks of the morning were beginning to wear off, and my brain was again taking precedence over my heart, or whatever organ was in charge of rampant emotions. "Tessa was pretty high on my list of suspects before," I mused aloud. "I'm not sure this changes anything."

"What do you mean?"

Plumping my pillow, I settled back to consider my new information. "Tessa insisted that she and Crawford were no more than friends, but Dorothy is certain they were having an affair. Who's telling the truth? According to Tessa, Crawford wanted a lot more from her, but she refused. She swears she loves Wood. But even Tessa admits Crawford hadn't given up on the idea of winning her back. And my arrival gave him additional ammunition. Tessa said she'd been terrified that—" I sat straight up.

"Terrified about what?" Cal prompted.

"Wait, I'm trying to remember exactly what she said. She was terrified Crawford would go to Wood and tell him everything. Everything about me is what she meant. I can see her point. It would be difficult enough to hear another man profess undying love for your wife. I think it might be a lot worse to learn, in addition, that the man and your wife shared a daughter, that your entire marriage had been constructed on lies from day one.

"Wood Potter seems like one of the kindest men I've ever met, but even he might not be able to overlook deceit of this magnitude." I shook my head. "Tessa's right, you know. If it all came out, she'd probably lose her husband, one way or another. If he didn't simply walk away, which he would have every right in the world to do, a blow like this might very well trigger another stroke. The question is, how far would Tessa go to keep Wood in the dark?"

"Taylor, you can't seriously suspect Tessa."

"Why not? Because she gave birth to me? Come off it, Cal. She's not exactly brimming over with maternal love. Blood ties never affected her before, so why would they now? Wood is the most important person in her life. She told me so straight out. I'm nothing but a past mistake."

"I don't know..."

"Hush, I'm moving on to someone else now. Dorothy told Wood her suspicions about Tessa and Crawford. If he believed that Tessa returned Crawford's feelings, would he be willing to kill in an attempt to save his marriage? And if he did, he'd sure want to get rid of me before I convinced anyone that Crawford's death wasn't an accident. Imagine how frustrating it would be to plan and execute such a perfect crime, and then have some nosy city girl arrive and spoil everything."

"Are you hearing yourself?"

"I'm trying. It would help if you'd keep your mouth shut." I thought back to my conversation with Dorothy at the dance, and relayed to Cal her description of events on the last evening of Crawford's life. The frantic phone call from a weeping woman. The woman who rang Crawford's doorbell later that night. "Tessa admits to being the visitor, but denies making the phone call. I'm not sure I believe her, though. From what Dorothy overheard, Crawford said, 'I know you love him. You don't have to keep telling me that.' If he was talking to Tessa about Wood, that fits, doesn't it? Tessa swears she loves Wood, and that she made it clear to Crawford."

Cal started to interrupt, but I held up a hand. "Wait. He said something else, too. 'I've tried it your way, God help me, but this can't be covered up anymore.' Don't you see? He was probably talking about me. Sounds like he had decided it was time to bring his bastard daughter out of the closet, doesn't it? It makes sense, Cal. Tessa would certainly have been in tears, probably begging him to reconsider. But, according to what Dorothy heard, he didn't back down.

"So, when Tessa dropped by later on, why couldn't she have been the one to murder him? As far as I've been able to find out, no one saw or spoke to him after that." I opened my mouth to tell him what Tessa had divulged about Lester and Paula, then changed my mind. Marriage counseling was a private thing, and I couldn't see that it made any difference in my speculations. It wasn't any of Cal's business either, though it would certainly have given him some mud of his own to sling during the election if he were willing to stoop that low. "Now, here's what I'm wondering—" I began, but Cal groaned and heaved himself off the bed.

"Enough. Please. I think it's time we go have a little fun at the festival."

Fun, he called it. I slumped against the pillow. "Oh, Cal, I'm not sure I'm up to that today. Couldn't I watch the phones again and let Billy go instead?"

"Guess so," he drawled. "But I'm gonna feel pretty silly buying him cotton candy and winning him a Kewpie doll."

"What are you talking about?"

"I figure we'll work until four or so, then hand things over to Billy and Lester. It's the last night and all the snakes are gone, so they can handle it. Do I have to spell it out? Okay. I'm askin' you on a date, Ms. Madison. What do you say?"

What did I say? "Make yourself useful and go rig me an ice pack," I commanded. "I'll be damned if I'm going out on my first date in two years looking like a chipmunk."

Chapter Twelve

FIFTEEN MINUTES WITH an ice pack, followed by an application of more makeup than I had worn since a college Halloween party, rendered me fit to be seen in public. I even changed into my least raggedy pair of jeans and wiped off my dusty sneakers with a wad of damp toilet paper. This was, after all, a date.

During the drive out to the festival grounds, I rediscovered how the word "date" can screw up an otherwise amiable relationship between members of the opposite sex. I found myself fidgeting with my hair and sneaking a finger to my mouth to check for smeared lipstick.

Cal noticed my odd behavior. "What's the matter with you?" he asked, finally. "Has Hazel given you fleas?"

I lit a cigarette, rolling down the window to let the smoke escape. The cigarette would ruin my lipstick and the open window would snarl my hair, and the best part was I didn't care. His typically snide comment had brought me back to earth.

"Why were you avoiding Sheriff Crawford the night he died?" I asked, pleased to note that the car swerved a bit.

"Where did you hear that? Never mind. Billy."

"Well?"

He scowled at the road for a moment, then sighed. "I knew he had been looking for Lester all evening, and I figured I was going to get pegged to play babysitter again. I just wasn't in the mood, okay?"

I studied his unsmiling profile. "You've said something before about Crawford expecting you to keep Les out of trouble. Exactly what kind of trouble was he in the habit of getting into?"

He shrugged. "You might have noticed that Lester has a quick temper. Sometimes he swings first and thinks later. Crawford hoped I could provide a calming influence."

It didn't sound fair to me. If Crawford had so little faith in Lester's abilities, why on earth would he have chosen the man to be his successor? And to ask Cal, who was also planning to run for the office, to be responsible for keeping Les's reputation untarnished, seemed not only ludicrous but insulting. I said as much.

Cal's tight jaw eased. "I appreciate the sentiment, Taylor, but family connections play a major role in small-town politics. My father didn't happen to be lifelong friends with the sheriff, that's all. And don't forget Les has a year's seniority on me."

"You're still going to run against him, aren't you?"

"Sure. I might even have a chance now." He saw my expression and groaned. "Oh, God, I didn't mean it that way. Did I just get added to your list of suspects?"

"No." I was able to say it truthfully because it wasn't a matter of adding him. He had been on the list from the beginning; I simply didn't enjoy being reminded of that.

Cal and I walked security patrol until four o'clock, then tucked our badges away and joined the crowd of merrymakers. A decent cloud cover kept the temperature comfortable without threatening rain and, despite my troubled thoughts, I felt my spirits lifting as we wandered among the booths. Cal shot a series of tin ducks with an air rifle, winning a tiny stuffed sheep with a jingle bell in its tail. I took a few shots myself, and was presented with a bright pink plastic snake. Fortunately, I was able to talk Cal into trading prizes with me.

We rode the carousel, then snacked on roasted peanuts; rode the miniature train, then snacked on cotton candy. We viewed an exhibit of cactus, watched a burly man juggle apples, bowling pins, and china plates, and tried our luck at pitching horseshoes.

By mid-evening, exhausted and a little queasy, we settled at a picnic table and ordered roast beef sandwiches and coffee. Cal's hair had escaped its tie some time back, and blew about his tanned face as he lifted his head to the cool breeze. He looked more like a happy little boy than a deputy sheriff, and I felt my heart skip a beat. He couldn't have done it. Please, God, he couldn't have.

Billy plopped down next to me, breaking into my reverie. Grateful for the distraction, I gave him such a warm smile he nearly backed off the bench. Les took a seat across the table, munching a candied apple.

"Howdy." His tone was friendlier than I had expected, or probably deserved. "Since I don't see any badges, I'm guessing you two are taking the rest of the day off."

"Didn't think you'd mind," Cal said easily.

"Not a bit. Things are slowing down some since they've closed off the snake tent. Folks can't get in a lot of trouble playing games and riding rides. We can handle it, can't we, Billy?"

"Yup."

"How's your father, Les?" I asked.

"He's in the hospital in Lubbock."

"Oh, no!" Guilt swept over me. "I'm so sorry. Is he going to be all right?"

"I think so. Doc said they need to monitor him for a while and get his insulin stabilized. He missed another dose this morning." He sounded irritated, though whether at his father, at himself, or at me, I couldn't be sure. I decided it was directed at me, and again admitted I should have sought help for his father sooner than I had.

"Your mind was on other things. Taylor, I need to talk to you in private for a minute. Billy, Cal, will you excuse us?" Les led me away from the table and around a tent until we found an unpopulated area. Figuring he was going to chew me out again about questioning his father, I braced myself for a lecture. But he surprised me.

"I owe you an apology," he said. "I wasn't very nice to you this morning."

"I probably had it coming."

"No, you didn't. Now, I'm still not convinced you're right about Crawford being murdered, but I seem to recall telling you it was okay with me if you wanted to snoop around. I wasn't really mad about that."

"Then what?"

He pulled off his sunglasses. "Shit, I'm mad at the world in general, Taylor. I'm worried about Dad, I've got that damned election coming up, and now Paula..."

"Paula? Isn't she back yet?"

He finally looked at me and I saw the pain in his eyes. "I'm not sure she's ever coming back."

"Oh, Les. Why?" Apparently, the marriage counselor Tessa had told me about wasn't doing much good.

"Am I interrupting something?" Cal stood a few feet away, watching us, his expression unreadable.

"Not a thing," I said lightly. "What's up?"

Cal glanced at Lester, and his jaw tightened. "We're on a date, remember?"

Lester's eyebrows rose. "You are?"

"Yep. So I think we'll take off now, okay?"

I hated to leave Les looking so sad, but Cal was right. 'Dance with the one that brung ya,' as the old adage went, so I told Les I'd see him later and followed Cal back to the picnic table. "Where's Billy?"

"Off patrolling. What did Les want?"

"He was apologizing about something he said to me this morning."

"Really? Looked like more than that to me."

Did he actually sound jealous? "Like what?"

"I figured he was telling you to drop this wild murder theory of yours. You've got the whole town stirred up, you know."

"Wild theory," I repeated. "That's how you see it."

Cal rolled his eyes. "Taylor, I think I understand what put the idea into your head, and I'll even admit that the thing with the lamp is a little weird, okay? But I want you to pay attention to what I'm going to tell you. Crawford was killed by a snake bite. Not a bullet, not a knife, not a blunt object or a rope around the neck. Now, I read a newspaper story a few years back about a snapping turtle being used as a weapon in a hold-up, but you're not going to convince me that someone could use a rattlesnake to murder someone."

He held up a hand as I opened my mouth to disagree. "I know what you're going to say. Doc had a little chat with me about some hinky questions you were asking him the other day, and it was pretty obvious to him the track your mind was taking. Well, you'll have to trust me when I tell you what you're considering is a darn sight less than unlikely. I learned how to milk snakes when I was fifteen years old, and it's not as easy as it may appear. Those critters are strong, they're heavy, they're ornery, and they don't like being handled.

"Maybe, and it's a big maybe, someone could've managed to control a baby rattler well enough to have actually forced it to bite the man, but there are two flaws in that scenario. The first is that I saw the remains of that snake with my own eyes, and the sucker was well over four feet long. Granted, it wouldn't have won our biggest snake trophy, but even an expert couldn't control it with one hand."

"What do you mean, one hand?"

"That's the second problem with your hypothetical crime. Seems to me the killer would've needed a hand free in order to hold Crawford down. I don't know about you, but I wouldn't sit placidly by while some lunatic attacked me with a rattlesnake. Matter of fact, I'm pretty doggone sure I'd have run like hell."

"Crawford could've been asleep," I pointed out. "Dorothy says he dozed off in that chair all the time."

Cal sighed. "Believe me, he wouldn't have stayed asleep for long. I'm not sure you're getting a clear picture of what would be involved here. I've never tried to milk a snake that big, but I can tell you that, even with a smaller one, it takes both hands—one to grip the head, and one to maintain some kind of control over the body. Snakes aren't real cooperative when it comes to holding still. They tend to flop around like beached fish. Manipulating a four-and-a-half-foot rattler would require two people to do it safely, much less as stealthily as you're suggesting. And please, don't tell me there could've been two murderers."

My sails were beginning to droop, but he hadn't knocked all the wind out of them. Not quite. "What about the sandbag? Even you were convinced someone tried to—to hurt me the other night. So, who would bother doing something like that unless I was on the right track?"

He shook his head. "It could've been an accident."

"Cow poop. Three witnesses confirmed the rope had been deliberately cut."

"That's not what I meant. It was cut, all right, but what makes you so sure you were the intended victim?"

"Huh?"

"Well, think about it. You were a judge, tucked away on the sidelines. No one could've expected you to be on that stage when you were. Maybe whoever did it was after Tessa, or Les, or even our newest Miss Snakeskin."

I briefly considered the possibility of the nasty, little, raven-haired beauty crowning her rival with something heavier than tinsel, but it didn't wash. "The only reason I was up there at all was because no one could find Tessa when it came time to crown the winner. Suppose she was hiding on the catwalk, waiting to bean me? Even if she didn't kill Crawford, she had good reason to want me out of Perdue."

Cal was silent for a moment, thinking it over. "Maybe," he said finally, reluctantly. "Would it make you feel better if I had a talk with her?"

"No, I'd rather do it myself. You can yell at me, but you can't stop me from asking questions."

"Not unless someone files harassment charges." He looked more amused than irritated. "Did anyone ever compare you with a mule?"

"More than once." I tried a smile. "Let's drop this for now, okay?"

Cal shook his head wearily. "Fine."

"Good. So, are we still on a date, or what?"

"Yep."

We started back toward the crowded grounds and when I realized he was holding my hand, I mentally vowed to keep the conversation casual for the rest of the evening.

I kept that vow, at least until our first turn on the Ferris wheel. I gasped in sheer delight as our car swung to the top, allowing an unobstructed view of yet another fabulous sunset.

I will swear to this day that the west Texas sun is not the same one that shines upon the rest of the world. Twice as large and more bronze than gilt, it broke free of the low clouds and dipped to touch Perdue's craggy blue hills. What had been a barren landscape blazed with sudden color, and the puffy clouds glowed from within as if the angels were lighting their candles.

Cal draped an arm around my shoulders and, as the car started back down, I caught a glimpse of the old gas station in the distance and thought of Jack.

"I hope he's all right," I murmured.

"Who?"

"Jack Forman. I didn't tell you what happened this morning, did I?"

When I had finished, Cal sighed. "You do get around, don't you? No wonder Les was a might upset."

"Don't rub it in, I feel guilty enough. I just wanted find out why Jack had said he was glad Crawford was dead."

"I sort of wondered about that myself. Did he give you a reason?"

"No. He didn't seem to remember saying it. As a matter of fact, he acted like Crawford was going to show up any minute for a game of cards and a glass of tea. He did say that he and the sheriff had exchanged a few harsh words about Jack's snakes." I looked up at Cal. "You know, it strikes me how really weird it is that Jack Forman, of all people, would choose to keep snakes."

Cal nodded. "Because of Les, you mean."

"Yeah. Hey, call it indulgent, but if my kid was terrified of spiders, I wouldn't raise tarantulas."

"Maybe Jack was practicing immersion therapy."

I slapped the hand hanging over my shoulder. "That's cruel."

"No, that was a joke. Sorry. I agree with you to a point, Taylor, but on the other hand, why should Jack be deprived of something that has supplied him with so much pleasure?"

"Have I told you how much I hate it when you shift into your lawyer mode? You may have dropped out of law school, but the urge to debate any issue seems to have lingered. I suspect you don't even care which side you take, as long as you can get a good argument out of it." I felt, more than heard, his low chuckle. "Okay, you'll have to explain to me how anyone could derive pleasure from cages filled with poisonous reptiles."

Our car picked that moment to lurch to a stop at ground level, and

Cal leaned into the growing darkness to say something to the operator. I glimpsed money changing hands and a moment later, we were lifted into the air once more.

"Venomous," Cal said.

"What?"

"I've told you before, plants are poisonous, and snakes are venomous."

"Oh. Right."

"You don't mind riding a little longer, do you? I like it up here. I It's peaceful. Someday I'll be rich enough to have a Ferris wheel in my back yard. Much more fun than a swing set, don't you think?"

"Much. But you don't have a back yard."

"So I'll have to work on that, too. Okay, we were talking about Jack, right? I guess I forgot that you didn't know him before his illness got so bad. Jack Forman probably knows more about rattlesnakes than anyone in Derrick County. As a matter of fact, he's the one who organized our first festival, back in the sixties. And although he's never had much formal education, he's done some impressive research over the years for the AITR. That's the American Institute for Toxic Research, located in Sweetwater. Doc told me he's written some amazingly detailed papers concerning everything from mating habits to hibernation."

"You're kidding."

"Nope. Raising rattlers in captivity is difficult and dangerous, and Jack is one of very few people who have been able to pull it off with real success. His snakes have actually bred in captivity into several generations. According to Doc, that's almost unheard of."

We were now illuminated only by the tiny fairy lights that rimmed the Ferris wheel. "You know what I hate most of all about your lectures? You lose some of your west Texas drawl."

"I do?"

"Yeah. And strangely enough, I miss it."

"Taylor," he said softly. "You're not trying to tell me anything, are you?"

"Like what?" I found myself whispering, too, but only because my breath seemed to be catching in my throat.

His dark eyes reflected a hundred multi-colored sparks. "Like, for instance, that a city girl wouldn't mind being kissed by a country bumpkin?"

"The thought never crossed my mind," I lied. We were so close, I couldn't tell whose heart I could feel pounding, but, as his lips touched mine, I discovered it really didn't matter.

An eternity later we came up for air, the car rocking gently beneath us like a boat on a lake. Cal looked every bit as stunned as I felt. It was as if a tornado had sucked us up, spun us until we were dizzy, then set us back down in the exact same spot where we'd started. *No,* I thought, as I reached to trace his strong cheekbone, *not the same spot at all.* I wasn't even sure we were still the same people.

Cal was the first to speak. "Wow."

"Ditto." I cleared my throat. "Um, haven't we been up here for an awfully long time?"

He smiled. A slow, sexy smile that almost made me forget my question. "It helps to have a friend at the controls."

I peered over the side of the car and Hank Barton gave me a cheery little wave as we sailed by him. I'm pretty sure he winked at me, too.

"Why do I have the feeling we're going to be a front page story in the next edition of the *Derrick Gazette?* Shit, Cal, let's get out of here."

We made it off the Ferris wheel and back to the car. I had never necked in a patrol car before, but I have to say I enjoyed myself thoroughly until my foot somehow made contact with the siren switch. It's uncanny how quickly a crowd can gather in a parking lot.

By the time we pulled up in front of the hardware store, things had cooled off enough that we managed a relatively sedate climb up the stairs, stopping for only three kisses along the way. I realized we had come to an abrupt halt in the hallway, inches from Cal's door, both of us out of breath. He made no move to let me into his apartment.

"What?" I asked impatiently.

"Maybe we're rushing this," he mumbled.

"We are?"

"Aren't we?"

"I don't know."

"Well," he said after a moment. "Good night, Taylor."

"Yeah. Good night." I hoped I didn't sound as baffled as I felt.

He unlocked his door and vanished inside. As I fumbled with my key, my mind flashed back to Tommy Finster, the boy I had gone steady with my senior year of high school. We'd shared some pretty steamy grope sessions in the back seat of his father's Lincoln Continental, but they had all ended the same way. I hadn't been ready to take the final plunge. Tommy, struggling to re-zip his tight jeans, would groan and say, "Damn it, Taylor, you're gonna strip my transmission." For the first time, I fully comprehended how he must have felt. Cal had ground my gears into full reverse so quickly, I was still shaking.

Hazel scampered to greet me and I scooped her up. "Men," I told her, "are bizarre creatures. Don't ever become involved with one." She nipped my thumb in response, indicating that she was more interested in her supper than she was in my love life.

As I bent to fill her bowl, I spotted a white envelope that had apparently been pushed under the door. It was from Les. "I'm going to sleep at the office again tonight. Come by if you'd like some coffee." While Hazel crunched her cat food, I crept through the bathroom and pressed my ear to the connecting door, though I couldn't have said what I was hoping to hear. The sound of Cal slamming his head against a wall would probably have made me feel better.

Too antsy to sleep and curious about what Les had started to tell me earlier, I decided to take a walk to the Sheriff's Office.

Perdue was like a ghost town at that time of night, and I didn't even have to pause before crossing the street to the courthouse.

Les was busy with a stack of paperwork, but pushed it aside as I walked through the door.

"I'm glad you came," he said. "How was the date?"

"Not bad." I poured both of us some coffee and sat down in Billy's chair.

"If I'd known, I wouldn't have dragged you away like I did. Cal must have been pissed."

"He'll get over it." I was eager to change the subject, because the thought of Cal still made my skin tingle. "Les, what you were saying earlier about Paula—do you really think she isn't coming back?"

Les rubbed the back of his neck. "I just don't know."

"Sorry, you don't have to talk about it. I didn't mean to be nosy."

"You're not being nosy, Taylor. It's sorta nice to have someone who'll listen." He sighed. "Paula's never been happy here in Perdue. She says the people are all busybodies, and complains there's nothing to do after they roll up the sidewalks at twilight."

"Well, that's true," I admitted, and he gave a weak grin.

"Guess it is. I'm not sure anymore that she should've married me in the first place. Her folks are well off, and Paula was an only child. I wish I could give her more."

A spoiled brat, I thought.

"Dad drives her crazy because he won't stay on his insulin unless she follows him around and gives him the shots, and he's out of his head half the time. And she just can't seem to forgive me..." He stopped.

"Forgive you for what?"

"The baby. It's my fault she lost the baby."

I blinked at him. "How is it your fault?"

Les stood up and paced to the door. "I'd been fixing the railing on our back porch. It was a hot day, so I decided to take a break, went inside for a beer. Unfortunately, I left the hammer lying on the top step."

I shuddered, remembering Jack telling me in a roundabout way that a fall had led to Paula's miscarriage. "Oh, no."

"And she's right I'm to blame. If she hadn't tripped over that damned hammer—"

I reached out and put a hand on his arm. "Don't do that to yourself, Les. It was an accident."

He grabbed my hand and held it like a lifeline. "Taylor, you don't know how much I needed to hear that."

As gently as possible, I pulled away. "Maybe if you continue with the marriage counseling..." The words were out of my mouth before I could yank them back.

His eyes narrowed. "How'd you know about the counseling? Shit, is the whole town in on it now?"

I tried to think of a convincing lie, but my brain was too exhausted. Besides, he'd shared something private and painful with me; I supposed I could return the trust. "Hell, sit down, Les, because it's quite a story."

I sketched out my encounter with Tessa and he listened with his mouth hanging open.

"Your mother? My God. And Sheriff Crawford was—?"

"Yes."

He let it all sink in for a moment. "No wonder you've got such a bee in your bonnet about Crawford's death."

"That particular bee was buzzing long before I found out about my relationship to him," I reminded him. "This only makes me more determined to find out what happened. But let's go back to Paula. Didn't the counseling help at all?"

"It might've helped her, but it just made things worse for me." He leaned back in his chair and propped one boot on the desk. "She got a kick out of taking potshots at me, and the counselor didn't try to stop her. Every time we went, I felt like a practice target someone had tacked up on the wall." He gave a short, bitter laugh. "Which is why I finally just decided not to go anymore."

"And that's what Crawford was so mad about? Billy thought you were skipping college classes of some kind."

"Yeah, the sheriff called the sessions classes around Billy and Cal. Didn't want to embarrass me, he said, but it was more because he didn't want my marriage troubles leaking out to the voters."

"Something else I don't get, though. Why was Crawford the one to arrange your marriage counseling? Seems to me like he was sticking his nose in where it didn't belong."

"Heck, the sheriff and my dad have been friends since they were kids. When Dad's health started failing, Crawford sorta stepped in as a substitute father. He was determined to make my marriage work."

"I'd think that'd be between you and your wife."

Les kneaded the back of his neck. "He thought Paula was the best thing that ever happened to me. Crawford was always telling me that I lacked ambition, and he was convinced a city girl would kick my butt into gear. Then, of course, he was grooming me to take over as sheriff, and even talk of a divorce so near the election wouldn't help my chances. He was constantly reminding me that people in these parts look for stability in their elected officials, and a scandal could blow my chance of winning."

"Divorce is still a scandal in Perdue?"

"You've probably noticed that the good folk of Derrick County haven't bothered to consult a calendar lately. Most of 'em still think it's 1930. Anyway, Crawford kept threatening to pull his support if I didn't make things work with Paula. He said he'd be damned if he'd back a dead horse in the election."

My pride in the man who had been my father slipped a little more. "I'm sorry, Les. That was crappy of him."

"He meant well." Les drained his coffee mug and went for a refill. When he returned, he sat facing me squarely.

"I'd better get this over with. Now that the festival is past, we really don't need you as a temporary deputy anymore. I wish I could keep you on, but the money isn't available for another full-timer." He reached into a drawer and pulled out a stack of currency. "Here's your pay for the past few days. Easier doing this out of petty cash than going through all the paperwork to cut you a check."

"Thanks." I thumbed through the bills and was stunned to find enough to get my car out of hock. "Wait a minute. This is way more than Crawford said I'd get paid."

Les flushed. "Call it a bonus. C'mon, Taylor, don't argue with me. According to Roger, you've been checking on your car every day.

He says it's like watching a mother hover over a sick kid."

"But..."

"Nope, it's done."

"Okay, okay. I appreciate it." I'd be sure to return the bonus as soon as I had my advance money.

Les rolled his chair closer to mine and put a hand against my cheek. "No, don't worry, I'm not gonna kiss you again. Can't say I wouldn't like to, but I understand. I'm still married after all." He slid one finger across my lips to keep me from speaking. "Taylor, I can't help worrying about you. Whether you're right about Crawford's death or not, you've clearly got someone pissed off. I really wish you'd consider going back to Houston, at least for a while. Let Cal and me poke around and get to the bottom of all this."

I moved his hand. "I can't do that, Les."

He looked into my eyes for a long moment. "No, I reckon I knew you'd say that." His dimples flared. "I've always liked stubborn women. Just be careful, damn it."

Pleading exhaustion, I hurried back to my room, my mind churning with problems. For one thing, nice as it'd be to have my own wheels again, I'd have to find another job if I wanted to stay in Perdue. Maybe Hank needed someone to keep track of inventory and sweep floors.

I crept into bed and closed my eyes, letting my thoughts to wander over the previous evening, starting at the point when things had begun to get interesting aboard the Ferris wheel. A few seconds later, my eyes popped open and I sat up, the thudding of my heart convincing me that these particular memories would not be conducive to sleep.

I thought about Lester instead. What he'd told me tonight explained a lot, even the kiss he'd surprised me with at the dance. He seemed to be developing feelings for me, whether out of loneliness or something more, I didn't know. I'd have to set things straight with him, and soon. Even if his marriage with Paula ended, I wasn't looking to become romantically involved with him.

Hazel crawled up next to me and I stroked her absently, considering another matter. Cal's arguments hadn't fallen on deaf ears. My inbred stubbornness aside, I conceded he had made his point, and made it well. My half-formed theory as to the mechanics of Crawford's murder crumbled to dust like a dawn-struck vampire in the harsh light of Cal's logic. I certainly couldn't doubt his expertise on the subject of snakes and their handling. Of course, I had to admit Hazel probably knew more about snakes than I did.

According to Cal, though, the real resident expert was Jack Forman. If only I had known that this morning, I could have asked more intelligent questions.

Sleep didn't come easily, but I finally slipped into a troubled doze. Dreams had always been vivid for me, and I used to feel sorry for people who said they never remembered their nighttime excursions into the subconscious. On that particular night, however, I would have traded places with any of them.

In my dream, I sat in the sheriff's recliner, a torn and tattered Christie novel in my lap. The reading lamp flickered on and off, on and off, until Dorothy passed by and whacked it with a fried chicken leg, leaving a greasy spot on the paper shade. I tried to thank her, but she told me to hush, she was trying to talk on the phone. Someone was crying; I could hear the wails emanating from the receiver she held pressed against her ear. "*Shhh*," she kept telling the caller. "Quiet, please. Taylor is trying to read."

Her words made me remember the book I held, so I opened it to the first page. An inscription, in bold, black handwriting, read, "To my daughter. I wish I had known you." It was signed by Miles Crawford. My vision blurring with tears, I turned to the next page. The severed snake's head from the paperweight sprang forth before I could react, sinking sharp fangs into my neck. I started coughing, and blood spattered from my mouth to speckle the pages of the book.

The dream's sharp images began to fade as I struggled toward consciousness. I was still coughing, my throat raw and constricted. As I edged out of sleep, I felt Hazel scratching at my arm and noticed that she was coughing as well.

I tried to draw a breath, and something thick and hot surged down my throat. Forcing my gummy eyelids open, I saw the yellow flames springing from the wastebasket beside the bed, already reaching to lick the hem of the curtains at the window.

Hazel was no longer moving; she lay limp across the corner of my pillow. I scooped her up, pressing her against my chest, and scrambled off the bed. The smoke was thicker when I stood up, stinging my eyes and obscuring the shadowy corners of the room. It was like being deep underwater, robbing me of any sense of direction.

Fuzzily recalling that since smoke rises, I would be safer on the floor, I dropped to my knees and began crawling away from the source of the fire. When I thought I had made it to the connecting door, I raised up enough to feel for the doorknob. It was there, thank God, and it even turned, but the door refused to move. Still clutching Hazel, I groped with my free hand and discovered that the trunk I had once used as a makeshift means of barricading the room had been placed to block my exit.

Turning so I was sitting with my back braced against it, I shoved, my feet sliding as they tried to find purchase on the old wooden floor. I felt a long splinter wedge itself into the tender arch of my left foot, and the sudden pain forced me to scream. Unfortunately, the scream expelled what breath was left in my lungs, and there was nothing but smoke to replace it. Gagging, I slipped closer to the floor, my ears buzzing like a nest of hornets.

The force of the door being shoved open propelled my limp body back into the room, slamming me against one of the larger pieces of junk that lined the walls. Pain flared in my jaw and in my upper right arm, but I didn't have sufficient strength or oxygen to cry out again.

I was groggily aware of someone standing over me, someone who said, "Holy shit," and then bent to grab me beneath the armpits.

I was dragged into the bathroom, collecting another splinter in my posterior along the way, relishing the cool tiles beneath me when I was eased to rest on the floor. Cal's face swam into focus, his hair standing straight out from his head as if he'd stuck his finger into a light socket, his eyes huge with the whites showing all around. He looked so funny I tried to laugh, but all that came out was another fit of coughing.

Before I could catch my breath, he was gone again, back into his apartment. Seconds later, he emerged with a red cylinder and vanished into the veil of smoke beginning to wend its way into the bathroom. I heard a hissing sound, and my barely functioning brain cried, "Snake!" When Cal returned, he found me inching frantically along on my side, trying to make it into his living room. I was still holding Hazel to my chest like a worn teddy bear, and as Cal bent to pick me up, he gently repositioned her across my stomach.

He laid me out on the threadbare couch and fetched a cool, damp cloth. I rolled to one side and vomited a mass of something black and smoky-tasting onto his rug. He didn't say a word, just ran the cloth over my mouth. Hazel picked that moment to recover from her near-death experience; she wobbled to her feet, shook herself like a wet dog, and bit my stomach.

I howled and sat up. Cal burst into laughter and I had to join him, relief generating a sensation of near euphoria.

"Am I all right?" I asked as soon as my hysteria had subsided a little.

"I was getting ready to ask you the same thing. I think you are.

Made a hell of a mess on my carpet, though, not to mention the storeroom. You little idiot, were you smoking in bed?"

I moved Hazel to one side and swung my legs off the sofa, the movement making me a little dizzy. "I'll take responsibility for your carpet," I told him. "I'll even clean it up. But I wasn't smoking in bed. Someone else started that fire, Cal. Deliberately."

He gave me one of his patented looks.

"Don't say it. Don't you dare tell me I'm imagining things, or try to make it into carelessness or an accident. Cal, where's my laptop? Did it burn?" I tried to stand up, but he pushed me back.

"Would you stop worrying about your stupid computer? You're lucky to be alive."

I took a deep breath, savoring the clean air, and tried to speak calmly. "Go get it for me. Please, Cal, it's important."

Chapter Thirteen

AFTER QUITE A BIT of nagging on my part, Cal finally fetched both my laptop computer and my backpack, the two items I had worried about most. As everyone has at one time or another, I had idly speculated about what I would most want to save if my dwelling caught fire. Now I had my answer, and she was crouched beside me on the sofa, placidly licking a scoop of ice cream. Cal had asked me to name her favorite treat, and had served it to her in one of his best, non-plastic bowls. I wasn't sure whether he was rewarding her for living through the fire, or for biting me. I suspected the latter.

My computer had survived without a scratch. My backpack, too, although it smelled strongly of smoke. Luckily, both had been near the hallway door, and the fire hadn't spread beyond the area surrounding the bed.

"Cal, someone moved that old trunk to block the bathroom door. That's why I couldn't get out."

"Trunk? There was nothing blocking the door when I came through."

"Well, of course not. I had managed to move it by then. Which is how I acquired this." I held up a filthy foot, and Cal winced at the sight of the protruding fragment of wood.

"We'd better get that out. Be right back."

He returned with two things that had long ago made my list of "least favorite first aid tools." A pair of tweezers, and a bottle of hydrogen peroxide. Tweezers inflicted pain, whether they were tugging on a splinter or removing unwanted eyebrow hair, and I hated the very sight of them. The brown-bottled antiseptic, through no fault of its own, had developed a reputation over countless decades of well-meaning mothers assuring their children, "This won't sting. It's only peroxide."

Determined to maintain my status as a grownup, I lay back, eyes squeezed shut and teeth clenched, while he pried a good inch of kindling from my flesh. As he wet a cotton ball, he patted my knee and said, "This won't sting now. It's only peroxide." And I nodded as the stuff bubbled and foamed and stung like an angry yellow jacket.

"Okay, all better. Was that the only one?"

"No, I've got another one—um, yeah," I amended hastily as I

recalled the location of the other splinter.

"You sure?"

"I can get the other one out myself. Shouldn't we call Hank?"

Thankfully, he accepted the subject change. "No. The fire's out and there's no structural damage. I don't see any reason to wake him up."

"But it was arson. Won't he have to file a report so his insurance will cover it?"

Cal looked at me for a long time, then rose and held out a hand. "Think you can walk on that foot if you lean on me?"

"Sure." I let him lead me back through the bathroom and into the haze of smoke. The window had been raised to let the room air out, but it hadn't helped much.

He opened the bathroom door wide, allowing as much light as possible to filter into the storeroom, explaining that the bulb in the floor lamp had exploded from the fire's heat.

"Look." He pointed. "The trunk is well behind the door."

"I told you, I pushed it away."

"Uh-huh. Let me get this straight, Taylor. What you're saying is that someone set the fire, and then made sure you were trapped inside this room. Is that it?"

"That's pretty much it," I agreed.

"Then explain this." He moved to the hallway door and pulled it easily open.

The stench of smoke, the pulsating aches in my jaw and arm, and Cal's accusing tone all combined to severely interfere with my brain function. It took me several long minutes to absorb that the hallway exit hadn't been blocked.

"Well?" Cal prompted.

I forced myself to think. "I don't know the answer. Maybe he lost his nerve. Wait." I limped to his side. "I noticed this before, and it struck me as odd at the time. Both doors open into the room, see? There would be no way to block both of them from the inside without trapping himself. It's possible he didn't even notice that until he had already started the fire."

I squinted around the dim room. "If that's true, he would have had to think fast, and he did exactly what I'd have done. He chose to jam the door nearest to the bed, the one I'd be most likely to try first."

"He?"

"Oh, hell, you know what I mean. He or she, is that better? I haven't had a chance to think about who it might have been." The fumes were getting to me, and I choked on the last couple of words.

"Let's get out of here."

I nodded, coughing, and we walked back through the bathroom.

Hazel had curled up inside her ice cream bowl and was snoring softly. Cal picked her up, bowl and all, and set her on the coffee table then we settled on the couch.

He launched into his debate mode before my rather sore hindquarters had made full contact with the cushions.

"I'm finding it hard to buy your theory."

"So, what else is new?" I grumbled, squirming around in an attempt to find a more comfortable position. I was going to have to get that other splinter out. Soon.

"You're telling me an arsonist would set the fire before he started looking around for ways to block the doors? That would be pretty poor planning."

"Sure it would, if the guy—or gal, okay?—was a professional. Not everybody has a steel-trap mind, Cal. Whoever this was wanted to get to me, whether to scare me or to kill me, I don't know. He or she definitely succeeded in the scaring part, I'll tell you that." I grimaced as my tender rump rubbed the cushion. "This makes twice. First, the sandbag, and now, the fire. Hell, Deputy, even you have to admit that I'm making someone nervous."

He chewed on his lower lip for a while, not looking at me. "Someone certainly set that fire."

I nodded. "And moved the trunk."

"So you say."

He spoke so quietly I almost didn't catch the words. Then their meaning sank in.

"Jesus, Cal, you think I did it myself? You've lost your mind. What possible reason would I have?"

"I didn't say any such thing." He reached to take one of my hands, but I snatched it away. "Calm down, Taylor. You've been under a lot of stress lately, and it's got to be upsetting when you're convinced of something no one else will believe."

"So I figure another attempt on my life will bring you around to my way of thinking, is that it? Well, if you really believe that, why haven't you called the men in white coats yet? Because I'd have to be completely around the bend to attempt something so utterly stupid." I leaned toward him, hooking his jaw with my finger and forcing him to meet my eyes. "Even if I was enough of an idiot to put myself in that kind of danger, do you really think I'd take a chance on hurting Hazel?

Okay, that might sound weird to you, but I'll tell you right now that she's my best friend. For longer than I like to remember, she was my only friend. I wouldn't do it, Cal."

He kissed me, very suddenly, very warmly, and I tasted apology on his lips before he actually drew back to speak it. "I'm sorry. No kidding, Taylor, I don't know why the thought ever occurred to me. This whole thing is so far out, I can't make sense of any of it."

"You think I can?" I edged away from him a little, trying to keep my mind on the problem at hand. It wasn't easy; my defenses were weakening. I had every reason to be furious with the man, but I couldn't seem to summon more than a spark of irritation. Possibly because, in all fairness, I had to admit that his accusing me of arson was peanuts compared to my past suspicions that he might have been responsible for Crawford's death. I sighed. "Forget it. If we're in agreement that I didn't start the damn fire myself, what we have to do now is figure out who did. We have to really think." I paused to smother a jaw-cracking yawn.

"Wrong." Cal got to his feet and in one motion, lifted me from the couch. "It's three a.m., and what we have to do now is go to bed."

As he carried me into the next room, I discovered there's nothing like the idea of sex to jump-start a weary body. The still-unremoved splinter wasn't even throbbing anymore. Much. I only hoped that what he had in mind didn't drive it deeper. The splinter, that is.

My heart was thumping almost painfully by the time he placed me gently atop the rumpled sheets of his bed, switched off the lamp, and leaned to kiss me again. I wanted to tell him to wait, to let me at least take a quick shower. I knew I reeked of smoke and sweat, and I couldn't remember when I had last shaved my legs. While I was still trying to determine how best to approach the subject, he picked up one of the two pillows, grabbed a blanket and left, after informing me that he'd be on the couch if I needed anything.

I stifled a scream of sheer frustration. If I needed anything? I wanted to march into the living room and show the big dolt, in no uncertain terms, exactly what I needed. Damn it, what was wrong with him? Or was it something wrong with me? I wasn't playing hard to get by any means; my signals were loud and clear, so why—?

I sat up in the bed. No. Oh, no. Cal had been the first to denounce my suspicions about Crawford's death. If it hadn't been for Bo's intervention, he might have gone so far as to convince Lester to fire me. Later, of course, his attitude had mellowed, but that could be explained, too. Good cop, bad cop. The bad cop routine wasn't getting him anywhere, so he switched to sweetness, listening to my 'wild theories,' but countering every argument I made with seemingly impervious logic. Suppose the date last night had simply been yet another attempt to distract me? Getting hot and heavy for a while was okay if it would take my mind off the issues at hand, but when it came down to the ultimate intimacy, he wasn't willing to go quite that far.

And how easy it would have been for him to set the fire. I shied away from thinking he'd actually intended to kill me, but another scare on top of the ones I'd already suffered might just push me into leaving town once the festival ended and I was out of a job. I crept out of bed, thankful to find that *his* bedroom door did have a lock. I made use of it then, shivering, huddled back under the covers and fell into a heavy sleep.

The aroma of fresh coffee woke me, dragging me into the kitchen over the protests of my stiff and sore body. Cal was nowhere to be seen. I put Hazel on the counter so she could nibble toast crumbs and spotted a note, tucked behind a refrigerator magnet.

T—Bad accident on the highway. Overturned RV. See you when I can get loose. Stay out of trouble. —CC

Mulling over my most recent thoughts of Cal, I poured myself a cup of coffee and reached to stroke Hazel. She backed away, wrinkling her nose. I sniffed the sleeve of my nightshirt and conceded that she had a point.

A long, hot shower did a lot to make me feel (and smell) more human. My hands, legs, and face were coated with a layer of soot that had adhered like paste during the night, but I scrubbed with a soapy washcloth and got most of it off. I even managed, with the aid of a hand mirror, to pluck the splinter from my posterior, though I was pretty sure there were still a few remaining slivers that would require a steady hand and a needle to extract. Maybe I'd prevail upon Doc. Then again, maybe not.

I dried off and encountered my next difficulty. My suitcase, which had been crammed beneath the bed, was in fair shape, a coating of soot the only real damage. However, my clothes reeked of smoke.

In the end, I rummaged through Cal's closet, borrowing a pair of his jeans and a short-sleeved shirt. Giving up on the idea of underwear after laughingly trying on a pair of his boxers, I rolled up the hems of the jeans and belted them tightly. Very punk, I decided after checking the mirror. It would do.

As I combed out my damp hair, I pondered the most recent events. If I was wrong about Cal—and I fervently hoped I was—then who remained on my suspect list? The first name that sprang to mind was, of course, Tessa. Even more than before, she wanted me gone. Crawford was no longer in a position to reveal her long-held secret, but I sure was. She had even offered to pay me to keep quiet, but I had refused, offering only a promise. I couldn't be offended if the promise hadn't reassured her since I had, after all, broken it already. But I could be, and was, mightily offended at the prospect of her trying to kill me.

While I was pulling everything out of the ruined suitcase, my hand closed around the damned paperweight that had found its way into my nightmares every night since Billy had given it to me. I placed it gingerly on Cal's dresser and decided it could stay there.

I stuffed my rank clothing into a couple of plastic trash bags, then headed for the laundromat I remembered seeing down the street from the café, and dug as many quarters as I could find out of my backpack. Fortunately, the soap machine accepted dollar bills. It was going to take quite a few of the toy-sized boxes of detergent to clean this load.

After I had three washers going, I ducked into the café for a cup of coffee and a pack of overpriced cigarettes from the vending machine.

Back at the laundromat, I sipped coffee and watched the vibrating machines, lost in thought. A shadow fell across me and someone peered through the smudged window. I hustled to the door.

"Hi, Wood, come on in. If you'll wait a few minutes, you can watch my clothes tumble in the dryer. Better than TV."

He came in, but he wasn't smiling. "Thought that was you when I looked through the window, but I wasn't sure. That a new style you're wearin'? Can't say I care for it."

I didn't want to explain, so I shrugged. "How's Tessa?" I asked, though what I really wanted to know was where Tessa had been around two o'clock that morning.

His tone was missing its usual friendliness. "That's what I wanted to talk to you about. Heard you paid my wife a little visit yesterday. She's pretty upset."

"I didn't mean to upset her," I said honestly, wishing I knew what explanation Tessa had given him so I could back it up. After shooting off my mouth to Les and Billy, I didn't want to repeat the mistake with Wood. "It was just, uh, something I needed to talk to her about. All cleared up now."

"Yeah." He sank down on the bleach-stained wooden bench and lowered his head. "Yeah, she told me. All cleared up now, even if it took nearly thirty years."

Stunned, I sat down beside him. "You mean, she——" I realized I might be jumping to conclusions. "What exactly did she tell you?"

He almost smiled at that. "It's okay, Taylor, you don't have to protect her. She told me everything about you. About Miles. Dorothy had said some stuff about Miles and Tessa sneakin' around. Scared me real bad, Taylor, I gotta tell ya. It's almost a relief to find out the real story. I only wish she'd told me sooner." He chuckled suddenly. "Well, listen to the old fart moan, will ya? It hit me hard, I can't deny that, but it probably wasn't real easy for you to hear either, was it?"

"I'm fine, Wood," I assured him, uneasily eyeing the grayish tinge of his skin. "Are you?"

"I'll get through it. I'm more worried about Tessa. She was afraid I'd leave her—can you imagine?"

He looked so disbelieving that, for a few seconds, I couldn't speak at all, thinking of the misery and fear Tessa had inflicted upon herself. All the wasted years, hanging onto her grim secret for dear life, terrified that this man wouldn't understand. This man who, upon hearing the whole sordid tale said, with childlike simplicity, 'Leave her? Can you imagine?'

"No, I can't imagine you ever leaving her. Or her you."

He heaved himself off the bench, leaning heavily on his cane. "Little gal, don't take this the wrong way, but it might be a good idea if you went on back home."

"What?"

"You found out what you came here to find out, didn't you? I tend to think it'd be better for everybody if you gave Tess some time to come to grips with all this. I promise you, we won't lose touch. I'm sure later on she's gonna want to get to know her little girl, but right now, it'd be too painful for her to bring all this out in the open. I think there's been enough pain for a while, don't you?"

I was so shocked by his joining in the contingent that wanted me out of Perdue that I almost let him leave. Then, it hit me.

"Wood, wait!"

He turned inquiringly.

"When did Tessa tell you all this?"

"When?" He looked puzzled. "Last night."

"What time last night?" I pressed.

He raised a fuzzy white eyebrow. "I didn't check my watch, but I'd guess about seven or so. She was pickin' at her supper and I asked her if she was feelin' bad, and—well, it all poured out."

"Seven," I repeated, more relieved than I could have expressed.

"Seven." Tessa would have had no reason to set the fire. She probably didn't have very kind feelings about me, but I was certainly no longer a threat to her.

Unless he was lying again, protecting his wife as he always had. And even if he'd been telling the truth this time, Wood could easily have set the fire himself.

Back in Cal's apartment, I said as much to Hazel as I spread my clean clothes over the bed and began folding them. "Don't you see, Hazel? Wood came out and admitted he believed Dorothy when she told him that Tessa and Crawford were having an affair. So, if Wood killed him—okay, I know Cal says it couldn't have been done, but forget that technicality for now—then it all fits. Even the fire last night."

Hazel, curled up on Cal's pillow, yawned and scratched her chin.

"I know what you're thinking," I told her as I crammed clean underwear into my freshly-washed duffel bag. "Wood doesn't seem capable of that kind of violence. But you don't understand how much he loves his wife. I'm not sure I understood it myself until today."

I returned Cal's shirt and jeans to his closet and began dressing in my own clothes, selecting a long-sleeved shirt that concealed the massive bruise on my upper arm. I sat at the dresser and was attempting to do something with my frizzy hair when I noticed a spot of soot on my forehead that the shower had somehow missed. Grumbling, I dampened a tissue with spit and rubbed it away, then rubbed at a second smudge on my jaw.

"*Ow!*"

This smudge wasn't soot...it was another bruise. Belatedly, I remembered skidding across the floor and feeling pain flare in my face as well as my arm. It didn't hurt unless I applied pressure to it, but it looked pretty awful, so I reached for my makeup case.

I had covered the bruise and was applying mascara to my pale lashes when the little light bulb in my brain hit me with about two hundred watts.

Long sleeves. Makeup. Oh, God.

I had to talk to Tessa.

She wasn't thrilled when I showed up at her door, but at least she didn't begin the conversation by asking me to leave. Clearly, we were making progress. I waved away her polite offer of iced tea, and got right to the point.

"How much did Crawford tell you about the problems Lester and Paula were having?"

She had already started pursing her lips, and I resisted the urge to shake her.

"Damn it, Tessa, this is important. I'm not asking out of curiosity. If I wanted gossip, I'd go to Rita or Dorothy." As briefly as possible, I filled her in on my recent brainstorm.

"You can't tell me that it doesn't add up," I finished. "The long sleeves and the makeup were hiding bruises, not a skin condition, weren't they? I've been told more than once that she was anti-social— 'stuck up' was Rita's description—and that she rarely came into town. That's a classic symptom of a battered wife, Tessa. I've read enough articles to know.

"Sometimes the reclusiveness is self-imposed in an attempt to hide what's happening, and sometimes it's due to possessiveness on the man's part. Rita told me the only time they ever met, Paula had a broken arm. And her miscarriage? Jack said she'd taken a fall down the stairs. Maybe she did, but if so, she probably had a little help.

"He also talked about all the 'noise' in the house. Poor man is out of touch with reality half the time, but I'm willing to bet he overheard some pretty nasty fights between Les and Paula." I drew a breath. "Am I right? Tessa, you've got to tell me what you know."

She had paled as I spoke. "He didn't go into detail, but yes, he knew Lester had hit his wife once. Only once he was aware of. Apparently, it happened about a month after the wedding, and Paula showed up at Miles' house, terrified. Les swore it would never happen again."

"And Crawford believed him?" I was shaking with pure rage. "He was going to help a man like that become the next sheriff?"

"Miles felt sorry for the boy."

"Sorry—?" I choked on sheer outrage.

"Yes, sorry," Tessa repeated firmly. "Jack was widowed when Lester was very young, and his version of discipline was to beat the poor child with a belt. Miles was close to Jack, and he saw what was happening. Talking to Jack didn't help, so Miles took Les under his wing, and got him out of that place as soon as he could. Found him after-school jobs and, when the boy was old enough, talked him into joining the Army.

"He hoped Les would never have to come back to Perdue, but Jack became so ill, and Les felt responsible for taking care of him. Don't you see, Taylor? The boy probably equates love with hitting."

"The Twinkie defense," I muttered. "Yeah, Tessa, I can see it, but grasping the underlying cause doesn't do Paula a heck of a lot of good, does it?"

"But that's why Miles signed Les up for those counseling sessions in Lubbock. He hoped a good course of therapy would keep the problem from escalating."

"Obviously it didn't." I stood up. "Miles Crawford was murdered, Tessa, and I think I know who and why. But I'm going to have to figure out how before I can convince a certain stubborn deputy I'm right. Les told me that Paula has been visiting her parents in Dallas. Do you happen to know her maiden name?"

"No, I can't remember ever hearing it. Oh, God, Taylor, do you really think—?"

"I don't think, I know. But I've got to find Paula. She's the only one who might be able to fill in the missing pieces. Thanks for your help."

At the door, she gave my arm a brief touch. "Taylor, please. Be careful."

Well, well, I thought. *We really have come a long way in a short time.*

I jogged back to the Sheriff's Office and was puffing like a locomotive by the time I opened the door.

"Is Cal back yet?" I asked Billy as soon as I could catch my breath.

"Uh, no, he's still workin' that wreck out on the highway."

"What about Les? Is he here?"

"Nope, he's out there, too. Most of the tourists are headin' home today, and there's lots of traffic out there. It's a real mess, what with the ambulance and the fire truck and all." He sounded halfway excited at the prospect, and more than a little disappointed that he was chained to a desk instead of in the middle of the action.

I bent over the water fountain, trying to determine how best to find out what I needed to know. Wiping my mouth, I turned to Billy. "Have you heard from Paula lately?"

He looked a little surprised, but answered readily enough. "Uh-uh. Why?"

I did my best to sound casual. "Oh, no special reason, just wondering if she was back in town yet. Thought I might invite her to lunch."

"Why?"

"To be friendly," I said in my most injured tone. "Something wrong with that?"

"No, I guess not. Well, I don't think she's back yet. I haven't talked to her since Wednesday night."

I was so busy trying to frame my next question I almost missed what he had said. "Wednesday? You saw her Wednesday night?"

"I didn't see her, just talked to her on the phone. She called to get the sheriff's home number."

I stalked over to his desk, flinging caution to the winds. "What time was this? Did she say why she wanted it? Did she sound upset?"

He had rolled his chair backward away from me, his eyes wide. "What's goin' on?"

"Answer me, damn it!"

"It was about seven, I think, maybe a little later." He hesitated. "I guess she might have been crying, now that you mention it. I figured she had a cold. Uh, what was your other question?"

"Never mind. Billy, do you know what her maiden name was?" He looked blank, so I rephrased it. "Her last name before she married Lester."

"I have no idea."

"Okay." I perched on the edge of the desk, trying to think. "Okay. Billy, I need to borrow the patrol car again."

His mouth dropped open. "Oh, I don't think I should let you. Les said you're not a deputy anymore."

"If Les asks, tell him I stole it. I've got to go."

Before he could add to his protests, I was out the door and inside Les's old car. It smelled as bad as ever, but I hardly noticed. The situation was beginning to smell a lot worse.

The keys, as usual, were in the ignition, so the theft presented no problem. Billy stood in the doorway screaming at me as I roared out of the parking lot, but I paid him no attention, already focusing on what I needed to do.

I squealed to a stop in front of the sagging gas station and stumbled through the weeds to the equally dilapidated house behind it. The front and back doors, when I tried them, were locked, and I found myself thinking how odd that was. Less than a week in Perdue, and I had been brainwashed into considering a locked door abnormal. I really did have to get back to civilization.

Wandering around the perimeter of the house, I finally located a window in the rear that was open about half an inch. It was the old-fashioned type, and the wood had warped, so it took me several minutes and a lot of shoulder straining to get it raised enough to permit me to wriggle inside.

I ended up in a tiny bathroom, dingy and dark and smelling of mildew. The rest of the house proved to be no better. Picking my way like a blind person, I made it into the shabby living room and stood for a moment, getting my bearings.

Where would Paula keep her address book? Did she write letters, or would she be more likely to use the phone to keep in touch with friends and loved ones? Assuming, of course, that she bothered to keep in touch at all. What does a battered wife have to say?

Dear Mom, Well, he only hit me twice last night, things are looking up.

Right.

But I had already broken and entered, so I might as well play out the hunch.

I started in the kitchen, where a yellow wall phone seemed to be the only appliance purchased after 1956 or so. A thin Perdue telephone directory hung from a cup hook screwed into the front of a cabinet, but none of the drawers yielded anything resembling an address book.

Her bedroom, then. Correction. Their bedroom. I wasn't sure I wanted to see it.

I cut back through the living room and started up the stairs, but halfway up, I paused, cocking my head. Had I really heard something, or were my nerves just hopping like Mexican jumping beans? I promptly scratched cat burglary off my list of possible professions and had lifted one foot to continue when I heard it again. A scratching, scrabbling sound from overhead.

Rats, I remembered with a combination of relief and distaste. Jack had said there were rats in the attic, said he heard them all the time. I had no sooner made this brilliant deduction, however, than the muffled scraping was joined by a thump loud enough to shake the staircase.

I told myself rats scratch. They scrabble. They might even scrape. But rats do not thump.

I wasn't alone in that house.

Chapter Fourteen

MY FIRST INSTINCT was to get out of there. Fast. So why weren't my feet moving? I scowled down at them, willing them to reverse direction, but they seemed glued to the step. A weaker thump sounded overhead, and I was horrified when my ignorant feet actually carried me all the way up to the second floor landing.

An open doorway on my right revealed another staircase, the steps uncarpeted and steep. I had no intention of climbing them, and mentally informed my feet of this rational decision. They might even have obeyed at that point, if it hadn't been for an entirely different noise from above. A groan. A very human groan.

I was beyond clear thought, but I somehow got a picture in my head of Jack returning from the hospital, making his way to the attic to poison rats, and falling, perhaps breaking a leg. This convoluted reasoning was enough to propel me up the wooden steps, only to find a locked door at the top.

"Jack?" I shouted. The doorknob was loose, and I jiggled it, mystified. Why would he lock himself in? "Jack, it's Taylor. Are you all right?"

The only answer was a louder moan, followed by a metallic clink. Good grief, maybe he'd set some kind of trap and gotten caught in it himself. A rather gruesome Stephen King story flashed through my mind, and I shuddered away an image of the old man attempting to chew off his own foot.

Like everything else in the house, the door was ancient and in poor condition. I braced my shoulder against the thin wood and shoved, startled at the ease with which it crashed open.

I caught myself before I had stumbled into the lap of the woman who huddled on the floor, her left hand raised above her head at an awkward angle. I was shocked to realize she had been handcuffed to a heavy, iron ring that protruded from the rough attic wall.

I hardly recognized her.

"My God," I whispered. "Paula?"

Her fine, dark hair was matted with sweat and plastered to her skull like an ugly cap. She was dressed in denim shorts and a t-shirt, an outfit that fully exposed the bruises covering her body. Some were dark purple; others were fading to a yellowish green, telling tales of many beatings both recent and past. Her lip was split at one corner; the line of dried blood curved upward, giving the grotesque illusion of a crooked smile. Her left eye was swollen nearly shut. Her right eye watched me warily.

"Oh, Paula." I crouched beside her, noticing as I did so that her ankles had been bound with silver duct tape. The room reeked of urine, and I tried not to gag.

The handcuff had been tightened to the point it bit into the tender skin of her wrist. I righted a fallen ladder-backed chair—she had obviously kicked it over, which accounted for the thud I had heard—and helped her into it, her new position lessening the pressure on the cuffs. The problem now was how to get her loose. Without a key, I wasn't at all sure I would be able to.

I pulled off my backpack and rummaged for my pocketknife, then knelt at her feet and cut through the tape. She grimaced as I ripped the sticky stuff off her unshaven legs, and I caught a glimpse of her teeth. Several in front were badly loosened; one incisor was missing altogether.

She mumbled something as I tossed the wad of tape to one side and rose to examine the handcuffs.

"What did you say?"

Her tongue shot out to moisten dried lips, and she tried again, lisping a little through the ruined teeth. "Jack. Jack okay?"

"I think so. He's in the hospital."

Her good eye widened, and I hastened to reassure her. "They're monitoring his insulin, trying to get him stabilized. I'm sure he'll be fine."

She snorted what might have been a laugh. "Nah effie cuns ack ear."

Not if he comes back here. I shivered, though the airless attic was stifling.

The iron ring had been screwed into the wall like an oversized cup hook, and I couldn't unscrew it without twisting her arm off. I scratched at the wood with my thumbnail and discovered that it flaked away easily, soft with age and incipient rot. Choosing the sharpest blade from my knife, I began digging around the metal ring.

Paula tugged at my sleeve with her free hand. "Wa'er?"

I was appalled to consider how long she might have been held prisoner in the stuffy attic, with no food or drink. Reluctantly, I shook my head. "In a minute, I promise. Let me get you loose first, okay? I'd hate for Les to show up."

At the mention of her husband's name, she shrank back into the chair. I patted her shoulder. "Sorry, I didn't mean to frighten you. He's out working a big wreck, and I really doubt he'll be finished anytime soon."

She remained silent, her head bowed, and I felt a jolt of such utter fury at the man who had done this to her that it was all I could do to keep chipping away at the wood. I tried to keep up a litany of soothing words, but they sounded hollow and meaningless, even to me. Paula was probably used to meaningless words by now. Words like, "I'm sorry," and "I'll never hit you again."

As I probed deeper into the wall, the soft wood became harder and the tip snapped off my blade. Cursing under my breath, I unfolded the second, smaller blade. It was sturdier, but not as sharp. Paula turned her head now and then to check my progress, but fortunately, she couldn't maintain that position with any comfort. I didn't want her to become aware that her potential rescuer was having problems.

"Why did you come here?" It sounded more like, "Wy id you cun ear?" but I was quickly getting used to her flawed speech.

"I was looking for you. Actually, I was hoping to find your address book. Les had told me you were visiting your parents in Dallas, and I wanted to call you there."

"No parents. Dead."

"Oh. I'm sorry."

"Why? Why looking for me?"

I was hesitant under the circumstances to raise the questions I needed answered. But since she seemed willing to talk, I figured I might as well.

"Paula, did you make a phone call to Sheriff Crawford on the evening he died?"

"Yes." It was a whisper, and I had to bend slightly to hear her. "God help me. My fault."

"None of this is your fault," I told her firmly. "Why did you call him?"

"Les." I could feel her trembling. "Tuesday night, he hit me again. It was my fault. No, really, it was," she assured me as I let out a grunt of disgust. "I forgot to iron his uniform shirt. He didn't hit me very hard, but it was the first time he'd hit me at all since I lost the baby. The counseling sessions were helping a lot, but he'd started skipping them." She swallowed. "He was so sorry afterward."

The forgiveness in her voice made me feel physically ill. When I thought of how easily he'd gained my sympathy, feeding me lies about a snobby, self-centered wife who blamed him for the accidental loss of their baby... I attacked the wood, pretending it was Lester's throat.

"He brought me an ice pack, and he cried," she continued softly. "He swore he'd start going to the counselor again." She squinted up at me. "You were at the Sheriff's Office Wednesday when I came by to remind him that he had an appointment that evening."

"I remember," I muttered through clenched teeth. I certainly remembered the heavy makeup she had worn that day to conceal her bruises.

"But I guess that wasn't a good idea," she went on. "Reminding him, I mean. He came home about an hour later and started in on me again. This time, he knocked me down and I hit my head against the edge of the kitchen sink. Must've passed out because when I opened my eyes, it was getting dark outside and he was gone."

"Is that when you called Crawford?"

She nodded. "That was a big mistake. I thought he'd just talk to Les, like he did before, but he got so mad. He said he'd done all he could, and it wasn't working." She rubbed tears from her good eye. "Not long after that, Les came home. I've never seen him so furious. Crawford had called him over to the house and told him to forget about being the next sheriff. Les hit me again. Really hard. I told him I was sorry, but he kept hitting me. Then he locked me up here. Said it'd keep me from making any more trouble for him."

"Where was Jack?" I couldn't imagine the older man standing by and watching his son do something like this.

"I don't know. Unconscious, probably. Les messed with his insulin dosage all the time, said it was the only way to control his father."

Control. That's what it all boiled down to, in the end. Control your wife by knocking her around, control your father by withholding his insulin. Tessa had said Jack used to beat his son, and I knew a psychologist would rationalize the resulting behavior. Being the sheriff would have given Les more control over more lives than any other job in the county, and when Crawford threatened to take it away from him, he lashed out—this time, with fatal results.

"I think Les killed Miles Crawford," I said bluntly.

Paula twisted in the chair. "So do I."

I tried wiggling the iron ring. It moved much more easily now, like a rotten tooth that only needed a good tug to come out. Wishing for a pair of pliers, I started digging into the wood again.

"I haven't quite figured out how he did it, though," I told her. "Paula, is Les really afraid of snakes, or is that an act?"

She shook her head. "It's no act. He's terrified of them. Unless they're dead. He helped the skinners at last year's festival."

"Well, so much for that idea then. He couldn't have killed Crawford with a dead—" I stopped, frozen by the force of the idea that sprang full blown into my head.

"Did you get it loose?" Paula asked hopefully.

"Huh? Oh, almost. Let's see." I hooked three fingers through the ring and leaned back, pulling with my full weight. The next thing I knew, my butt made painful contact with the hard floor and Paula was on top of me, jerked out of the chair by the handcuff chain as I fell.

We managed to get to our feet.

"Think you can walk?" I asked.

"Yeah. Can I have some water now?"

"Of course you can."

I helped her down the stairs and she pointed to one of the bedrooms. "Is it okay if I change clothes? I, um, don't smell very good." She lowered her head, and my heart ached for her embarrassment.

"Go ahead. But try to hurry, okay?"

She nodded.

"Paula, wait. Do you know where Jack keeps the key to the shed?"

"Yeah, sure. It's hanging on a hook by the kitchen window."

"Okay. While you're getting cleaned up, I'm going out there to take a look around. Meet me out front when you're ready."

I located the key and crossed the yard to the shed. A light breeze stirred the tall weeds and cooled my cheeks. I sucked in fresh air, erasing the foul smells of the attic.

The padlock opened easily and I stuck a tentative hand inside, searching for the light switch. I could hear the snakes stirring in their beds of shredded newspaper, and though the sound made my flesh creep, I found myself wondering who was feeding them since Jack was in the hospital.

A small refrigerator was tucked beneath the air conditioning unit. The shelves inside were lined with small vials, some clear, others tinted brown. The brown ones were marked with prescription labels and obviously contained insulin. The clear ones were full of murky fluid. The same murky fluid, I was horrified to remember, that Jack had brought to me when I asked for his insulin. I knew, now, what it was, and I couldn't bear to think what would have happened had I gone ahead with his injection. Hypodermic needles, wrapped in cellophane, were stacked along one side of the bottom shelf. I slipped one into my pocket with a vague notion that I needed to collect evidence.

I crouched to peer into the cages. The snakes seemed to be all right, but then, what did I know about snakes? None of them were lunging at me. None were even coiled and poised to strike. At rest, I had to admit they were beautiful, in their own deadly way. The diamond patterns along their backs stood out sharply in the bright light, glistening as if etched in gold and ebony. I pulled the keys to the patrol car from my pocket and studied the key ring. There was no doubt in my mind. I knew how Les had done it.

Sighing, I turned to leave.

"Hi, Taylor." Les leaned against the doorjamb, oh, so casually blocking my exit. "Having fun?"

My pulse pounded into rapid action, but I tried not to let him hear my panic. "I, um, got to worrying no one was feeding the snakes."

"That was nice of you. So, did you feed them?"

"I'm afraid not. I realized after I got here that I have no idea what rattlesnakes eat." Was I really going to pull this off?

"Rodents, mostly. Usually alive, though they can be conditioned to accept dead food. Dad told me that." He shifted his position slightly, but he was still blocking the door. "I'm sure they'd love to get hold of that ferret of yours. Billy told me about it."

I flinched at the thought.

"Billy also told me that you had stolen my old patrol car, and that you'd been asking a lot of questions about Paula. Did you manage to find her?"

"Paula? How could I? I mean, she's still in Dallas, isn't she?" I hadn't known until that moment how fluently I could lie, given the proper situation. I met his eyes boldly.

"Nope, she's not in Lubbock. She's right here." He reached behind him and yanked Paula into view.

She had changed into long pants and a loose-fitting top; a red scarf hid her filthy hair. Her eyes met mine, wide and hopeless.

"Let go of her." My teeth were so tightly clenched I could barely force the words out.

He shrugged. The bastard actually shrugged. "Sure. Paula, get your ass back to the house and stay there."

She looked at me, so many emotions flickering that it was hard to read them all. Fear, helplessness, apology, shame. A hint of anger, hastily suppressed.

"Paula." Les spoke softly, but she jumped as if he had slapped her. Which, of course, he had. Many times. She ducked under his arm, glancing back at me once more before she turned in the direction of the house. I heard her shoes crunching through the weeds.

Les watched after her for a moment. A muscle twitched in his jaw as he turned back to me.

"You couldn't leave it alone, could you?" His soft tone frightened me more than a fit of rage would have. "My little wife tells me you've decided I killed the sheriff. Oh, don't act so surprised. Paula knows better than to try to hold back when I ask her a question."

His insufferable pride turned my fear to fury. "You son of a bitch."

He smiled thinly. "You could be right. I don't remember my mother very well, so I couldn't say for sure. But let's get back to the so-called murder. Cal said he thought he'd convinced you that your theory was impossible."

"He almost did."

"But you're still sure I killed Crawford."

"So what if I am? No one believes me, not even Cal." I took a deep breath. "Just get out of my way, Les, and I'll leave. I'll even go back to Houston. That's what you want, isn't it? That's why you made sure I had enough money to get my car back?"

In one swift motion, he pulled his revolver free of its holster. I swallowed. The hole at the end of the barrel looked like a black, malevolent eye.

"You don't really think I can let you go? It's way too late for that now. This murder talk aside, I'm not gonna let you start flappin' your gums about Paula and me. Not that it's anybody's business what goes on between a husband and wife, but I've got the election to think of."

The derringer was still in my backpack, which I had left behind in the attic. Not that it mattered. In the time it would have taken me to dig it out, Les would have emptied his revolver into me.

I backed away, but the shed was small and I couldn't go far enough to make any difference to a bullet. "For God's sake, you can't just kill me."

"Really? Why not? No one will know." He smiled again. I was beginning to hate that smile, dimples and all. "I was really hoping that fire last night would scare you into leaving. But I found out from Roger that you still hadn't gone by to pick up your car. So I sneaked into his shop and grabbed your keys." With his free hand, he reached into his breast pocket and produced my silver key ring.

He jangled it playfully. "Tonight, when it's nice and dark, I'll get the car. There's a very deep lake on the outskirts of the county, and even a Volkswagen will sink if you open all the windows and help it along a bit. I doubt if anyone will ever find it. I know no one will ever find you. Sixty acres go with this house, and I won't have a lick of trouble finding a nice, remote place to bury your body. Folks will think you shafted Roger out of the repair bill and hightailed it back to the big city."

I licked my dry lips. "It won't work."

"Don't be stupid, Taylor. Of course it'll work." He straightened from his half slouch and moved farther into the shed. "This is your own fault, for sticking your nose where it didn't belong."

My back was against the wall, and something was jabbing me in the spine. "My fault?" I repeated to keep him talking as I inched my right hand behind me.

"Yes, damn it!" He was finally showing some anger. "You're the one who started spreading all that crap about murder."

"But it wasn't crap, Lester, and you know it." I kept my eyes locked with his. My fingers found what was poking me. The object was long and thin, a stick of some sort. Suddenly, I knew what it was.

Keep him talking, I told myself. *If you lose his interest, he'll pull the trigger.* "Crawford found out you were still abusing your wife, and he decided not to support you for sheriff. As a matter of fact, he probably would've ended up supporting Cal instead, wouldn't he? That really would have ruined your chances." Slowly, carefully, I moved my hand along the wooden shaft, trying to determine how it had been secured to the wall. "So you killed him."

Lester's green eyes glinted. "You're crazy."

I ignored that. "It's funny, really, considering you didn't even stay on my first list of suspects for long. I crossed you off as soon as I remembered how frightened you are of snakes. Just about everyone else in this town seems to know how to handle snakes, but not you." My groping fingers located a simple metal bracket on the wall behind me. The broom handle—the one with a hook screwed into one end so Jack could use it to lift snakes from their cages—was in my hand. Now, it was a matter of timing.

"When I finally put two and two together about you and Paula, I knew you'd killed Miles. Your motive was strong, and you certainly had the opportunity, but it took me a while to figure out how a man who was phobic when it came to snakes could manage to do something even an expert swore couldn't be done." I had a firm grip on the stick, but Les was still watching me much too closely. There had to be some way to distract him for a few precious seconds. "Then Paula said something that made me realize what I'd been overlooking all along."

He growled at the mention of his wife's name, and I knew if I failed, if Les got away with killing me, he would surely kill her too.

"She said you weren't afraid of snakes as long as they were dead. And that's how you did it, isn't it?"

He lifted an eyebrow.

"It should've hit me before now. I think I've known for days, really—at least my subconscious did. I kept having nightmares about the damn paperweight Billy gave me, the one with the snakehead inside. I dreamed it was biting my neck." My left hand curled into a fist, and something bit into my palm. The car keys. I had forgotten I was holding them. I considered springing at him, going for his eyes with the keys as I had once been taught in a self-defense class. But no, he was too far away. I'd have a bullet in me before I was halfway across the shed.

"You killed Crawford with a dead snake, Les. A dead snake and a hypodermic needle loaded with venom. That's what's in the other vials in the refrigerator. I don't know why it took so long for me to realize that a man who studies snakes like Jack does would surely collect their venom as part of his research."

My right arm was going numb from its awkward position behind my back, but I didn't release my grip on the wooden pole. Sweat was dripping into my eyes, despite the air conditioner. I was running out of time. "I'm guessing you sneaked into Crawford's house—not a difficult thing to do since no one in this backwater town seems to believe in locked doors—and waited until he fell asleep. An injection of venom in the jugular would've killed him almost instantly. After he was dead, it was a simple matter of pressing the dead snake's fangs into his neck."

Les's lips pulled back from his teeth. "Smart little bitch, aren't you?"

"Smart enough." I didn't feel all that smart at the moment. "You left the dead snake in the living room. Carefully hidden underneath the couch, of course, because you had to be the one to find it and 'kill' it the next morning. That's why you slept on the cot at the SO, isn't it? You wanted to be close by when the call came in, and you knew Dorothy got to Miles' house early every morning. But you slept right through it, and Billy ended up calling me instead. I'll bet that really got your shorts in a knot."

"I couldn't sleep," he muttered. "Drank some bourbon to relax me. I guess I drank too much. I never even heard the damn phone ring."

"Well, I have to admit it was a good plan. You sure fooled me, and Dorothy, too. We'd have sworn in court that you killed that snake. Especially after..."

Les moved a little closer. "After what?"

I was such an idiot. The keys had been in my hand all along. "Um, after the great act you put on, pushing us out of the house and running for your shotgun. We were convinced you were really being brave." It was lame, but it worked. Even under the circumstances, I could see him preen a little.

Sending up a quick prayer, I fumbled with the key ring and managed to press the button, at the same instant yelling, "Shit, Les, watch out! A snake is loose!"

An angry buzzing echoed through the shed, and Les's expression rapidly changed from skepticism to pure terror. He stumbled backward toward the door. The pistol and his eyes moved wildly from side to side, seeking the source of the noise. I turned and yanked the pole from its brackets, then swung it at Les with all the force I could muster. He saw it coming and brought the pistol up, twisting to avoid the blow.

The gun went off with a deafening roar and I felt a sharp sting in my upper arm. At the same instant, the broom handle skimmed across Les's knees and smashed into one of the cages. Glass shattered.

Striving to keep his balance, Les reached out blindly and his hand plunged into the broken cage. A small snake shot forward and sank its fangs into his wrist. He screamed, the sound reverberating off the tin walls. I dropped the pole and clamped my hands to my ears.

I should have covered my eyes instead. I still dream about what happened next. Les fell heavily, his upper body smashing through the remaining glass. I saw a triangular shard pierce his neck, just above the Adam's apple. Another snake slithered forward and latched onto his cheek, but I'm pretty sure he was already dead. That's what I keep telling myself anyway.

Chapter Fifteen

I WAS PROPPED UP in a hospital bed, a situation made tolerable only by the small computer that rested on my lap. Doc had reluctantly consented to let Cal bring it by the clinic, and had even helped me hook up the modem to the bedside phone. In return, I had allowed the old doctor to clean and bandage the scratch on my upper arm. He tsked and muttered and grumbled and generally behaved as if the bullet had pierced my heart.

The clinic had two rooms set up for patients, and these were used only for overnight observation. Serious illness or injury warranted a trip to the hospital in Lubbock, so I supposed I was lucky to be where I was. My room shared a wall with the veterinary hospital next door; muted barks, growls and meows accompanied my taps on the computer keys as I composed a letter to my agent, Annie. Despite everything, the thought of the e-mail I had received from her made me smile.

The door eased open and Doc poked his white head inside. "All right," he said, irritably. "She's awake. Five minutes, that's all you get."

"Nonsense." Dorothy Stenson elbowed him aside as she carried a laden tray into the room. "I'll stay and make sure she eats her dinner." A swarm of people followed in her wake, all of them ignoring Doc's heated protests.

"We ganged up on him," Rita explained, handing me a strawberry malt. "I was gonna bring you some food from the café, but Dorothy wouldn't let me."

"The last thing you need is a pile of greasy junk," Dorothy put in sternly. "Home cooking's what you need. Here, now, this'll fix you up. Put some meat on those skinny bones of yours." She pulled aside the towel that covered the tray, exposing enough roast beef, mashed potatoes, salad and rolls to feed an army.

Billy approached the bed and gave me a shy hug. Wood brushed past him to set a bouquet of spring flowers on the nightstand. Bonita Posey gave me a congratulatory whack on, unfortunately, my sore shoulder, then dropped a pack of cigarettes and a pint bottle of Chivas Regal into my lap. "Vices are comforting," she told me with a wink.

Cal, after checking to make sure Doc had left, reached inside his jacket and pulled out a squirming Hazel. "I had to smuggle her in," he whispered. "Doc is sure she's crawling with germs."

"I'll take my chances." I cuddled her against my shoulder. "Thank you. All of you. I'm overwhelmed."

"Eat," Dorothy said gruffly, so I dug in, sneaking Hazel a bite of roll now and then.

Wood leaned against the wall and watched me. "Cal told us part of what happened. Hard to believe."

"Believe it," I mumbled around a mouthful of salad, then pushed the tray away, my appetite suddenly gone.

Cal cleared his throat. "Maybe she's rather not talk about it, folks."

I groaned. "Might as well. Rita and Dorothy can make sure the truth gets out." Neither of the two women even pretended to be affronted.

They all paid rapt attention until I reached the part about Lester's behavior on the morning Crawford's body had been discovered.

"Wait a minute," Dorothy interrupted. "I was there, remember? That snake couldn't have been dead, Taylor. I heard it rattle."

I slid open the nightstand's drawer. "Here's what you heard, Dorothy." Holding up the key ring, I pushed the button.

Rita let out a shriek at the sound and covered her ears. "Put that horrible thing away," she begged.

"This horrible thing, as you call it, saved my life. There's not a doubt in my mind Lester Forman would've killed me."

When I had finished my story, the room was quiet for a moment.

Bo broke the silence. "Poetic justice, I call it," she muttered.

"I heard that Cal showed up just as you came out of the shed," Rita said. "How did he know where you were?"

I looked at Cal. "I never got around to asking you that."

"Paula called the SO," Billy put in. "And I started trying to get Cal on the radio right away, but it took me a while to raise him." He sighed. "We've gotta get some portables."

Paula. I was ashamed to realize that I hadn't asked about her.

"She's going to be fine," Cal assured me before I could frame the question. "Physically, anyway. Besides the bruises and the loose teeth, she's got a cracked collarbone and she's pretty dehydrated. Doc sent her on to Lubbock. She'll probably need some counseling, too."

"But she called," I marveled. "As frightened as she was, she picked up the phone and called for help. That's a good start, don't you think?" A sobering thought crept in. "What in the world is she going to do now?"

"Well, I had an idea about that," Cal said. "She told me she wants to go on living here, so she can take care of Jack when he comes back home. How do you think she'd feel about being a dispatcher? Billy's going to start the academy soon, and I'm gonna need someone in the office."

Everyone discussed that possibility for a while, then Bo scooped up the tray and signaled Rita and Dorothy.

"Let's get out of here. Taylor needs some rest."

I thanked them again and they left, trailed by Billy. Wood and Cal lingered.

Wood sat on the edge of the bed and took my hand in his. "Could I ask you to excuse us for a minute, Deputy?"

"Uh, sure." Cal raised an eyebrow at me, but slipped out of the room.

"Little gal, I can't say that this town gave you a real friendly welcome, but you've done us all a great service. Come November, we probably would've been stupid enough to vote that scoundrel into office if it hadn't been for you. And poor ol' Miles sure wouldn't be restin' easy, either, with his murderer walkin' free."

I squeezed his hand.

"Tessa's feeling mighty bad about how she's treated you, too." He hung his head. "I'm right sorry myself about what I said to you this morning."

"Don't worry about it. You were probably right. I should head on home for a while. Let things settle down." I was surprised at the tears that stung my eyes as I said the words. 'Home' was a concept that Houston didn't fit anymore, if it ever had. I'd made friends here, real friends, for perhaps the first time in my life.

As if he had read my mind, Wood raised his head and looked into my eyes. "No, honey, that's just it. Tessa and I and probably a lot of others hope you'll stay in Perdue. See, Miles' lawyer came by this afternoon. Turns out the good sheriff left everything he owned to the woman he never stopped loving."

"He left it to Tessa?"

He nodded sourly. "Guess it shouldn't bother me, but it does. 'Course, Tess was real flustered. She said she'd sell the house right away and send everything else to Crawford's sister in Chicago, and then we could get on with our lives."

"Makes sense," I soothed him. "Now, Wood, don't go getting jealous again. She couldn't help what Crawford wrote in his will."

"Oh, I know, I know. You're missin' the point, though. I talked her out of sellin' the house."

"You did? Why?"

"Well, we talked it over and decided it might be better if she gave it away. Maybe to one of Crawford's relatives, see? Like, for instance, his daughter." He beamed at my expression. "What do you say, gal? Don't ya think you can write them mystery books just as well here as you can in the city?"

My mouth was still hanging open when Wood pushed out of the room and Cal came back in.

"You're gonna catch flies," he drawled. "What's going on?"

I told him and he grinned ear to ear.

"So you're going to stay? You mean it?"

"I don't see why not," I said happily. "Especially now I've got a new project to work on. Hand me the laptop. I want you to read the e-mail I got from Annie."

True to her nature, Annie's letter read like a telegram. "Great stuff. Waiting for more. Send complete outline ASAP. Brinkly interested. Annie."

Cal looked up from the screen. "I have no idea what this means."

I started laughing all over again. "Right in the middle of this mess, I sent Annie some notes I'd made about the circumstances of Crawford's death, along with a list of suspects."

He still seemed puzzled. "So?"

"So, Brinkly is a publisher, and Annie is waiting for a complete outline to send them. Don't you get it? She thinks I sent her an idea for a new murder mystery."

"As long as you stay here to write it," he murmured, pulling me into his arms.

"Cal," I murmured, after a few kisses that would have popped my stitches, if I'd had any. "We really need to get something cleared up." I backed away a little so I could read his eyes. "There's no way to put this delicately, so I won't even try. Why don't you want to make love to me?"

He gaped. "Who said I didn't?"

I felt myself blushing. This wasn't easy. "Well, you had the perfect opportunity the other night."

"Oh." He bit his lip. "Listen, Taylor, I believe in practicing safe sex, you know?"

"Yeah? So?"

"So, the only place in this town to buy protection is at Posey's and

I—well, hell, Taylor, she knew my mother. I'd planned to make a run to Lubbock, but...why are you laughing?"

I wiped my eyes. "You idiot. Did it ever occur to you that a woman might carry her own supply?"

His eyes widened. "You're kidding."

"Not that I've had an opportunity to use them for quite a while, but I still keep 'em around." I lowered my voice. "Um, Cal? Does the door to this room have a lock?"

Texas Fried Rattlesnake

1 cup corn flake crumbs
1 tsp paprika
1/2 tsp garlic powder
1/4 tsp ground thyme
1/4 tsp red pepper
1 large rattlesnake, skinned and chopped into sections *
1/4 cup low-fat, cultured buttermilk

Combine corn flake crumbs and seasonings in plastic bag, mixing well. Dip snake meat in buttermilk, then place in bag with crumb mixture, shaking to coat. Deep fry in vegetable oil until browned and tender. (* The faint of heart may substitute chicken)

Elizabeth Dearl

Elizabeth Dearl is a former Texas police officer who also owned a small bookstore for several years. Her short mysteries have appeared in many magazines and anthologies. Her story "The Way to a Man's Heart" won a Derringer Award, and "The Goodbye Ghoul" has been optioned for a short film (for which Elizabeth is writing the screenplay).

Elizabeth's mystery novels, DIAMONDBACK (an EPPIE Award finalist which has recently been optioned for a feature film), TWICE DEAD (2002 EPPIE Award winner for "best mystery"), and TRIPLE THREAT (2004 EPPIE Award winner) are set in West Texas and feature amateur sleuth Taylor Madison, who is assisted in crime-solving by her ferret, Hazel. "Buyer's Remorse," a novella which also stars Taylor Madison, in included in the print version of TRIPLE THREAT, and was also included in BLOOD, THREAT and FEARS: Four Tales of Murder and Suspense (2002 EPPIE Award winner for "best anthology"). MALICIOUS INTENT (DiskUs Publishing) is a collection of Elizabeth's mystery/horror short stories.

Elizabeth is a member of Sisters in Crime and The Short Mystery Fiction Society, and is an instructor for Writer's Digest School's Writers Online Workshops. She lives in the Houston area with her husband, a fraud investigator, and two fur-children of the canine variety.

Website: http://www.elizabethdearl.com
Email: elizabethdearl@mail.com

More Taylor Madison Mysteries

TWICE DEAD

More than thirty years ago, a minister named Ralph Posey absconded with the church funds, abandoning his wife and daughter. At least, that's what everyone in Perdue thought, until a startling discovery makes it obvious that he never left town at all - he was murdered, and all evidence implicates his wife as the killer. Bonita Posey admittedly detested her husband, but she denies taking his life. Can Taylor uncover the truth in time to keep her octogenarian friend out of prison?

TRIPLE THREAT

Triplets, a tornado, and twisted lies add up to trouble for Taylor Madison as Perdue's townfolk gather for Hank Barton's funeral. Why do the three identical sisters dislike each other so much? Why did Hank put such an odd codicil in his will? Throw in swaggering new deputy, a citizen's police academy, and an amateur tornado hunter, and Taylor finds herself longing for the comparative peace of big city life!

Both available in eBook and Print from
Hard Shell Word Factory
www.hardshell.com

Printed in the United States
30226LVS00003B/321